Her Fifth Husband?
by Dixie Browning

Jake gave her a look that defied interpretation.

Placing baby, cradle and all on the coffee table, he turned to where she stood surrounded by an assortment of baby gear, plus her usual clutter.

Sasha forgot to breathe. Was it only her imagination that made her feel as if every cell in her body turned his way, like a sunflower following the sun?

All it took was the slightest encouragement and she was off on another fantasy, inventing a happy ending that wasn't going to happen.

Jake placed his hands on her shoulders and pulled her into his arms. With her face against his hard, warm chest, she inhaled the scent that was pure Jake Smith.

"Fair warning. I'm about to kiss you," he said calmly.

"Go ahead," she said in a voice only an octave or so higher than normal. "I dare you."

The Last Reilly Standing
by Maureen Child

ꙮ ꭓꞁꭉ ꙫ

"You don't know me well enough to know I have an ego."

"Please." She gave a short laugh. "Look at you. Of course you do."

"I think that was a compliment."

"See?" she said. "Ego."

"Touché. So, how are you going to help me with the bet?" She smiled, and he felt the powerful slam of it hit him like a sledgehammer.

"Why, First Sergeant Reilly, if some gorgeous woman shows up, I'll just throw myself on you like you were a live grenade."

Aidan looked up and down slowly, completely. Then he shook his head. "Terry Evans, with that kind of help, I'm a dead man…"

Available in April 2006 from Silhouette Desire

Her Fifth Husband?
by Dixie Browning
&
The Last Reilly Standing
by Maureen Child
(Three-Way Wager)

ᓱᐑᐎᐯᓇ

Baby at His Convenience
by Kathie DeNosky
&
Out of Uniform
by Amy J Fetzer

ᓱᐑᐎᐯᓇ

Business Affairs
by Shirley Rogers
&
Riding the Storm
by Brenda Jackson

Her Fifth Husband?
DIXIE BROWNING

The Last Reilly Standing
MAUREEN CHILD

SILHOUETTE®

Desire™

First published in Great Britain 2006
Silhouette Books, Eton House, 18-24 Paradise Road,
Richmond, Surrey TW9 1SR

The publisher acknowledges the copyright holders of the
individual works as follows:

Her Fifth Husband? © Dixie Browning 2005
The Last Reilly Standing © Maureen Child 2005

ISBN 0 373 60309 6

51-0406

Printed and bound in Spain
by Litografia Rosés S.A., Barcelona

HER FIFTH HUSBAND?

by
Dixie Browning

DIXIE BROWNING

has won numerous awards for both her paintings and her romances. A former newspaper columnist, she has written more than one hundred romances. Browning is a native of North Carolina's Outer Banks, an area that continues to provide endless inspiration.

One

Stealing a few moments from the job, Sasha lay back on the chaise longue, closed her eyes against the late-afternoon sun and savored the warm sea breeze that fluttered her georgette camisole. She might not have a regular salary, much less benefits, but this beat a desk in a cramped, windowless cubicle all to pieces.

The sound of distant traffic merged with the nearby sound of the surf to become a soothing lullaby. "Five minutes," she murmured.

Five minutes and then she would jump up, finish checking off her list, think of anything she might have forgotten and then stop by another client's new office complex to see how long before she could get started there.

As an interior designer, her bread and butter consisted of professional suites—usually law, real estate or medical. Occasionally she did between-season patch jobs for rentals in the various beach communities along the northern Outer Banks, but her real love was having a brand new McMansion to do from scratch. Any budgetary limits only stimulated her creativity.

She sighed in contentment. When the soft southeast breeze blew her hair across her face, she smoothed it back, still without opening her eyes. If she had the energy she would take off her shoes, but that would require sitting up and bending over to unfasten the ankle straps. She should have worn mules.

"Vanity, thy name is Sasha," she murmured. The trouble with pointy-toed, stiletto-heeled shoes was that they were so darned flattering she couldn't *not* wear them, even knowing she'd be climbing up and down all these wretched stairs.

She actually owned a few pairs of flats, though she seldom wore them. At home she went barefoot and wore shapeless tents, but anytime she went out in public she took pains to look her best in case she ran into a potential client. Her friends, knowing her background, called it the Cinderella syndrome.

Sasha had never denied it. Underneath the careful makeup, the streaky cinnamon-tea hair and the fashionable outfits bought at end-of-the-year sales—not to mention the jewelry she adored—Sasha Combs Cassidy Boone Lasiter was still plain old Sally June Parrish, oldest daughter of a dirt-poor tobacco farmer turned preacher.

At times like this, she almost wished she didn't give a damn. She wondered if Cinderella's feet had hurt in those miserable-looking glass slippers.

"Relax, feet," she murmured drowsily. "Once we get home you can let it all hang out, I promise."

The sun felt marvelous now that it had lost most of its midday heat. A natural redhead—sort of—Sasha freckled whether or not she wore foundation with a serious SPF.

One more minute, she promised herself. After that she would go back inside and finish her check-off list. The cleaning crew had come and gone last week, but the place still reeked of cigarette smoke. Not only that but one of the bedspreads was rumpled, as if whoever had made it up had been interrupted before they could finish the job. King-size beds probably required a team to do the job right.

Housekeeping, however, was not her responsibility. She had listed the items that needed replacing. Chair cushions, flatware and a few dishes that had probably been taken out on the beach and lost, one chair with a broken leg, a stained lampshade and two leather-topped bar stools that looked as if they'd been used as targets in a game of darts. Normally the owners would have handled it, but according to Katie McIver, who managed several cottages in the area, the owner of Driftwinds had called at the last minute and asked her to find someone else to bring the cottage up to standard for the upcoming season.

Sasha had worked with Katie before. This was a peanuts job, but small jobs lead to larger ones and she was in no position to turn down any commission, no matter how small. In the case of the Jamison cottage, if the owners wanted their investment to pay off, Katie or someone needed to screen their clientele, if that was legally possible. The last tenants had waxed surfboards in one of the showers, leaving an unholy mess for the poor cleaning crew.

Sasha massaged her temples, taking care not to involve her long, acrylic nails. The headache that had been threatening all day was getting closer to a reality. She'd counted on a few minutes of complete relaxation to take care of it, but so far it wasn't working.

One more minute, she promised herself. After that she would go back inside and finish making the rounds. She'd already noticed what looked like a red-wine stain on one of the bedspreads that the cleaners had missed. People who had everything—people who could afford to rent one of these million-dollar-plus rentals—too often valued nothing.

Think peaceful thoughts, she willed silently. Think of bittersweet chocolate melting on your tongue. Alan Jackson singing softly in your ear. Nordstrom's and a no-limit charge card.

Here she was in a beachfront cottage—if a six-bedroom, seven-bath house complete with two hot tubs and a swimming pool could be called a cottage—and her blasted sinuses refused to allow her to enjoy it.

She was still attempting to talk herself into relaxing before her headache got any worse when a shadow passed over her. Without opening her eyes, she frowned. A shadow of what? According to Katie, this entire row of cottages was empty until Memorial Day weekend.

Opening her eyes, she blinked against the late-afternoon sun. There wasn't a cloud in the sky, not even a vapor trail. Yet even with her eyes closed, she could've sworn a shadow had just passed over her.

Probably a pelican, she thought, and relaxed again. Sasha hadn't grown up in this part of the state, but she did know that long before the developers had taken possession, these dunes had belonged to sea birds, sand fiddlers, a few hardy fishing families and a herd of wild ponies.

Sighing, she let her eyes drift shut again, conscious now of the reddish-brown color of sunlight seen through mauve-shadowed eyelids. She was almost asleep when it happened again. Reddish-brown briefly turned dull black and then back again. Warily, she opened her eyes, lifted her head and looked around.

Nothing moved. Not even a mosquito.

More curious than afraid, she tried an experiment, closing her eyes, she passed a hand over her face, just to be sure.

There it was again—that momentary darkening. Something had definitely blocked the sun for one split second. A fast-moving airplane? Flight-seeing tours were common in the area, but usually not until the season got underway. Besides, unless it was a glider, she would have heard it.

She struggled to sit up, because whatever it was, it wasn't her imagination. There was simply nothing up there to cast a shadow. No birds, no planes—not even a flying superhero. Whatever it was that had passed between her and the sun was gone.

And dammit, so was any chance of relaxing.

She was still struggling to get up off the low chaise longue when she heard a soft thump and what sounded like a muffled exclamation. Pulses pounding, she glanced over her shoulder. Sunlight reflected off the sliding-glass doors behind her, blocking her view of the interior. Logic told her that no one inside could have cast a shadow over the outer deck, but logic was the first victim when a woman was truly spooked.

Had she locked the lower door when she'd let herself in? With her mind on so many things at once, details occasionally escaped her attention. Katie could have seen her car and dropped by to check on her progress. Maybe one of the cleaning crew had left something behind. Or maybe they hadn't finished, which would explain the stained bedspread and the cigarette smell.

But that still wouldn't explain a shadow crossing over the upper deck.

Gripping the sides of the low chaise, Sasha called out, "Dammit, who's there?" Bracing her feet, she readied herself to dash inside and lock the sliding doors. "Listen, whoever you are, I'm tired, my feet hurt and I've got a killer headache. You don't want to mess with me!"

Okay, so she'd been reading a lot of thrillers lately—crime was a sad fact of life, even here in an oceanfront paradise. Like most of the upscale cottages, Driftwinds had a state-of-the art security system.

Which she hadn't bothered to re-arm....

Well, shoot. She had the instructions written down somewhere—what numbers to punch in and how long to wait and what to do next. But she hadn't planned on being here long today, so it simply hadn't seemed worth the effort.

Uneasiness gave way to alarm. Oh, God—what if she had to run for it? She wasn't exactly one of the kick-ass heroines that were so popular now. As much as she abhorred exercise, she had to admit there were times when physical fitness came in handy.

Crossing to the nearby wooden rail, she peered down at the paved parking below. The only car there was her own red convertible.

So it wasn't Katie, and it wasn't one of the cleaning crew. Warily, she glanced over her shoulder toward the outside stairs, half expecting to see someone step out onto the upper deck. The lack of logic didn't bother her—she'd figure out later how someone downstairs could cast a shadow upstairs.

What was it everyone said? Get real?

Real fact number one: a work crew armed with pneumatic hammers had invaded her skull.

Real fact number two: she'd just finished her period, so her hormones were probably involved, too. Which didn't help matters.

Real fact number three: she had probably imagined the whole thing.

Sighing heavily—again—she turned to go inside. That's when she saw the figure silhouetted against the sunset on the upper deck of the cottage next door. The cottage that was supposed to be empty.

They stared at each other across the fifty or so feet of beach sand that separated the two elaborate cottages. He was holding something in his hand—something that was aimed directly at her.

A *gun?*

She swallowed hard and forgot to breathe. It was impossible to tell what it was from this distance. The only gun she'd ever met up close and personal was the old .410 her father used to use for squirrel- and rabbit-hunting.

The thing she was staring at now was small and squarish. Actually, it looked more like some kind of a camera than a gun, but then, there were all sorts of weird weapons in use these days. Tapers—tasters—something like that.

Common sense—admittedly not her greatest strength—said that if he'd meant her any harm, he would have made his move when she'd been lying there half-asleep and helpless. He was probably just taking pictures for one of the rental agencies. She would never even have noticed him if his shadow hadn't passed over her.

Against the low-angled sun, she couldn't make out his features, but his silhouette indicated broad shoulders that tapered to narrow hips before his body disappeared behind the deck railing. Before she could clamp down on it, her imagination supplied a few more details, and she turned away in disgust.

"It has to be these flaming hormones," she muttered. For all she knew he could be an escaped prisoner who'd spent the winter hiding out in a closed cottage, which was a whole lot more comfortable than hiding out in the mountains like Eric whatsisname, that guy who had eluded the FBI for about a dozen years. Only now that the season was about to get underway, he had to get out and find another hiding place. As for those shoulders, he'd probably developed them busting rocks on a chain gang. Maybe that thing he was holding was one of those gizmos that broke glass or read the combination on a wall safe, or—

She simply *had* to stop reading so much romantic suspense!

What was that old saying about the better part of valor? In the stress of the moment it escaped her, but right now the better part of valor was slipping inside where she'd left her purse and dialing 911 on her cell phone, just in case. Like any sensible woman, which she devoutly hoped she was, but secretly suspected she wasn't, Sasha had the emergency number on speed dial.

Pretending nonchalance, she crossed to the sliding doors, slipped inside and looked around frantically for her purse, breathlessly watching over her shoulder for someone to burst through the door.

"Hello? Yes, this is Sasha Lasiter. I'm at Driftwinds cottage in Kitty Hawk." She gave the milepost and the street number—at least she remembered that much. "Look, there's a man in the cottage next door that's supposed to be closed, and either he's pointing a weapon or taking pictures of me. Yes, I'm sure!" she replied indignantly when asked. "Well, whatever that thing is he's holding, he was aiming it at me."

Maybe he was—maybe he wasn't, but if she wanted help she needed to make out a worst-case scenario. "Look, I know—" She broke off in exasperation. "No, I am *not* in the hot tub! I am fully dressed, but I *happened* to be outside on the upper deck, and—" Impatiently, she explained what she was doing in an unoccupied cottage. "I don't *remember* if I locked up behind me or not!" She was pretty sure she hadn't. She listened as the flat voice gave instructions, then broke in and said, "Look, I am not about to take a chance on reaching my car and risk being mugged, so could you please send someone to check him out?"

Feeling discouraged, a little bit frightened and in no mood to finish what she'd started earlier, she refused to stay on the line. Instead, she headed for the kitchen and located a block of kitchen knives. Armed with a filet knife that she would never have the nerve to use, she made her way back upstairs and looked around for the most defensible place to wait. She hadn't been lying when she'd told the dispatcher she was afraid to go outside. A friend of hers had recently been mugged in a parking lot not two miles from here. Her own car was parked close enough to the house so that she could probably unlock it with a remote, jump in and lock it again before anyone could grab her, only her remote didn't work anymore—she wasn't even sure it was still in her purse.

Besides, how safe was a convertible? The top was aluminum, not rag, but even if she got away, who was to say the creep wouldn't follow her home?

Who would ever have thought that being an interior decorator at a beach resort could be a hazardous occupation?

"Hey, Jake. We just got a call from some lady that says you're spooking her out." The lanky deputy stepped onto the upper deck from the outside stairway.

"Hey, Mac. How'd you know it was me?"

"Call came from next door, but I saw your wheels parked outside, figured you'd know what was going down. You working?"

"I was. Sorry if I upset the lady. I yelled at her, but she'd already gone inside."

"Oh, yeah—like yelling at a woman always sweetens 'em up. So, you want to tell me what you're doing? She said you were either aiming a gun at her or taking her picture."

"Pictures. Hell, Mac, you know I can't tell you who I'm working for." John Smith, otherwise known as Jake, squinted against the low-angled sun. "Divorce case. Woman thinks her husband's got a little something going on the side. She wants some backup evidence before she files. I figured I'd check out their cottage first since it was empty. The guy's pretty well known in the area, so I figured he wouldn't risk being seen at a motel with another woman."

"Any luck?"

"Not yet. I just started today."

The deputy nodded. Mac Scarborough had been three years ahead of Jake's son, Tim, at Manteo High, but they'd known each other the way people in small towns did. Then, too, being in the security business, Jake knew most of the lawmen in the surrounding area.

"How's Timmy? He gone over there yet?" the young deputy asked.

"Shipping out any day now." Jake shook his head. "I don't mind telling you, I wish he'd joined you guys instead of the army."

"Yeah, well…wait a few weeks till the season cranks up. You'll be glad he's over there working on heavy equipment in a war zone instead of rounding up DUIs and busting up drug deals and trying to untangle pileups at every intersection between Oregon Inlet and the Currituck Bridge." The deputy shook his head. "Ah, hell, man, I'm sorry."

Jake ignored both the reminder of his loss and the apology. "You wouldn't trade your job for one any place else in the world, and you know it."

Grinning, the younger man removed his hat and raked his fingers through short, sun-bleached hair. "You got that right. I guess nothing goes on here on the Banks that don't go on a whole lot more in the big cities. Leastwise, here we get to go surfing on our day off." He replaced his hat, angling the brim just so. "Reckon I'd better go next door and let that poor lady know you're one of the good guys."

Knowing that whatever chance he'd had of collecting evidence was shot for the time being, Jake said, "Might as well, now that you've scared my red-feathered pigeon off."

"Hey, at least I didn't use my lights and siren." Mac grinned and turned toward the outside stairway. "You take care now, Jake. Tell Timmy I said hey and don't go upsetting any more ladies, y' hear?"

Just then they heard a door slam. Mac hesitated, and then both men leaned over the rail in time to see the shapely redhead run that awkward way women did when they were wearing those ridiculous shoes. She unlocked the door to a fancy red convertible and climbed in, her miniskirt-covered hips being the last thing to disappear before she slammed the door, backed out of the driveway and scratched off down the beach road.

"Well, hell," the deputy muttered.

"Guess that takes care of that," Jake said.

He'd just have to try again tomorrow. Waste another day, probably. Common sense told him if anything was going on over there, as his client seemed to think, it would be during the day, not at night when lights might arouse curiosity in a supposedly empty cottage. The day wasn't a total loss, though. The redheaded woman had obviously been waiting for someone.

He packed away his digital camera, shoved his sunglasses back on his face and jogged down the outside stairs, his mind on the comely redhead. Except for the hair, she reminded him of that classic poster of Marilyn Monroe, especially the ankles. A little shorter—maybe a little rounder. Whoever she was, she had what it took to tempt any man between the ages of can-do and can't-do.

On the other hand, he mused as he climbed into his middle-aged, slightly rusty SUV, since she'd called the law, there was some room for doubt as to her identity. Would she have done that if she'd just stopped by for a little afternoon delight with Jamison?

Either way, pictures of the woman alone weren't going to do Mrs. J. any good. He must've snapped off a dozen shots from different angles before she'd wakened up and caught him at it.

At age forty-one, Jake Smith, owner of a small security business, had allowed his PI license to go largely unused while he was single-handedly raising his son. A few years ago he'd taken a refresher course at Blackwater, one of the world's best security training outfits, which happened to be just up the road in the next county. But as there was far less demand for private investigators than there was for security engineers, he'd concentrated on the latter. Even so, as a spook, even a slightly rusty one, he knew enough to take down the license number of any potential suspect.

Which he had—and which he should have asked Mac to run for him. They occasionally traded favors, JBS Securities and the sheriff's department.

She'd cut over to the bypass and headed north. So did Jake, even though it was getting late and he lived in the opposite direction. On the way, he placed a call to his second-in-command. "Hack, I need some information quick. Red Lexus convertible, I make it about an oh-two model, vanity plate S-A-S-H-A."

"Gimme a minute." The nineteen-year old electronics whiz snapped his gum and ended the call.

Hack was as good as his word. By the time Jake

reached the point of decision—whether to take a right and head toward Southern Shores and points north, or turn west, cross the Wright Memorial Bridge over Currituck Sound and go from there, he had an address.

Muddy Landing. Slapping his hand against the steering wheel, Jake didn't even try to come up with a logical reason for what he was doing. There was a good barbecue place on the way, and he hadn't taken time for lunch.

As for what he hoped to accomplish, that was another matter. The sexy little redhead might or might not have been waiting to meet Jamison, who might or might not have been delayed, scared off or otherwise held up. In an area where either of them might have been recognized, it stood to reason they wouldn't risk meeting in a more public place, not when Jamison owned a big empty cottage with all the comforts of home.

On the other hand, the woman could have had legitimate business there. She might be a rental agent, or even a potential renter. Before he dumped the pictures he needed to find out whether or not she was involved. She was definitely tempting enough, especially compared to Jamison's wife.

But no matter how great the temptation, carrying on an affair in a property you owned was pretty stupid.

He passed the barbecue place, inhaled deeply and promised himself to stop in on his way back. More an overgrown community than a town, Muddy Landing was small enough so that he had little trouble locating the address, even without the gizmo Hack had installed in the SUV.

Nice place, he thought as he pulled up two houses down on the other side of the street, although he wouldn't have chosen to paint a house light purple—orchid or lavender, whatever the color was called—with dark green trim and a red car parked in the driveway. But what the hell, no one had ever accused him of having good taste.

Jake considered the best way to approach her. "You looked like a hot number, so I decided to follow you home," probably wasn't going to cut it. She'd slam the door and call the cops, same as she'd done before, and this time he couldn't blame her.

On the way up the front walk, he tucked in his shirttail and ran a hand over his thick, dark hair. While he waited for someone to answer the doorbell, he took in the details of the well-kept two-story house. He liked the fact that not all the houses were the same style or color. From here he could see three whites, two yellows and a blue. When it came to color, the influence of the nearby beach had evidently spread inland. Over on the Banks, the county commissioners had actually considered limiting the colors a property owner could use. Talk about government running wild. At least on his own two properties in Manteo, some 40 odd miles south, he stuck to plain white, inside and out. Nobody could complain about that. He was in the process of having the duplex repainted and the roof re-shingled, partly because of storm damage, but mostly on account of it was long overdue.

He pressed the button again and was about to give it another try when the door opened. "Ma'am, my name's Jake Smith and I—"

He got no further than that when a short creature with raccoon eyes growled at him. "Leave me alone, I don't want any, I'm not interested, and I don't do surveys."

"Oh, hey—" Jake had the presence of mind to wedge his foot in the opening before she could slam the door shut. "I'm not—that is, I've got credentials." When he reached for his wallet, she lunged and stomped on his foot. Pain streaked all the way up to his groin. "Legitimate business," he grunted through the pain. Quickly, he flashed his PI license and the sheriff's courtesy card he'd been given years ago, that had no official bearing, but hell, he'd have shown her his mama's recipe for cornmeal dumplings if he thought it would help.

"Ma'am, I just wanted to apologize—to explain in case you were still worried."

Was this even the same woman? Same height, same hair color, but instead of that hot little number she'd been wearing less than an hour ago—red miniskirt, thin flouncy top and a pair of sexy spike-heeled ankle-strap shoes—she was covered from the neck down with what looked like a deflated army tent. Her feet were bare, with red toenails and red places on the sides where those pointy-toed shoes had rubbed. As fetching as they were, shoes like that were a crime against nature.

He lifted his gaze to her face while his own throbbing foot held the door open. When a hint of some exotic fragrance drifted past, he inhaled it, eyes narrowing in appreciation.

"You're dead meat," she said flatly. "There's a deputy living two doors away. All I have to do is call him."

"You want to use my cell phone?" He made a motion as if to get it, although he'd left it in the truck.

She blinked and relaxed her death grip on the door. At least, her fingers were no longer white-tipped. Actually, they were red-tipped to match her toenails. "Just state your business and leave," she said grimly. "I'll give you thirty seconds and then I'm calling Darrell."

He might have taken her more seriously if she didn't have eye-makeup smeared halfway down her cheeks. At least he hoped that's what the black and blue stains were, otherwise this might be a worst-case domestic situation. The hair that reminded him of the color of heartwood cedar was mashed flat on one side, standing up on the other. His wife used to call it bed-head.

Hell, maybe this was where she was meeting Jamison. Could they have got their signals crossed? That perfume she was wearing smelled like torrid sex in a tropical garden.

But then, why would she be dressed like this to meet a lover?

Not that even dressed in what looked like a Halloween costume gone wrong, she wouldn't make any normal man think of tangled sheets and damp, silky skin.

"Would you please remove your foot?" she demanded.

Khaki-colored eyes. He could've sworn they were some shade of blue, but then, at any distance of more than a dozen feet, eye color was hard to discern. "Ms. Lasiter, I just wanted to reassure you that—"

The black-rimmed, khaki-colored eyes widened. "How did you know my name?"

Jake thought, I'm too old for this. No matter how good she looked under that disguise—no matter how good she smelled, it just wasn't worth the wear and tear.

But she deserved an answer, and he'd come here expressly for that purpose. Among other things. "I'm in the security business and I was on a job I had to check out your license I'm sorry if I upset you I just wanted you to know you're in no danger from me." He said it all in a single gust of breath, hoping she wouldn't finish breaking every bone in his foot. Now he knew how a fox felt when it was caught in a steel trap.

Jake Smith, Sasha thought. A variation of John Smith. Right. How likely was that? Staring through bleary eyes, she tried to convince herself that the man who called himself Jake Smith was on the level. Silhouetted against the sunset he'd been impressive enough. Up close and personal, he was—

Yes, well regardless of what he was, she didn't need any. Didn't need it, didn't want it, knew better than even to think about it. By the time she'd got home her headache had grown to the four-alarm stage, which meant pills alone weren't going to do much good. Nevertheless, she'd downed three with a swallow of milk from the carton. Then, not bothering to remove her makeup, she'd shed her clothes, pulled on her oldest, most comfortable caftan and fallen into bed with a package of frozen peas over her eyes.

"Just so you know," he said, "I'll probably be there again. I'm not finished with my job."

Even in her semi-demented state, she couldn't help but notice that he was sort of attractive, his tanned, irregular features bracketed by laugh lines and squint lines. Under a shadow of beard there was a shallow cleft on his square jaw. A few strands of gray in his dark hair. Obviously he'd reached the age where a man either started to fall apart or ripened into something truly special.

This one was ripe.

"Well, just so you know, neither am I," she warned,

belatedly coming to her senses. "Finished with my business, that is."

He stepped back, freeing his foot. She didn't wait for him to turn away before slamming the door.

Two

Distracted enough without trying to drive and eat at the same time, Jake ordered a barbecue plate to go and drove the rest of the way to Manteo, a distance of some forty miles, listening to a Molasses Creek CD and thinking about the unusual woman he'd just met.

Sasha Lasiter. It had a ring to it. He wondered if it was her real name. The first thing he'd noticed about her back at the Jamison cottage was her shape. That thing she'd been wearing when he'd tracked her down might have covered her curves, but he'd already seen 'em first-hand. The short skirt and that wispy thing she'd been wearing on top, while it was a lot more than most women wore at the beach, barely covered the essentials. His imagination had filled in the rest.

A guy didn't see curves like that every day. Jake had heard about hourglass figures. Hers fit the description, with maybe twenty-minutes more sand in the bottom than in the top. The fact that those same generous curves extended all the way down to her ankles meant it was probably genetic and not silicon.

Damned fine genes, he mused.

The scent of barbecue drifted up to his nostrils as he crossed the Washington Baum Bridge over Roanoke Sound and headed home. He had a feeling that it might take more than 'cue and fries to satisfy him tonight. His sex life had died of neglect while he was single-handedly raising his son.

Almost as tall as he was, Jake's wife Rosemary had been a local track star and dreamed of making the Olympic team. They'd gone to school together, K through twelve. In the tenth grade Jake had made up his mind to marry her. They'd eloped the week they'd graduated—by that time she had given up on her Olympic dreams. Neither of them had ever regretted it.

Seven years later Rosemary had been killed by a drunk driver at one of those intersections Mac had mentioned. Because of their son, Timmy, Jake had managed to hold it together—just barely. After a year or so of fighting the memories, he had rented out the house he and his wife had bought cheap, decorated on a shoestring and shared, and moved himself and his son into the other side of the duplex where his office was located.

God, how long ago had it been? Sometimes he had trouble visualizing her face. Looking at the pictures—which he hadn't done lately—no longer seemed to help. Not that the styles back then had been all that different—blue jeans were blue jeans; shorts were shorts. But the goofy, self-conscious grins on their faces, especially after Timmy had been born seven-and-a-half months after they'd been married, were hard to relate to after all these years. There were pictures of the tree house he'd built when Timmy was six months old and of the rust bucket they'd bought as a second car and been so proud of.

Somewhere over the next dozen or so years, his memories had turned to memories of photographs instead of memories of the real thing.

"You're getting old, man," he muttered as he let himself into the empty duplex, dodging around a folded drop cloth and two ladders. Funny thing, though—he didn't feel old. As tired as he was and as much as his right foot was starting to ache, he felt younger than he had in years.

Sasha woke when early sunlight slanted through the window across her pillow. Without opening her eyes she lay there for several minutes, thinking of yesterday and the color of light and shadow seen through closed eyes. Holding her breath, she waited to see if her headache was going to smite her again.

The word *smite* reminded her of her father, who had frequently smote with his fists, even after he'd gotten religion. It also reminded her that the church-sponsored box suppers would soon be starting up again, which steered her thoughts directly to the matchmaking game she and her friends had played for the past several years. Daisy had married and moved to Oklahoma. Marty had married, too, but still lived on Sugar Lane. Faylene, the maid they shared, was an invaluable member of the matchmakers, and the weekly box suppers were one of their favorite venues for getting two people together.

They still hadn't found anyone for Lily, the CPA who had moved to Muddy Landing a few years ago. The yachtsman they'd tried last fall hadn't worked out. He'd sailed away; she'd stayed put. Faylene, who cleaned for Lily, had mentioned the letters she got weekly from somewhere in California, that she always put away in a bedroom drawer instead of her desk.

Not that that meant anything, especially as Faye said the letters were written in pencil on lined paper. So maybe she had a child by a previous marriage. Or maybe a niece or nephew…

One who wrote once a week?

Sasha thought of her own nieces and nephews. She was lucky to see their signatures on the birthday and Christmas cards her sisters sent.

Rolling over onto her side, she thought about Jake Smith, wondering if he was married or otherwise involved. If not, they might want to add him to their list of candidates. Whatever else he was, he was definitely one studly hunk.

As random thoughts came and went—she was always at her most creative early in the morning—she made a mental note to check with Katie at Southern Dunes Property Management to see if there were any new cottages going up. Might as well get her bid in early.

Satisfied that her headache was gone, her sinuses no longer in rebellion, she sat up, did a few minimal exercises and headed for the shower.

Jake Smith had said he wasn't finished with whatever it was he'd been doing in the cottage next door. Adjusting the water temperature, she wondered idly what he'd been doing when the deputy she'd called had showed up. She'd seen the two of them together just before she'd made a run for it. Whatever it was, he hadn't been arrested, so it was probably nothing illegal, after all.

My mercy, that felt good! Hot water beat down on her shoulders, softening the muscles where stress always grabbed her. She could do with a good deep-tissue massage if she could ever find time.

He'd said he was in the security business. He'd probably been either installing a new system or repairing an old one, in which case he was probably one of those technical types who spoke a language she'd never even tried to master. She used a computer only because she had to, but she wouldn't know a RAM from a nanny goat, a gig from a crab-net. She read instructions only when she was forced to and even then she rarely understood a word. When it came to disarming and re-arming the gizmos people used to protect their property, she usually managed to follow simple written instructions of the do-this-and-then-do-that variety, but occasionally she screwed up and had to call for help. Basically she was a big-picture woman in a small-picture world.

So he was a security man. Big deal. He and Lily would probably find loads of things in common to talk about in intricate detail.

Increasingly relaxed, Sasha worked coconut-scented, color-care shampoo through her thick, wavy hair. She was still toying with questions and answers concerning yesterday's mini-adventure when she dried off, lotioned generously and dressed for work in a long skirt topped with a yellow T and a gauzy camisole. Her skirts were getting just a wee bit snug in the hips. Not in the waistbands—whenever she gained a pound, it went straight to her hips, never her waist or her boobs. If she'd been born a century earlier she'd have been right in style, complete with a built-in bustle.

Unfortunately, long, lean and selectively silicon-enhanced was today's style. As she was none of the above, she was forced to make the best of what she had.

Which she did with—she hoped—style, taste and panache.

By the time she had breakfasted on a doughnut—just one, as she was dieting—and a homemade latte and gotten dressed, the temperature had climbed into the low seventies. As there wasn't a single cloud in the sky, she put down the top on the convertible that had been her thirty-fifth birthday gift to herself. Her foundation was a high SPF, but even so she tied on a wide-brimmed hat, letting the scarf-ends trail out behind her.

Hadn't some famous actress died that way when her scarf got tangled around a wheel? She might not have a college degree, but she prided herself on having a wealth of trivia at her fingertips.

Just past the bridge over the Currituck Sound, she stopped at her favorite coffee shop and ordered a hammerhead to go. In case her headache threatened again— and even if it didn't—she could do with the double shot of caffeine.

Several minutes later she pulled into the paved parking area beside the Jamison cottage. A single glance told her that the parking area next door was empty. She refused to admit to being disappointed. Judging from what she knew about men—and she could have written a book on the species—the studly security man was probably still in bed.

A morning person herself, Sasha had practically been forced to pry all four of her ex-husbands out of bed. Frank had been born lazy. Barry had worked nights, which gave him a legitimate reason, she admitted reluctantly. But Rusty had simply preferred to sleep late and play late, gambling and partying till all hours, usually without her.

As for Larry, her first husband, met and married in a mad, mad weekend the month before she'd turned nineteen, she couldn't even remember what his excuse had been, unless it was because he knew it drove her crazy. Even as a child she'd been up with the sun, bursting with energy.

The truth was that not a single man she'd made the mistake of marrying had possessed anything resembling a work ethic. Even her father, redheaded, stern-faced Addler Parrish, had sold his tobacco farm and taken up preaching.

Not that he was very good at that, either. Everyone said old Ad was mean as a snake, and she could personally vouch for that. But at least the hours suited him better, giving him plenty of time to lay down the law to his family and punish anyone who broke his rules. Which Sasha had consistently done.

She'd been plain Sally June Parrish back then. Her overworked mother had lacked the strength to defend either herself or her children from her husband's vicious tongue, much less from his belt and his fists. As soon as Sally June could escape she'd left home and found a job stocking and clerking in a furniture dealer's showroom. Within a few years, she began taking night classes at the community college and attending the International Furniture Market in High Point with her employer.

By that time she'd been married to Larry Combs, a Jude Law lookalike who couldn't manage to hang on to a job for more than a few months. He'd claimed to be overqualified. What he'd been was under-motivated. Larry had been the first. Her second husband had been even better-looking, and witty, besides.

Unfortunately, he'd also been a crook.

With two brief marriages behind her, she had left the Greensboro area and started her eastward migration, eventually leaving behind two more ex-husbands. None of her marriages had provided her with what she so desperately needed—a close and loving family. And none had lasted much longer than a year. By the time she'd moved to Muddy Landing and set herself up as an interior decorator, Sally June had become Sasha. She had stuck with her fourth husband's name because it was easier than changing everything again.

Besides, it sounded good with Sasha.

She'd chosen Muddy Landing because at the time, property in Currituck County had been comparatively cheap. That was rapidly changing as more and more of it was developed, but the location was perfect, being little more than an hour from the Norfolk shopping area and less than half that from the Outer Banks where building was booming and decorating jobs were plentiful.

That had been eleven—no, nearly thirteen years ago. Once it gathered momentum, time seemed to fly. At the age of thirty-eight, thirty-five years of which she admitted to, Sasha was single for keeps. Each time she'd married she'd been certain she'd finally found her prince.

Instead she'd found another poor jerk who thought that learning to dress and speak well would alter who he was. Underneath the designer sportswear, the fancy colognes and the rip-off Rolexes, they'd all been every bit as insecure as she had once been, the difference being that they'd lacked her guts, her brutal self-honesty and her relentless drive to succeed.

She might joke with her friends about looking for number five, but before she would ever allow herself to get involved with another man, she would let her hair go natural, dump all her makeup in the North Landing River and turn her jewelry into fishing lures.

Parked in the shade of the Jamison cottage, she sat outside for a few minutes, savoring the perfect spring weather and the last of the double-strength coffee. She should be able to wind things up here in an hour, with some time to spare.

Opening the door, she swung her legs out and sat there for a moment, savoring the relative quiet of the early morning. A week from now, traffic would have doubled and most of the cottages would be filled, but for now the quiet cul-de-sac was almost like a private retreat.

Leaving the top down, she trudged up the first flight of outside stairs, unlocked the main door and disarmed the security system. The place still smelled of stale cigarette smoke, so she left the sliding glass doors open to air it out. Mosquitoes weren't yet a problem as they'd had a record dry spring. On the next level up, she opened another door, drawing air from below.

At least she didn't turn the air-conditioning full blast with all the doors and windows open the way too many thoughtless tenants did.

Humming under her breath, she began double-checking the list she'd made yesterday to make sure that everything that had been lost, stolen or damaged had been replaced. The new bar stools had been delivered. She checked that off her list. Climbing to the top level, she took a good look around to confirm that she hadn't overlooked anything. Once she was done, she slid open the glass doors on the top floor and stepped out onto the sundeck, her favorite place of all. Ignoring the spectacular view of dunes and ocean, she glanced at the cottage next door.

Not that she'd expected to see him—the parking area next door was empty. Not that she even wanted to see him, but he'd said he wasn't finished with whatever it was he was doing over there—installing, updating or repairing a security system.

She told herself she wasn't disappointed, and really, she wasn't. Not for herself. But for months now she and her friends had been looking for a candidate for Lily Sullivan, the beautiful blond CPA with the sad eyes who lived a few streets over from Marty's house. So far as anyone knew—Faylene could find out more about a person from their garbage alone than any CIA agent— Lily had no social life at all.

The trouble was that there were so few available men around—certainly none who might interest a woman who was both attractive and intelligent. The best had already been taken; the rest were too old, too young, too dull or too dumb.

Ironically, over the past couple of years it had been Daisy and Marty, two of the original matchmakers, who had skimmed the cream off the top, with Daisy marrying Kell Magee when he'd come east to check out a relative, and Marty marrying the yummy carpenter she'd hired to renovate her house.

And she wasn't envious, she really wasn't! As she turned to go, one of her heels slipped between two boards. Flailing her arms for balance, she grabbed at the chaise longue, which slid away from her, throwing her even more off balance. Pain shot up her left leg. Trying to catch herself as she went down on her behind, she jammed her fingers on the sun-warped deck.

"Oh, help, oh, shoot, oh, damn, damn, *damn!*" She rocked back and forth, clutching her ankle with one hand and waving the other hand in the air, her shoe heel still trapped in the crack between boards.

Seeing that the pink suede covering the five-inch heel was ruined, she cried out in frustration as well as pain. She'd paid dearly for these shoes, knowing that nothing flattered a woman's legs like a good pair of spike heels. Especially a woman who had stopped growing—at least vertically—in the fifth grade. Having been told at an early age that redheads shouldn't wear pink, she'd gone out of her way to wear something pink on every possible occasion, even if it was only pink tourmaline jewelry.

With trembling fingers, she managed to unbuckle the ankle strap, unwrap it and ease her foot from the arrow-shaped toe that looked so gorgeous she usually didn't even notice the torture.

Oh, gross! Her ankle was already starting to look like an overstuffed sausage. Not only that, she had popped three fingernails and collected a handful of splinters that would probably give her blood poisoning. Didn't they use arsenic to treat the lumber for these beach houses? Did that include the sundecks?

At least she managed to unfasten her gold ankle bracelet before it cut off circulation. Oh God, she was going to die right here on the top deck of an empty cottage. The sun would turn her red as a boiled crab. Her nose would blister, seagulls and ospreys would drop disgusting things on her body—

Her cell phone—she'd left it in her purse inside. If she could just get up she could use one of the plastic chairs as a walker and hop inside to call 911. Although after yesterday…

Maybe a different dispatcher would be on in the mornings.

Tears streamed down her cheeks, leaking trails of mascara through her blusher, dripping off her chin onto her Tilly MacIntire blouse. She unfastened her other shoe and tossed it aside. What good was one shoe when its mate was ruined? If it weren't for the fact that nothing flattered a woman's legs like putting them on a pedestal—and she was just vain enough to want every advantage she could possibly get—she'd burn the treacherous things the minute she got home.

But first she had to get there.

She was on her knees, trying to grab the leg of a chair and drag it closer when she heard someone step out onto the sundeck behind her.

"What the devil have you done to yourself?" a familiar voice boomed.

Startled, she twisted around and stared up at the voyeur—the man who had scared the wits out of her just yesterday.

Oh, please, her inner woman groaned, not like this!

"Help?" she said weakly.

* * *

By the time they were in Jake's SUV on the way to the hospital in Nags Head, Sasha had set aside her misery to make three firm vows. First, no more five-inch heels—at least not when she was working. Second, starting now she would cut her carb count in half. No more Krispy Kremes, no more double lattes.

In other words, no more anything worth eating.

Jake had insisted on carrying her down the stairs. As her only option was bouncing on her butt all the way down, which would've left her rear end in the same shape as her right hand, she'd let him sweep her up into his arms. As if pain alone weren't bad enough, the feel of being cradled against a hard, warm body had rattled her to the point that she hadn't even argued.

She'd already forgotten the third vow, but it probably concerned steering clear of any man who could melt her resistance with no more than a growl, a glower and the way he smelled. Like soap, toothpaste and coffee, plus something earthy and essentially male.

Not to mention the fact that his touch alone was like poking her finger into a light socket.

She'd still been quivering inside when he'd settled her onto the passenger seat and arranged something to prop her foot on. He'd reached for the seatbelt and she'd brushed his hands away. "I can do it myself."

"Then do it," he'd snapped.

What the devil did *he* have to be angry about, she wondered, feeling sorry for herself and, oddly excited at the same time. She was the one with a broken ankle, not him. She was the one whose right hand was probably going to get infected and swell up and have to be amputated. Plus, she'd probably end up with blood poisoning. For all she knew she might be allergic to antibiotics. So she'd die of anaphylactic shock or whatever grisly symptoms that sort of allergy caused.

He drove fast, easing off each time he approached the stoplights so that he wouldn't have to slam on the brakes if a light suddenly changed. Grudgingly, she appreciated it. Her ankle throbbed like a bad toothache, and she hated pain, purely hated it. Always had. A stoic, she was not.

"You all right?" he asked as they passed the Wright Brothers Memorial at Kill Devil Hill. At least he'd quit growling. In fact, he sounded almost concerned.

"No, I'm not all right, I hurt," she snapped. Childish, but then, what did she have to lose that she hadn't already lost? Her dignity?

Ha.

"We'll be there in a few more minutes," he said. "This time of year, you probably won't have to wait. They'll give you something for pain and then do X-rays, my guess." He had propped her foot up on a plastic carton he'd padded with a folded shirt. She was cradling her splintery hand in her other hand on her lap. "What's wrong, did you hurt your hand, too?" he asked.

Well, shoot. Now he even sounded sympathetic. She couldn't handle sympathy. It had been in short supply back when she could have used it—back when she'd spent her lunch money on cheap makeup to conceal bruises inflicted by her father's fists, only to have him accuse her of painting her face like a hussy. Which often as not earned her a few more bruises.

Jake pulled up in front of the beach hospital and said, "Wait while I go get a wheelchair."

"Don't be silly, I don't need a wheelchair." She had never even been to a hospital before, except as a visitor.

"Okay then, put your arm over my shoulder." He leaned into the open door and eased his arm under her knees.

If she'd had a single rational thought in her head before, it was gone by the time he carried her inside. The man was definitely high-voltage.

"You'll have to do the paper work," he told her, "but I'll see if I can't speed up the process."

Two women behind glass windows stared. Several people in the waiting room glanced up from their outdated *People* magazines.

"Oh, for heaven's sake, put me down," Sasha muttered. At this rate she wouldn't even need a doctor's help. Being this close to Jake Smith, whoever he was—whatever he was—was distracting enough that she hardly even noticed her throbbing ankle, much less her stinging hand.

Just under two hours later an orderly wheeled her out to the waiting room. Laying aside the newspaper he'd read without retaining a single word, Jake stood to meet her. "All done?" he asked. No cast, just a wrap job, which meant a bad sprain, not a break. "What's with the hand?" Her right hand was bandaged, all but two fingers and her thumb.

"Splinters. I lost three fingernails, too."

His eyes widened. "Good God, that's awful!" he swallowed hard, fighting back nausea.

"I think another one's loose and I just had them done last week. Now I'll have to get the whole right hand done over." Glancing over her shoulder, she thanked the orderly. "I can make it from here just fine," she assured him with a smile that was undiminished by chewed-off lipstick and smeared mascara.

"It's the rules, ma'am," the orderly said, refusing to dump her out of the wheelchair.

Jake shook his head. He crossed to the double glass doors and held it wide. "Come on, don't be so stubborn."

Together, the two men eased her from the wheelchair onto the front seat. Jake slipped the orderly a few bucks—didn't know if it was proper or not, but the kid was about Timmy's age. Might even have been a classmate.

They drove several miles in silence except for a few heavy sighs coming from the passenger side. The first time they stopped for a red light, Jake tried to get a handle on how bad she was hurting. "We'll stop by and get your prescription filled, then we'll cut over to the beach road and put the top up on your car. It should be all right there for a few days until you can drive."

"Oh, wait a minute—just hold on, I'm not leaving my car unattended."

"You feel up to driving?" He looked pointedly at her ankle, which was once again propped on the padded carton.

"It's not a stick shift."

"Sasha—Ms. Lasiter—look at it from my perspective. If I dump you out in Kitty Hawk, I won't sleep a wink wondering if you made it home all right. It'd be criminal negligence at the very least if anything happened to you." They must've given her something for pain. From the way she was blinking her eyes, the lady was floating around in la-la land.

"I can call a taxi."

"That won't help you move your car. Look, I got you safely to the hospital, didn't I? Don't you trust me to get you home?"

Another milepost zipped past. He turned off onto the street that dead-ended at a row of oceanfront cottages that were identical but for color and the placement of a few exterior details. Driftwinds, where she'd left her car, was the next to last one on the cul-de-sac.

"You shouldn't have to drive me all the way to Muddy Landing."

She was softening, he could tell. Truth was, he didn't know why he was going to all this trouble. He should be working on the Jamison case, especially since so far his stakeout had produced zilch.

"You like barbecue?" he asked, climbing back into the SUV after pulling her car into the paved space underneath the cottage, putting the top up and locking it.

Nice wheels. The lady had good taste. He handed her the keys and backed out onto the street.

"Who doesn't?" She was picking at the bandage on her hand, and he reached over and covered both of hers with one of his.

"Leave it alone," he said. "Didn't your mama ever tell you not to pick at stuff like that?"

That warranted a fleeting smile. He had a feeling she was hurting more than wanted to let on, even after whatever they'd given her at the hospital. Which was kind of surprising, because judging by her looks alone he'd have figured her for a complainer.

Not until some ten minutes later when he came out with two barbecue plates and climbed back under the wheel did it occur to Jake that either they were going to share a late lunch or he was going to eat his share cold somewhere else. "Should I have gotten some drinks to go with it?" he asked as they rolled onto the bridge over Currituck Sound.

"I've got iced tea," she said, which pretty much answered the question.

"Tea's good." Jake pushed in a CD and whistled under his breath, keeping time with the music with his thumb tapping against the steering wheel.

With work piling up, his home and his office in a mess and the Jamison case going nowhere, he had no business being where he was, doing what he was doing. He'd never been the impulsive type.

On the other hand, when he started something, he always liked to carry it through. In his business, following procedure was the only way to get the job done.

Oh, yeah? And what have you started this time?

Three

Sasha desperately needed to reach her own front door unaided, if only to assert her independence, but after the first few steps she grudgingly accepted Jake's help. This had definitely not been one of her better days. Awkwardly, she dug out her keys. He took them from her uninjured hand. "It's the key with the fingernail polish," she told him.

Independence could wait another few minutes.

Without releasing her, he managed to unlock the front door. "Want me to carry you over the threshold?"

Her look said it all. Over my dead body. Sprained, splintered and disheveled didn't count.

Once inside, he steered her toward the three-cushion sofa. "First, let's get you elevated. Then if you'll point me to the kitchen, I'll make you an ice pack."

"How do you know what I need?"

This time it was *his* look that said it all. "Trust me, I've seen a sprain or two. Underneath that bandage you're probably already turning purple."

Sasha wanted to tell him to take his sympathy and his barbecue plate and go back to wherever he came from, because she didn't need him.

Only she did. This was Faylene's day to work for Lily, and Marty was just back from her honeymoon, still busy washing sand and salt out of her trousseau.

"The doctor called it a type-II sprain. He said something about torn ligaments, but I wasn't really listening." Admittedly, she had a few bad habits, one of them being deflecting bad news by concentrating on something else. In this case, she'd been focused on the possibility of insuring her more expensive shoes. "He mentioned ice. I think there's a gel pack somewhere in the freezer, but I usually use frozen vegetables."

"You do this often?"

While she gave him her patented supercilious look— naturally arched eyebrows tinted half a shade darker than her hair helped—he eased her down onto the sofa and gently lifted her legs up onto the cushions, which involved a lot more touching than she needed at the moment. Her skirt twisted around her hips and she tugged at it with her good hand, wishing she'd worn something longer. She had mini and maxi, nothing in between.

"Here, let's lift your foot up and slide a pillow under your heel." His voice was like blackstrap molasses— rich and sweet, but with a definite bite.

While she wondered where he came by his expertise, he slipped another pillow under her knee, which involved more touching. Considering she was still in ap-preciable pain, even after a dose of prescription-strength anti-inflammatory medication, she shouldn't even have noticed. If she didn't know better, she might think her whole body had been sensitized. The slightest brush with sumac and she broke out in a rash. The slightest brush of Jake Smith's hands on her thigh or the back of her knee raised goose bumps in places he hadn't even touched.

Granted, she'd been on a self-imposed diet these past few years, but she wasn't *that* starved for mascu-line attention.

He stepped back and looked her over. "There, that better?"

Wordlessly, she nodded, feeling her cheeks burn. The curse of a redhead's thin skin. "This is so embarrassing."

"No need to be embarrassed, it could happen to anybody."

If she read him right—and she was good at reading people—he might as well have added, Anybody crazy enough to wear skyscraper shoes lashed to her ankles. Was there such a thing as breakaway ankle straps?

"How's the hand?" His were on his hips. Tanned, ca-pable hands planted firmly on narrow masculine hips.

Just quit thinking what you're thinking! "It's fine." She looked down at the fingers she'd jammed. Her newly exposed natural nails looked like naked little orphans.

"Sit tight, I'll be back with your ice pack in a minute."

"No hurry. I think I'll get up and tap dance on the cof-fee table."

He shot her a quick grin as he headed for the kitchen. Distracted, she almost forgot her misery. He had a nice smile. He had a *really* nice backside, which she noticed only because it was more or less at her eye level as he left the room. Strong legs, too—at least he hadn't dropped her when he was carrying her down all those steps.

Not that she would have fallen too far, the way she'd clung to him with both arms.

"Peas or corn, either one will do fine," she called after him.

"Got it."

"You do this a lot?" he asked again a few moments later as he shaped a bag of frozen peas around her bandaged ankle. "Use ice packs, I mean."

"Headaches," she said, and then snapped her mouth shut. Just because he happened to be there when she'd needed a hand—just because he'd driven her to the hospital and waited for her, stopped at the drive-in window of the pharmacy while her prescription was being filled, taken care of her car for her and then driven her home after stopping to get barbecue—that didn't mean he needed to know her entire life history.

On the other hand, there was Lily, who definitely needed a man if Faylene could be believed. This one just might fill the bill if he happened to be available. The fact that he wasn't wearing a wedding ring didn't mean he was single. Some men didn't.

"Won't your wife be worried?" Well, that was really subtle, wasn't it?

"I called the office to say I might be late."

Was that a yes or a no? Even if he was single, he might not be right for Lily. Men who stayed single past their midthirties were usually confirmed bachelors. She'd read that somewhere.

On the other hand, Muddy Landing's primo match-makers never actually forced a couple to the altar. They simply engineered meetings between needy people in a setting that ensured they'd have to spend a little time together. Not all relationships had to end in marriage. The truth was, marriage itself ended many a good relationship, as both Sasha and Marty could confirm. Between them they'd gone through six husbands, Marty's current bridegroom not included.

"Nice pictures," Jake said, glancing around the cluttered living room.

The rest of her house was even worse. Her personal art collection, which could best be called eclectic, hung in a haphazard pattern on the lime-washed cedar paneling—haphazard because whenever she added to it, she was forced to shift things to make room. Stacked on the floor were nine framed reproductions for two offices she was presently doing.

"Food and a cold drink coming up," Jake said.

In the kitchen, humming under his breath, Jake took a moment to get his bearings. The lady sure did like color. Nothing matched except for a couple of the appliances. One red wall, a couple of pink ones. No curtains at the window, but a bunch of vines hanging down both sides that looked more like sweet potatoes than flowers. But then, he was no gardener—that had been Rosemary's department.

He filled two tumblers with ice, covered the ice with tea from a pitcher in the refrigerator and looked around for a serving tray.

Two o'clock on a workday—not that every day

wasn't a workday—and he was goofing off as if he had all the time in the world. The last time he'd had lunch with a lady was—

Hell, he couldn't even remember the last time.

"Here we go, two barbecue plates, two iced teas," he said, sounding like a snake-oil salesman as he walked into the living room. "You want your barbecue reheated?"

"No thanks, it's fine this way."

"Me, too. Reheating always does something to the flavor."

His social skills had grown rusty with disuse. Small talk defeated him. Besides, what could a hot babe who lived in a lavender house and drove a red Lexus convertible possibly have in common with a middle-aged widower who lived in a half-furnished white-on-white duplex—one who drove a six-year-old SUV with a primer-coated fender he'd never gotten around to repainting?

He watched as she reached for a hush puppy with her good hand. "Why don't I bring a towel to spread over your lap? Eating sideways is kind of awkward."

What was awkward was his being here. He should have just brought her home and left her. Although if he'd done that, she might have gone without lunch. Supper, too.

Ah, hell, she had plenty of friends she could've called on for help. With her looks she probably had to beat off men with a stick. "Look, I can eat in the kitchen if you'd rather be alone. Or leave and take mine with me."

"Oh, for Pete's sake, pull up a chair and use the coffee table. Move the rest of that stuff onto the floor."

He slid her magazines, books and mail to one side to clear a space on the table and drew up a cane-bottomed chair that had two monkeys carved on one of the back panels. She had unique tastes, he'd say that for her. Colorful, too. The rug was one of those oriental types, mostly orange and black. As for the pictures on the wall…yeah, *unique* just about covered it.

"It's an Eisher," she said, following his gaze. "The one beside the escritoire."

As he didn't know an escritoire from an estuary, Jake only nodded. "Interesting," he said, which was usually a safe comment. "You want catsup for those fries?" That was even safer.

Condiments at hand, they applied themselves to the late lunch. It was getting on toward three. Oddly enough, the silence wasn't all that uncomfortable. At least it wouldn't have been if he could have stopped watching her trying to manage with one injured hand and the other one handicapped by long, red fingernails and several rings.

He'd have offered to feed her, but he didn't trust himself to get that close. As it was, it might take a while before he could forget the way she'd felt in his arms when he'd carried her down the outside stairs at the cottage, and from there in to the hospital. As small as she was, there was nothing fragile about her. She was firm, but soft where a woman should be soft.

And then there was the way she smelled, like orange blossoms and incense with a few exotic spices tossed in. Under the right circumstances something like that could easily set off a riot.

In other words, look, but don't touch.

So he looked. The suntan stopped a few inches from the bandage on her bum ankle. Did that mean it was one of those spray-on jobs?

Yeah, probably. With legs like hers, she could've painted them blue and it wouldn't have mattered. Her lips were shiny from the fries and the hush puppies and those thick black eyelashes made her eyes look like the color of the surf in August, before the storms got it all churned up.

Hmm, that was odd. He could've sworn they were tan just yesterday.

Oh, man. That perfume must be messing with his head.

He cleared his throat. "If you're finished, I can take your tray. You want your cell phone handy?" Rising, he looked around for her purse.

"Why would I want that?"

"In case it rings so you won't have to get up? Or to call someone to come stay with you?"

"If it's important they'll call back, and I'm not in the mood for company."

"I just meant—" He started to explain and gave up on it. When it came to defenses, the lady could give lessons to a porcupine.

So he took her leavings to the kitchen, refilled the tumbler with ice and sweet tea and brought it back. Then he removed the cold pack, which was mostly melted, anyway. "Wait a little while, then ice up again. In the meantime, keep your foot elevated. I'll put your prescription here where you can reach it. Let's see…you took the last dose about two." He glanced around for a clock. She looked at her wrist. One of her several bracelets turned out to be a wristwatch. "Every four hours or as needed," he reminded her.

Sasha was glad he'd turned away. She hated being seen at a disadvantage, she purely hated it! She must look like a lump of raw dough with her clothes all twisted around her; with her hair falling out of the carefully casual do she'd started out with this morning and her lipstick chewed off. Heaven only knew what had happened to her eye makeup. At least she'd done nothing to smear her eyeliner or dislodge any of her eyelashes.

"You moonlight as a nurse, right?" she snapped, and was immediately ashamed of herself. She refused to apologize, and that bothered her even more, because she knew better.

Without a word he blotted the rings of moisture from the coffee table, then replaced her magazines and sample books. That mouth of his that could look so sensuous in unguarded moments had tightened into a grim line.

Sasha felt lower than dirt, yet she couldn't bring herself to apologize for her rudeness. God, she was wicked! That saying about pride going before a fall had been one of her father's favorite quotations, usually uttered right before he attempted to beat the pride out of her.

Obviously it hadn't worked.

Jake stepped back, his face expressionless. "If you're sure you don't need anything else, I'll be leaving. Don't forget to ice up again."

"Hand me my purse before you go, I haven't paid you for lunch. I owe you gas money, too."

He looked annoyed, but his voice remained calm. "Just make sure you call someone to sit with you. Tell 'em to bring a book so you won't have to entertain them if you'd rather not, but you're in no shape to take care of yourself."

"Oh, go to hell," she shot back. This time she really would have apologized, but before she could find the words, he was gone. Twisting around to look through the front window, she watched him stride down the front walk. Lordamercy, he looked like a storm waiting to happen. Not that she could blame him.

"Why do I do these things?" she moaned, flopping back onto the cushions. Talk about being your own worst enemy.

Jake was halfway across the Currituck Sound when his cell phone sounded reveille. He punched on and before he could say a word Sasha started rattling off what sounded like an apology, with a garbled explanation that he was in no mood to hear. He broke in, reminding her that she would need someone to take her to Kitty Hawk for her car once she was able to drive again.

"Don't you worry about that one bit," she said earnestly, "I have lots of friends."

He assured her he wasn't worried in the least.

So how come, he wondered as he replaced the phone in its holder, he was trying to think of some excuse to turn around and go back to Muddy Landing?

As to that, how the hell had she gotten hold of his number?

"Dammit, Hack, you know better than to give out my number," Jake said some forty-five minutes later as he slammed the door of his office. The whole damn place reeked of paint. No wonder Miss Martha found so many reasons to stay away. He'd have opened all the windows and cut off the air-conditioning, but Hack insisted the ever-present humidity was lethal to computers.

"The Lasiter woman? Hey, she called here and shot

me this line of bull about leaving something in your car. How was I to know she wasn't on the level?"

"You're paid to know, dammit."

"Whoa, I'm paid to put together the stuff you design and then see that it works. Miss Martha's supposed to handle the phone—that's what you hired her for—only she left early today to go to a funeral. Where you been, anyhow? The Jamison woman called a few hours ago, said for you to call her right back. I tried to get you."

Jake expressed himself in a single succinct oath. A few hours ago he'd been on his way to the emergency room. Hack could have reached him easily…except that he'd left his cell phone in the car.

He had already punched in the first three digits of the Jamison woman's number when it hit him. He didn't have a damn thing to report—at least nothing that was going to help her case.

He replaced the phone without completing the call while Hack looked on, his thin face showing equal parts of amusement and curiosity. Without a word, Jake opened the door to his private office, which was roughly the size of three phone booths and was currently crowded with five phone-booths' worth of stuff that had been shifted from room to room as the painting pro-gressed. The entire duplex was undergoing repairs that had been put off too long. The roof had been damaged in last fall's hurricane and a tree had damaged it further when it had fallen on one corner of the house during a hard northeaster. Things were generally in a mess.

And so was he.

Her shoe. When he'd carried her downstairs from the sundeck, he'd scooped it up and stuck it in his hip pocket, then tossed it onto the back seat. No way was she going to get those straps around her ankle anytime soon, but if she wanted the thing, he could drop it off tomorrow. Or the next day. No hurry, he told himself as he reached for the Jamison file.

On the other hand, it wouldn't hurt to call and let her know he had it.

Sasha hobbled to the bedroom and changed into something more comfortable, then took out a bag of corn from the freezer and settled back on the couch to call her friend. Marty and Greg had just returned from honeymooning at a place called Isla Mujeres, otherwise known as the island of women, in the Mexican Caribbean. "Hi, you rested up from all those sleepless nights yet?"

She switched the phone to the other ear and adjusted the cold pack on her ankle. Earlier she'd removed the bandage to see how bad it looked, as if she'd needed the reminder of just how stupid she could be when she put her mind to it. From now on whenever she had any more than three steps to climb, she would wear sensible shoes if it killed her—as it probably would. Anything labeled *sensible* was definitely lethal to the ego.

"Look, I might have somebody for Lily," Sasha said without preamble, and then had to wait through another rapturous description of everything from the Mexican cuisine to the music to the local legends. She'd heard it all yesterday. "About this man for Lily?" she said when her friend paused for breath. "I'm pretty sure he's single. He's about an eleven on a scale of ten, and—"

She listened to a spate of questions and a recipe for

huevos rancheros, Isla-style. When she could squeeze in another word, she said, "Thanks, hon. Compared to Faylene I'm a regular Julia Child, but I'm not about to try to cook anything I can't spell. Now, back to Jake— I don't know if he's currently involved or not, we'll need to check on it, but—"

Sasha tapped her remaining acrylic nails on the coffee table as her thoughts returned to the man who had taken her other shoe and thrown it away, for all she knew. He hadn't called back, but then, she'd been on the phone practically ever since he'd left. First she'd called her friend Daisy to see when the baby was due, then she'd called the hospital to ask how long before she could drive again.

Evidently the hospital wasn't about to invite a lawsuit by offering an opinion without another on-site examination, which wasn't even a faint possibility. She had several hundred dollars more out-of-pocket expense before her high-deductible insurance would kick in. She wasn't even certain how her policy treated emergency-room visits, as she hadn't bothered to read the fine print.

"Who, Daisy?" she repeated as Marty's excited voice recalled her to the present. "She's due in about three weeks, I just talked to her. Greg promised to let me know, and I'll fly out."

"But you hate flying," Marty reminded her.

"My sinuses hate flying. The rest of me can take it or leave it, as long as it's in first class." For Daisy, she would risk a monster headache. The third member of the original matchmaking trio, Daisy was expecting in June, and Sasha had promised to stand as the baby's godmother. A godchild, even one out in Oklahoma, might help fill the sense of emptiness that been growing inside her for years.

It was that same feeling of emptiness, not to mention a ticking biological clock that had driven her through four marriages in search of a prospective father for the child she wanted so desperately. She'd been married to husband number four when she discovered that, thanks to an early bout of endometriosis, her prospects for motherhood were dismal, at best.

"Okay, hon, then I'll see you in a day or so," she promised and laid her cell phone on top of a wallpaper sample book.

The antique monkey chair made an acceptable walker as long as she took care to plant all four legs squarely on the floor. She hadn't mentioned her accident to Marty, knowing her friend would drop everything and rush over. If there was one thing Sasha didn't need, it was hovering friends. She'd been called the proverbial hog on ice more than once, but she prided herself on her independence. It hadn't come easy.

She was halfway to the kitchen to exchange defrosted corn for frozen peas when the phone rang again. She was tempted to ignore it, but she'd been expecting a call from the Driftwinds property manager.

Instead of Katie McIver, she heard a male voice that affected her like velvet sliding over naked skin. "Hi, Cinderella, you missing a slipper?"

Four

"**Y**ou have my shoe?" she said breathlessly. Sasha was never breathless, not unless she'd just dashed up three flights of stairs. Definitely not over the mere sound of a voice—or even over half a pair of shoes that had cost far more than she could afford. As miserable as they were, the suffering was worth it when it added five extra inches to her height and called attention to her best feature—her legs.

"The heel's pretty messed up," Jake told her, "I guess you could peel off the rest of the leather and paint it to match the other one. Want me to bring it to you?"

"Oh, that's too much trouble." Unconsciously, she smoothed her disheveled hair. She was wearing her comfortable old caftan and hadn't bothered to put on her face.

"I'll be up in your neck of the woods this afternoon."

He paused, as if testing the atmosphere. "I could drop it off then."

She wanted to tell him not to bother, but even more than she wanted her ruined shoe back, she wanted to see him again. Considering the way they'd met—considering even more her deplorable record with men—it didn't make a speck of sense. But there it was. All she had to do was look at Jake Smith to forget everything she'd ever learned about men. He wasn't even all that handsome, technically speaking. But then, fancy looks, fancy clothes, fancy cars and fancy manners weren't worth a lick of spit when push came to shove.

At least nothing about Jake Smith was fancy.

Nothing except for the way he made her feel.

Besides, he'd already seen her at her worst, looking like a raccoon with eye makeup smeared over half her face, wearing an ancient caftan that should have been relegated to the rag bag years ago. And that was even before he'd risked a hernia by carrying her down all those stairs.

Had anyone ever noticed that good Samaritans could be sexy as well as useful?

"I suppose as long as you're coming this way, you might as well drop it off," she said as graciously as possible.

"See you in about an hour, then. You need anything I could pick up for you? I'll be passing by a couple of shopping centers."

Her mind fogged out on her. All she could think of was her hair, her face—the awful thing she was wearing.

"No? Okay, see you later then. If you think of anything you need, call me on my cell phone, all right? You have the number."

He waited. She waited. Neither of them spoke until he said, "Where are you, anyway, lying down?"

"I'm halfway between the living room and the kitchen," she told him as she clumped her way toward the sofa.

"Have you iced up lately? Look, the sooner you quit fooling around, the sooner you'll be able to drive again."

She was tempted to ask if that meant she had a choice between driving or fooling around. Fortunately, common sense intervened, because the choice was not even close.

He's for Lily, you dunce!

Nearly two hours passed before Jake pulled up in front of the lavender house with the dark green trim. He glanced at the rearview mirror and raked a hand through his hair. He was overdue a trim, but at least he was freshly shaved. Restless, he'd woken about five and gone next door to the office, where he'd made inroads in the stack of paperwork on his desk until the roofers had started hammering.

Shortly after that, Hack and Miss Martha had come in and he'd gone next door to shower and shave before the crew arrived to finish painting. A few more days, he thought as he headed north on the bypass, and the old place was going to look pretty damn good, if he did say so himself.

He happened to be wearing the new polo shirt Timmy had given him for his last birthday. Jake had taken it as a hint that his wardrobe could use some attention—at least the kid hadn't given him a necktie. He'd even splashed on a little cologne, God knows why. Keep the stuff from going bad in the bottle, probably. He never used it.

Some forty-five minutes later he reached into the back seat for the paper cone of flowers. They'd been right beside the checkout counter at the grocery store. He'd made a quick stop, figuring Sasha probably needed a few basics—more frozen vegetables, maybe some juice, a six-pack of canned drinks and a box of doughnuts. Milk, too, because bones needed calcium. And flowers because—because, well, why not?

He punched the doorbell and then tried the knob. It turned and the door opened. "Sasha? Don't get up." A security specialist, he thought about mentioning her unlocked door but decided against it. Right now she didn't need to be jumping up every time the doorbell rang.

With two plastic sacks and the six-pack in one hand, the flowers in the other, he peered into the living room. "There you are," he said, stating the obvious.

And there she was, looking even better than he'd remembered.

Jake had never been partial to redheads—he'd never been partial to any particular type, for that matter. Rosemary had been tall, lean, blond and athletic. But the way Sasha looked with her hair all soft and coppery around her face and her eyes shining like emeralds—

Emeralds? Yesterday they'd been blue.

The day before that they'd been tan.

"Those are lovely," she said, her full red lips widening in a smile.

Jake stared at the bouquet he was holding as if he'd never seen the thing before. "Uh—yeah, they caught my eye, too, so I thought I might as well…" He shrugged. "You got a vase or something? They probably need some water."

Damn, he thought as he ran water into a tall crystal vase he'd found following her directions, you'd think he was Timmy's age instead of old enough not only to have sown his oats, but harvested the crop.

He put the drinks in the refrigerator, the frozen vegetables that he'd selected by feel and not by label, in the freezer. The doughnuts, he left on the table. "You need more ice on your ankle?" he called.

"I guess so. It's been a while."

"How about something cold to drink? Or I could make coffee."

"Yes to the first two offers, but not the coffee. Did you bring my shoe?"

Jake nearly dropped a tray of ice. Her shoe. He'd left it on the dresser in his bedroom. Like a damned trophy.

Nothing to do but admit it. "Look, I know this is crazy, but I walked right out and forgot the thing. I can go back home right now and get it if—"

She waved him to a chair. "Don't be silly, it's not like I'll be wearing it anytime soon."

"Good thing, too. Shoes like that are just asking for trouble."

Ignoring him, she said, "First I'll have to get the heel repaired."

He shook his head. Women. "Why do you wear those things, anyway?"

"You mean ankle straps?" She batted a set of black eyelashes that had to be at least as long as her red fingernails.

"I mean ten-inch heels." A grin tugged at the corner of his mouth. She was teasing him, and damned if he didn't like it.

"In case you hadn't noticed, I'm slightly height-challenged."

"Short, you mean."

"Well, if you insist on being literal, I'm short and dumpy. And as long as I'm in confession mode, I wasn't born with this shade of hair, either." Laughter trembled on her lips and sparkled through her green contact lenses.

He crooked a grin. "Neither was I. The hair thing."

"You mean you weren't born gray?" she asked, all innocence.

"Believe it or not, I started out as a blond. By the time I was twenty it had turned dark. And yeah, lately the colors have started to change again."

"I started out the color of broom sedge, which is sort of red, I guess. Once I discovered my creative side, I started playing around with colors."

He looked pointedly at her hair. It was currently somewhere between spice-red and maroon and had been cut in varying lengths and gathered up so that it looked carelessly disheveled. "I look ghastly as a brunette," she admitted cheerfully. "I tried several shades of blond, but you know what? I don't care what they say, I never had that much fun as a blonde."

"And fun's the name of the game, right, Ms. Napoleon?"

"Nope. The name of the game is power," she said gravely, and then burst out laughing. "You're fun, did you know that?"

"Oh, yeah—everybody says so. Regular life of the party. Here, let me refill that glass for you." He stood, knowing he should leave before he got in any deeper.

What was it about this woman that made him want to explore every inch of her devious mind?

Her mind. Right.

And that wasn't Jake Smith the private investigator speaking, it was Jake Smith, the man.

She leaned back against a pile of oversize pillows, reminding him of a poster he'd once seen of Mae West. Had the come-up-and-see-me-sometime expression down pat, too.

"Did you play sports in school?" she asked. "Is that where you broke your nose?" Her gaze strayed from his nose to his mouth and back again.

"How'd you know it had been broken?"

"Just a lucky guess. My brother played football. He was a quarterback."

"Pro?"

She shook her head. Her playful look faded. "Just high school. He went to a community college and then joined the sheriff's department. He was killed the first year in an attempted jailbreak."

Jake sagged in his chair. What did you say to something like that? While he was still trying to come up with a response that didn't sound trite, she said, "I'm sorry. You're hardly interested in my family. I don't know why that popped out—frustration, probably. Being stuck here thinking about all the things I need to be doing."

Which made about as much sense as anything else she could come up with, Sasha told herself. The man was like a blotter, inviting all sorts of confidences. If he hung around much longer there was no telling what she might decide to share.

She smoothed her skirt over her knees. After he'd called she had hobbled to the bedroom and changed into a long flower-sprigged yellow skirt and a pale green silk cami—last year's styles, but still flattering. "Do you know many people in Muddy Landing?" she asked brightly.

He hesitated, then said, "I know several deputies— used to know a guy who ran a bait-and-tackle place down on the river. He moved away a few years ago."

"How about your taxes?"

"My what?" He did a double-take.

"Taxes. You know, those things we all have to pay to fund schools and roads and congressmen's junkets?"

"Oh...*those* taxes." He made a face, part amusement, part puzzlement. She was getting so she could almost read him until he put on his detective face. "Yeah, I pay taxes. Property, income, the whole shebang. You need to know how much, I guess I could get you the figures."

Sasha thought he was joking. *Hoped* he was joking. Embarrassed, she hurried to apologize. "I'm sorry, I didn't mean it that way. It's just that I know this CPA who lives not far from here. Her name is Lily Sullivan, and—"

"And?" he said after a while.

She shrugged. And what? For all she knew, Lily had all the business she could handle. For that matter, she might not even be interested in dating. It wouldn't be the first time the trio had goofed. "It's just that I happen to know that she's an excellent CPA, and I thought maybe—" She shook her head. "Forget it. You and your taxes are none of my business."

Rising slowly, Jake towered over her, yet oddly

enough, he wasn't the least bit intimidating. "You want to hand me your corn, I'll put it back in the freezer. Ten minutes, okay? If you've got a cooler I could put it here beside you with a few cold drinks and another bag or two of frozen vegetables."

Embarrassment was her worst enemy. Sasha felt her face growing warm even as she heard herself saying, "No thanks, it's royal blue—my ice chest, that is. I couldn't possibly use it in this room."

He looked at her, and then he looked around the room. "Yeah, now that you mention it, I can see how blue would be a problem."

Obviously, he thought she'd lost her mind. For all she knew, he could be right. "Sorry, I'm not used to being out of action. I tend to get frustrated—my tongue runs away from my brain."

He nodded as if he knew exactly what she was talking about.

Even *she* didn't know just what she was talking about—which was part of the problem.

"You need to stay off that leg as much as possible for at least another day or two. The sooner the swelling goes down, the sooner you can bring your car back home. I don't think it's in too much danger where it is, but you never can tell with a holiday weekend coming up."

She closed her eyes. "Gee, thanks, I really needed that."

"I can have it towed home for you if you're worried. Or if you give me the keys, I can get someone to drive it here for you. Hack—this kid who works with me—"

"No way is any kid named Hack getting his grubby hands on my car," she declared. "Tomorrow I'll have a friend drive me to Kitty Hawk. I'm sure my ankle will be well enough by then."

Jake shifted his weight, wanting to defend his young friend, but then he thought about the rebuilt TR-5 the kid drove. There was probably a reason he'd had a roll bar installed across the top.

He glanced at the flesh-colored bandage, thought about unwrapping it to check the swelling, and backed away, literally and figuratively. Instead of the small metal clip, she had used a gaudy brooch to secure the end. Shaking his head in reluctant admiration, he said, "It's your call. Just remember to pick a time when traffic's light, maybe around supper time or early in the morning."

She nodded and solemnly promised, although they both knew she would do things her way, on her timetable. She'd already proved she wasn't into obeying orders, even when they were in her own best interest.

Stubborn woman, Jake thought half admiringly. Climbing behind the wheel a few minutes later, he told himself to put her out of his mind and get on with his business. He'd done his good deed and that was enough. Hell, he'd even gone the extra mile and brought her flowers.

In exchange, she had screwed up any chance of catching Jamison and his side dish in a compromising situation. He'd tried to call his client, missed her and left a message. He would have liked to have good news—or at least *some* news to report—but as long as that red car was parked outside the cottage, the game was on hold.

Marty and Faylene converged on the lavender house early the next morning. Sasha hobbled to the door to meet them after seeing Marty's white minivan and Faylene's pink Caddie pull up in front of her house.

The night before, she had finally told them about her temporary indisposition, assuring both women that she was on her way to bed and the last thing she wanted was to have to get up and answer the door. That had staved off the visitation until this morning.

"You look bright-eyed and bushy-tailed considering you're just back from your honeymoon," Sasha said, greeting Marty, then laughing, she held up a hand. "No details, please! Just tell me this much—was this one an improvement over the last two?"

Faylene snorted as she strode directly to the kitchen to start a pot of coffee. "Tell you one thing, she's not stopped humming since she got home. 'Nuff to drive a person batty." But her faded blue eyes, set in a bed of wrinkles and frosted turquoise eye shadow, twinkled with amusement.

Five minutes later all three women were seated in the living room with coffee and doughnuts, ready to sift through the local gossip for any snippets that might be useful in their matchmaking games.

Sasha said slyly, "You're obviously getting plenty of sleep." Marty was infamous for her early-morning grumpiness. It was still not quite nine o'clock.

"Quality sleep," the new bride said smugly. "Makes a big difference. And before you take out your crowbar and start prying, that's all I'm saying. So—what's this about a new man for Lily?"

Sasha stirred a second spoonful of sugar into her cup. "He's only perfect, that's all. Like I told you over the phone, he's at least an eleven."

"And that's his shoe size, right?" Marty asked, tongue firmly planted in cheek.

"Uh-uh. His shoes are at least size twelve."

Faylene cackled and Sasha stretched out on the sofa and kicked a pillow under her ankle with her good foot. "Look, I'm just guessing, okay? Lily's tall, right? Jake's taller. He's big, but not too big—attractive without being blatant about it."

"What's wrong with blatant?" asked Faylene, whose Bob Ed was gray-bearded and beer-bellied, and according to the housekeeper, the sweetest man you'd ever hope to meet.

"Well, at least he's not vain. Remember that lawyer we introduced Lily to at the Christmas party? The one who couldn't pass his reflection in any shiny surface without preening?"

"Ask me, I think he used more wax on his hair than he did on his fancy car." Faylene snorted. "And how 'bout the guy that gave her that cheap box of candy that still had the sale sticker on it?"

"Hey, we tried. A good man is hard to find," Sasha said.

"Ain't the way I heard it," Faylene remarked dryly.

"Okay, so the thing is, how are we going to get them together? The box suppers won't start again for another few weeks, and I already asked him about his taxes."

"And?"

"And I botched it. He thought I was being nosy."

"You were, but you're usually slick enough to get away with it," Marty said with a laugh. "You're slipping, honey."

"You try being crafty when your ankle looks like a stuffed sausage and you've got three broken nails on one hand."

"Why don't you go natural? Nobody wears long red nails now. It's not even considered retro. Besides, think of all you'd save in maintenance alone." Marty admired her own French manicure.

"Terrific. Next you'll be wanting me to start wearing gingham."

"I can see it now. A ruffled gingham apron worn over a matching garter belt and bikini top." Marty giggled.

Marty never giggled. Now she not only giggled, she glowed.

Sasha studied her frosted cherry nails—the ones she had left. "Do acrylic nails come in short natural? I told you about my shoe, didn't I? The pink ankle-straps?"

Marty shook her head. "I warned you about those things. This time it was only a sprain, but next time you might break your neck. Shoes like that weren't even meant for walking, much less climbing stairs. And we're talking sun-warped, outdoor stairs with cracks between the boards, right?"

Faylene offered her own advice. "Be like me. I know how to dress sensible for work."

For as long as anyone could remember, the housekeeper's summer uniform had been white sneakers, white shorts and suntan support hose worn, more often than not, with a pink shirt.

"We all have to make the most of our natural attributes. Mine just happen to be small feet, nice ankles and good hair," Sasha said.

"Natural?" Marty jeered. "Yeah, like Mount Rushmore is natural."

"Besides," Sasha continued, ignoring the interruption, "I don't climb all that many stairs. I just had a few more of those three-story cottages this season on account of all the storm damage. And who'd trust a shabby-looking interior designer?"

"We're talking sensible, not shabby. White jeans and a halter, flip-flops and maybe a Hermes do-rag and you've got instant chic."

"Right, and I'd look like every other woman on the beach. Well...maybe not the Hermes scarf." Sasha sighed.

For as long as she could remember she'd loved playing dress-up, her imagination turning her mother's faded cotton dresses into fancy ballgowns. Having been accused more than once of never having met an artifice she didn't like, she'd never bothered to deny it. After dozens of makeovers she had found a style she really liked and stuck to it ever since. And while she might draw the line at silicon and botox, if dewlaps or wattles or cellulite ever seriously threatened, she would definitely go for liposuction—maybe even plastic surgery.

Faylene said, "Long's I'm here, I'll just put in a load of laundry. Be back later this evening to put it in the dryer, so don't you go messin' around in my utility room, y'hear?"

"When did I ever?" Sasha replied.

Marty said, "You know, I've been thinking...that fund-raising yard sale that's coming up? You reckon we could get them together there? There'll be food stands and tables, almost like the box suppers."

"Jake lives in Manteo. He'd hardly come all this way for a local fund-raiser."

"Manteo's not all that far. Besides, it's for an underprivileged kids' summer camp. Betcha he'll go for it if he's as good a guy as you say he is."

"Did I say that?"

In the background, the washing machine began churning.

"You sort of implied," Marty said with a lift of one eyebrow.

"I don't know how you do that." Sasha shook her head. "That one-eyebrow thing."

"It's easy. You could do it, too, if yours were real instead of penciled on."

"Bless her heart," Faylene said, drying her hands on the seat of her shorts as she rejoined them, "It comes from all that waxing she gets done. Last time they slipped up and did her eyebrows along with her legs and I don't know what-all. You get you one o' them Brazilian jobs?"

Sasha tossed a teal-and-orange linen pillow at her. All three women began to giggle, and then the phone rang. Faylene was closest. "Want me to get that?"

"Would you please?"

"Lasiter residence, Faylene speaking."

"Who is it?" Sasha whispered. No matter how many quit-bothering-me lists she signed up for, she still got calls from tour groups, resort salesmen and political surveys.

Faylene held the phone against her pink sequined chest. "Man says his name's Smith. I think it's *him*," she whispered loudly. "He says he's coming this afternoon to take you to get your car." When she hung up, her smirk said it all. "Didn't you say that guy's name was Smith? The one you got picked out for Lily? He sure sounded like a twelve to me. I better go add the softener, I forgot to fill the cup."

"Way to go, gal!" Marty jabbed a fist in the air. "While you've got him here you can tell him about the kids' day-camp fund-raiser and get him on the hook." She gave her a knowing smirk. "Some folks believe in catch-and-release. Me, I never did."

Jake brushed a hand over his newly trimmed hair as he left the barbershop. His client, when he'd finally been able to reach her, had called off the dogs. All a big misunderstanding, according to Ms. J.

Yeah. Sure it was.

All the same, with the holiday weekend bearing down on them, the car wasn't safe where it was.

Which was how Jake came to be driving to Muddy Landing for the second day in a row, neglecting two new commissions, not to mention keeping up with the paint crew that was finishing up work on his side of the duplex. He put it down to a natural talent for procrastination, along with worrying about his son, who was shipping out any day now, and worrying about the Jamison case. Something didn't feel right about it, but at this point it was out of his hands.

He made a mental note to have Miss Martha return the retainer, and then his thoughts veered back along a familiar path.

The phrase, "Out of the frying pan, into the fire," came to mind. He switched on a Molasses Creek CD and tried to focus on the lament of a crabber's woman.

Five

Marty had brought a cold pasta dish earlier and put it in the refrigerator. A size six, Marty had never met a carb she didn't adore. Faylene had brought a can of corned beef hash and a bunch of loose-leaf lettuce from Bob Ed's garden. Her culinary skills were notorious.

So there was no real reason for Sasha to accept Jake's offer of lunch at a seafood restaurant on the way to Kitty Hawk. "I had breakfast early," he said. "Are you sure your ankle's good to go?"

Ignoring the question, she said, "So did I. I'm an early riser."

The truth was, her ankle still bothered her. As for her sleep patterns, those had been crazy for the past three days. Yesterday she had dozed on the sofa during the day, then lain awake half the night. When she finally fell asleep she dreamed.

Oh, how she dreamed…!

Jake had looked her over when she'd first let him in, his gaze moving slowly down her body to settle on her feet. She could have swatted him. For a change, she was wearing one of her few pairs of sensible shoes. Her three-inch cork platforms with flowered straps were the only shoes she could get on over her bandage.

From the way he'd looked at her, she might as well have been wearing stilts.

It had to be her imagination. Too much time on her hands.

After carefully helping her into his SUV, his hands lingered on her arm. He said, "Listen, if you're not up to this, just say so. Like I said, I can get Hack to drive your car to Muddy Landing. It's practically on his way home since he lives in Moyock. The logistics might take some arranging, but we can work it out."

Sasha assured him she was feeling loads better. Actually, she was, until she'd overdone it. Just climbing up and down the stairs was exhausting enough without plowing through the spare room that doubled as a warehouse, looking for the set of framed patent medicine advertisements from a 1920s magazine she'd bought at a yard sale last year. Matted and reframed, they'd be perfect for the suite of doctors' offices she was doing.

They talked shop on the way to Kitty Hawk. Her shop, not his. As it turned out, Jake was a private investigator as well as a security expert. Evidently, private investigators discussed their work only on a need-to-know basis.

It wasn't his work she needed to know about as much as it was the man himself. For all her experience with the opposite sex, she had never met any man who affected her the way this one did. He was sweet, but not smarmy sweet. Sexy without even trying. She could hardly look at him without wondering what he would be like as a lover.

The curse of an inquiring mind!

By the time they were shown to a table in the beach-front restaurant, Sasha was practically salivating, which wasn't like her at all. It must be a lingering side effect of the painkillers she'd taken the first day and then dumped.

Once seated, she announced to the waitress, "I'll start with dessert. Then, if I'm still hungry, I might have something healthy. Lemon chess pie, please."

Jake looked at her across the table, scattering her feeble defenses with a lazy grin. "Why am I not surprised?"

Judging from the looks the waitress was giving him, Sasha wasn't the only one who'd like a large serving of Jake.

Without even glancing at the menu he ordered the fried oyster basket. She opened her mouth to ask if it was true what they said about oysters, then closed it before she could make a fool of herself. Any more of a fool, that was.

"You were serious," he said after the waitress left. "About having dessert first."

She fluttered a battery of false lashes. "I'm always serious."

He stared at her. She fluttered again. And then they both started laughing. "Don't make me wrinkle my eyes," she protested, "these things aren't foolproof."

"You mean those centipedes circling your eyes aren't real?"

"Absolutely, they're real. They're the best money can buy, but the glue's not guaranteed against squinting or crying."

Jake shook his head admiringly and Sasha preened. Flirtation was a game she always won, even though the prize was rarely worth the effort.

"Coffee with the pie, Miss?" Plopping the plate down in front of her, the waitress addressed Sasha while she looked ready to melt all over Jake. Sasha found it irritating in the extreme. With all the bronzed, sun-bleached surfers running around with their trunks at half-mast, what was so hot about a fully dressed guy with laugh lines, squint lines, and a sparkling of gray?

Sasha sighed. Jake nodded. "Bring her a decaf."

She waited until the girl left and then said, "I never drink decaf."

"You need to decompress. About your car—it's a little soon, so if you're not up to driving yet, we could—"

"I'm perfectly capable of driving." She was a big girl now; she could stand a little pain.

"Do you have an alarm?"

"A car alarm? I had one, but it got to be such an annoyance I had it disabled."

"An annoyance how?"

"It went off every time I forgot to click the little whoosie."

Jake sighed. And then he grinned. "Lady, you need a keeper."

"Thanks, but I already tried that. Four times, in fact."

He choked on a swallow of ice water. "Four times you did *what?*"

"Four times I thought I'd found a keeper, only I ended up having to throw him back."

He took a few seconds to process her claim. "You mean you had four, uh—relationships? That's not too surprising, I guess. Be more surprising if you hadn't." All the same, he looked as if he'd bitten into a particularly sour pickle.

"Not relationships. Husbands."

He shook his head slowly, but said nothing. The waitress brought Jake's oysters and looked questioningly at Sasha, who was only half finished with her pie. "I should have ordered it à la mode. Anything this sweet needs to be diluted with ice cream." When the girl continued to hover uncertainly, she said, "Oh, I guess you can bring me a salad. Any kind—just something disgustingly healthy."

She should have known Jake wasn't going to let her off the hook that easily. Once the waitress left, he leaned forward, forcing Sasha to look at him. "Now repeat what you just said. You've had four *husbands?*"

She did the eyelash thing again, trying for a look of innocence, but he was on to her now. "You make me sound like Lizzie Borden, or that Borgia woman. I didn't kill anybody, I just divorced them." She tilted her head to one side. "Why are you looking at me like that? I made four mistakes, okay? What's wrong, haven't you ever made a mistake?"

"More than my share, I just never married 'em."

"Then you're not married?"

"I was once, but it was no mistake. Rosemary was the best thing that ever happened to me. If it weren't for her, I wouldn't have my son."

She looked at him wistfully. "You have a son. You're incredibly lucky, but I guess you know that. I've always wanted one."

Jake accepted the remark with a nod. Then he started to ask her why she'd never had kids with any of her four husbands, but decided it was none of his business. Besides, it was hardly the sort of question a man asked of a woman he'd known casually for only a few days. A woman he had no intention of getting to know any better.

"Tell me about him—your son." She touched her lips with the napkin and crumpled it beside her plate.

Why not? Jake thought. It was safer than talking about what really interested him, such as why none of the men she'd married had been able to hang on to her. "I could start by saying he's everything any man could want in a son." His gaze moved past her shoulder to a wide, salt-filmed window, where a glimpse of the ocean could be seen between the dunes. "I just wish he weren't heading overseas."

Knowing she was staring at him, he tried to erase any hint of what he was thinking, but it was probably already too late.

"I told you about my brother," she reminded him quietly.

Jake nodded. For some crazy reason he found himself wanting to confide in her. To share not only his pride, but his very real worries. He'd never been the kind of guy who opened up to every stranger who came along. Besides, they weren't even friends. His mother would probably have labeled her fast, any woman who'd been married and divorced four times.

His grandmother would have called her a hussy, a painted lady—maybe even a scarlet woman.

The trouble was, Jake had a feeling that under all that paint and polish there lurked a very different kind of woman. A woman with weaknesses and vulnerabilities she tried a little too hard to conceal. One his mother and even his grandmother would probably like if they ever got to know her.

"You want more coffee?" he asked, reaching for any safe topic.

"Did I mention that I have twin sisters, too? Annette and Jeanette. They're almost ten years younger than I am and both happily married, with children." She waited a beat and added, "One husband apiece, in case you were wondering. We don't all run to multiple unions. Mama remarried after Daddy died, but then, she was barely fifty at the time. Her new husband raises llamas out in Colorado. He's gentle as a lamb."

All of which was far more than he needed to know, Jake mused, but judging from the way it had come out, like a faucet turned on full-blast, she'd needed to tell him. Odd comment, though—that part about her step-father being gentle as a lamb.

"The only trouble is, they all live so far away," she said with a sigh. "Anne lives in Birmingham, Jeanie in Tampa. I haven't seen either of them in more than a year." She toyed with her fork, making tiny squares in the sticky stuff on her pie plate. "And you know what's so funny? Now that I'm finally in a position to help, they don't need me anymore." She rolled her eyes, a look of disgust on her face. "That sounded so awful. Can I please take back my whine?"

Jake started to laugh, but didn't. He started to say something—God knows what—when his cell phone vibrated at his waist. One glance at the number and he swallowed hard. Timmy was probably calling to say goodbye. His unit had been day-to-day ever since their orders came down.

"Excuse me, will you?" he murmured.

Meaning to go the ladies' room and allow him some privacy, Sasha started to stand, grabbed the chair back when her ankle protested, and plopped down again. Instead, she reached for her half-eaten pie, pretending a fascination with the too-sweet confection while she tried not to listen.

A long pause and then, "Jesus, son, this is—"

Son? This was Timmy, then, not a business call. And Jake was frowning. Sasha's mind immediately manufactured a dozen possibilities, all of them tragic. At least the boy was able to call—that was a good sign. But if Jake's brows lowered any more, he wouldn't be able to see.

Her pie was suddenly tasteless, the crust leathery. She took a sip of her tasteless coffee only to find it was barely warm. Murmuring an excuse, she started to rise again just as he said, "What if I talk to your commanding officer?"

Oh, God, this was serious! Could the boy have been arrested? Had he deserted? Going AWOL—that was a court-martial offense, wasn't it?

"All right, give me her name and tell me how to get in touch with her. I'll call you back as soon as I know something positive. Within the hour if I'm lucky—I'm on the beach, not too far away."

His commanding officer was a woman. Did that help or hurt? Sasha was undecided whether to disappear, ignore the call or ask if there was anything she could do to help. She knew two county commissioners personally, but they probably didn't have a whole lot of clout with the military.

"Don't worry, son, I'll handle it. You just keep your head down and your mind on what you're supposed to be doing. Leave everything else to me."

He shut off the cell phone, laid it on the table and stared blindly at a salt shaker for a full minute—a minute during which Sasha ran through every possible way in which a teenage boy, even if he was a soldier, could get in trouble. "Can I help?" she finally asked.

"I should have given him a refresher course, like maybe about nine months ago." Rising, he pulled out his wallet and tossed several bills on the table.

Sasha wasn't about to mention her car, which happened to be in the opposite direction, nor was she about to ask any questions. From the look on his face, he had enough on his mind without adding her tiny problems.

Not until they turned off the bypass and headed toward one of the older soundside villages did Jake break the silence. Dropping back to the slower speed limit, he drove past several small houses, a few of which looked as if they hadn't been repaired since Hurricane Isabel. "She says she needs the money because she hasn't been able to work for the past few months."

She? Who was *she?* And what did she have to do with Jake's son? More to the point, what did she have to do with Jake?

Questions swarmed like a school of minnows, but as much as she wanted to help, she hesitated to pry into his personal business.

Jake slowed down to check a street marker. "Here's

what I don't get," he said as if they were in the middle of a conversation. "She didn't ask him for money. Didn't ask for a damn thing, she just said she wanted to let him know what happened and what she planned to do about it." He turned right and cruised down a narrow black-top street at about five miles an hour.

Looking as pale as a perennially suntanned man could possibly look, he swore softly under his breath. "She waited five and a half weeks to call him—five and a half damned weeks! Tim said he told her that as long as she'd waited that long, to hold off until he talked to me. I just hope to God she did—that she's still there."

He obviously didn't expect a response. In fact, Sasha wasn't certain he realized she was even here. If he was working things out in his own mind, the last thing he needed was questions—although sometimes a sounding board could help.

"You know what?" he asked suddenly, still without looking at her. "I'm not buying it. Tim said they spent last Labor Day weekend together at Virginia Beach, but he claims he hasn't seen her since then. I've never known him to lie, not even when a lie would have got-ten him out of trouble."

"They've obviously been in touch," Sasha ventured. "She knew where to find him." She still wasn't quite cer-tain what the problem was, but she was beginning to think it had nothing to do with the military. Evidently, Timmy and an old girlfriend had a problem. And now Jake was involved.

They passed a shoebox with weathered siding and tarpaper patches on the roof, and then Jake backed up, pulled off the pavement and opened the driver's-side door. Near the wooden steps an enormous gardenia bush in full bloom layered the air with its fragrance.

"You want to wait out here?"

It was the first time he'd actually acknowledged her presence. "Can you give me a quick rundown on what's going on? If this is a hostage situation, I'd just as soon wait outside, but I'll keep the car running in case you need to make a quick getaway."

Still holding the door open, Jake leaned back in his seat and closed his eyes. "Sorry. Communication's obviously not one of my skills. In a nutshell, my son impregnated a girl last Labor Day weekend. They've talked a few times since, but Tim says he hasn't seen her since then. Five and a half weeks ago she had a baby and she swears it's his."

"Do you think she's telling the truth?"

Jake's shoulders drooped. Suddenly he looked his age. It should have diminished his sex appeal, yet oddly enough, it didn't. She wanted nothing more than to gather him into her arms and offer comfort. In whatever form he preferred.

Girl, you just never learn, do you?

"Short answer—yes, I think she's probably telling the truth."

"Why is that?"

"Like I said, she didn't ask for anything—no money, no wedding ring. She was just reporting in, letting him know what she planned to do. According to Tim, she's been talking with a woman in Norfolk who takes unwanted babies and places them in good homes."

"You mean an adoption agency?"

He shrugged. "I guess. Probably a private one. Tim

made her hold off until he could get in touch with me. He's in no position to take care of a baby. Hell, neither am I, for that matter, but I'll tell you this much—nobody is going to sell my granddaughter."

"How long do we have?"

He turned to her then. "There's no 'we' about it. There's me and this woman and my granddaughter. Look, Sasha, I'm sorry about all this—the delay. I promise you, once I get things settled here, I'll see that you get to your car."

"Oh, bull pucky!"

For the first time since he'd received the call from his son, Jake looked almost amused. "*Pucky?* I haven't heard that one, is it original?"

"I doubt it. My daddy started out as a farmer. Once he switched to preaching, we all had to clean up our language."

"Yeah, well…while I go inside, how about making a list of everything I need to buy to take care of a baby. Diapers, bottles—a car seat."

He swung open his door, then turned and said, "Dammit, didn't those kids ever hear of birth control? Tim says she was seventeen when he knew her. That's barely legal."

As if knowing she wasn't going to stay put, he came around just as she opened the door and started to slide to the ground. Catching her, he steadied her against his chest, holding her closely for a moment as if he needed the brief contact as much as she did.

"Four-wheel-drive SUVs aren't designed with the vertically challenged in mind," she said breathlessly as she backed away. The man generated enough voltage to jump-start a battleship.

Leading the way across the unkempt yard to the shoebox house, he said gruffly, "Come on, let's get this show on the road."

They stepped up onto the porch where two pairs of sandy flip-flops straddled a potted tomato plant. Sasha caught his arm and said, "Look, this might be out of line, but just so you know, I have lots of money."

The look he gave her might have withered her on the spot if she didn't know how concerned he was. Turning away, he jabbed the buzzer and then rattled the screen door. From inside the house came the sound of a radio playing loud rap music. Jake's look darkened.

Sasha said, "You were expecting what, lullabies? Mother or not, she's still a teenager."

The girl who materialized on the other side of the mended screen looked as if she could do with a few pounds, a few hours in the sun and a few hours of sleep.

"I'm Tim's dad. He told you I'd be here. Where is she?"

The young woman looked them over thoroughly before she opened the screen door. "I guess you might as well come in. Is this Tim's mother?"

"I'm a friend," Sasha answered before Jake could explain that she was practically a stranger who just happened to come along for the ride. "Could we see her?"

"She spit up and I've not had time to change her shirt."

She led the way to a room that was even more depressing than the one they were in, and there in the middle of an unmade bed was a banana box stuffed with a pillow. Tiny pink feet kicked at a confining yellow spread. A small pink fist waved in the air as a red-faced infant vented her displeasure.

"That's her. I named her Tuesday on account of that's when she was born. Tuesday Smith," she added defiantly.

"And your name is?" said Jake, who looked tense enough to shatter at a touch.

"Cheryl," was the reluctant response. "Cheryl Moser."

Torn between reaching out to Jake and scooping up the fretful infant, Sasha chose the safest option. She leaned over and cupped a small foot in her hand. "Hello, sweetheart. You just fuss all you want to, I don't much blame you." She turned to the tired-looking blonde. "How old did you say she was?"

"Five weeks. And a half."

Jake said tightly, "You could have called sooner."

"I didn't think you'd be interested."

"What about your parents?"

She shrugged. "Mama's dead and Daddy said don't come crying to him if I got myself in trouble."

Sasha opened her mouth and then shut it again. Nothing she could say would help out in this situation. This was between Jake and the thin, pale teenager and a baby whose name was the same as a movie star this poor girl had probably never heard of. So much for originality.

Frowning, Jake said, "About this place in Norfolk—"

Sasha broke in. "Whatever that woman offered, we'll double it." She hadn't planned to say anything, the words just popped out.

Jake shot her a look that clearly questioned her sanity. To Cheryl, he said, "Why don't we go in the next room and talk this over?"

Not to be left out, Sasha scooped the infant from her makeshift bassinet, making crooning sounds she hadn't uttered in more than twenty years, and followed them into the living room, carrying the wet, fussing infant against her shoulder. Oh, how good it felt to cradle a baby again.

Jake turned to glare at her. Cheryl sighed and shifted her weight from one bare foot to the other. "Look, I mean, I just need to get back to work full-time, okay? Starting when I got too big to work tables, they put me in the kitchen. The pay stinks. I been taking her with me, but my boss don't like it. How much did you say you were willing to give for her?"

On the verge of saying something she probably shouldn't, Sasha felt a warm damp patch on the shoulder of her eighty-nine-dollar-on-sale, dry-cleanable blouse. It smelled like sour milk and probably was. "Judge not lest ye be judged" had been one of the favorite quotations of Addler Parrish, who had set himself up as judge and then proceeded to mete out whatever punishment he saw fit.

She'd been nine and a half when the twins were born, eleven when her brother came along. Her mother had been sickly after Buck, whose real name had been Robert, so Sasha had done more than her share of babytending. The warmth of the slight bundle and the familiar smell brought back a mixture of bitterness and nostalgia.

Speaking in a quietly controlled voice, Jake named a figure. While Cheryl gnawed on a hangnail, evidently considering his offer, Sasha cleared her throat loudly. When Jake glanced at her she waggled her eyebrows to remind him that she had money if his offer wasn't enough.

She knew very well she had no business meddling in his affairs, but the only thing that mattered here was this baby. If there was anything she could do to help smooth the way, she intended to do it, no matter whose toes she stepped on.

The baby whimpered, and she held her up and sniffed at her diaper. "Where do you keep her things? I can change her for you—her shirt, too."

"She spits up all the time. Over there." The girl pointed to a scarred table that held a folded towel, two packages of disposable diapers, a tin of baby powder and a half-empty nursing bottle.

"Come on, sugar pie, let Sasha make you feel better, hmm?"

Humming under her breath, she located the pitifully small stack of undershirts and took care of business while trying to overhear the negotiations going on in the next room. Cheryl was insisting loudly that the baby was definitely Tim's, and to prove it she'd put his name on the birth certificate.

Jake, in a voice even more controlled than before, said, "I'm not questioning your word. If you'd asked him for money or a wedding ring, I might've have had my doubts, but since you didn't ask for anything, I'll give you credit for playing it straight."

Reentering the living room, Sasha thought of the twins and how lucky they'd been to marry decent men the first time around. They could easily have ended up in the same situation as this poor girl.

The baby was trying to cram Sasha's finger in her mouth. "Oh, honey, sapphires don't taste all that good— this one's not even real. Let's find you a pacifier, hmm?"

Just then Jake spelled out his terms, naming a generous figure. "I'll write you a check for half today—I've got a checkbook out in the truck. You'll get the other half once we get things wrapped up legally."

"Look, I already told you, I'll sign whatever you want me to sign." She sounded close to tears.

Sasha thought that of all the painful things a woman could do, giving up her baby had to be among the worst. Cradling the infant, she said, "I know you want what's best for her."

Cheryl turned to Jake. "You're her granddaddy. You'll take care of her and nobody would try to take her away from you, would they?"

Sasha waited to hear his reply. He might be an expert in his field, but outnumbered by emotional females in a room that smelled of baby powder, soiled diapers and sour milk, he was obviously out of his element.

He fished out his wallet, extracted a card and wrote his cell-phone number on the back. "Here—you can see her anytime you want to once we get things settled, as long as you call first. You'll get the rest of your money as soon as we meet with the lawyer, but I'm taking her with me now."

"Today? Can't I get the rest of my money today?"

"I doubt if I can get an appointment that soon, but—"

"I can," Sasha said.

They both turned to her. "Let me make a call. This lawyer I know owes me a big favor for getting him— well, never mind that. He specializes in real estate, but considering nobody's contesting the adoption, it should be enough to get by on, don't you think?"

Later she would wonder how in the world she'd gotten involved in the matter, but at no time could she have stepped away. Blame it on missing her own family, remembering the time when Buck and the twins had depended on her. Blame it on the hopes she'd once had of having children of her own.

"Sasha's got you now, sweetheart. You're going to be just fine, you wait and see," she whispered.

Six

"Well, that went pretty well, don't you think?" Sasha leaned forward from the back of the car, one hand on the infant car seat that was secured with a seatbelt.

Neither Jake nor Cheryl said a word. After explaining the situation to the lawyer, they'd spent less than an hour in his office. Jake and Cheryl had signed an agreement, with Sasha serving as a witness. The small act of signing her name on little Miss Tuesday no-middle-name Smith's adoption papers had set her eyes to watering. Jake had written two checks, one for the lawyer and one for a tearful Cheryl.

The drive back to the house on Low Ridge Road where the young woman lived was largely silent. As they pulled up in front of the house, Jake said quietly, "Starting today I'll be putting money into her college fund."

Sasha thought that was probably as reassuring as

anything he could possibly have said. She hadn't missed Cheryl's occasional sniffle. And while her heart ached for the girl now, she had an idea that Cheryl Moser was a survivor.

While Jake got out and came around to the passenger side, Sasha whispered, "Call me if you ever need someone to talk to. I have two younger sisters." Granted, the twins were a lot older than Cheryl, but the sentiment still held. "That's up to you, but Jake's a wonderful man—he'll take good care of her, you'll never have to worry about that."

Just before Jake returned from seeing the young woman to her door, she carefully blotted her eyes with a tissue. It came away smudged with black and taupe.

Oh, well, she thought, resigned. It's not as if he hadn't seen her in even worse shape. "We'll probably need to make a stop at the nearest outfitters," she said. Except for the basics, Cheryl had improvised. Even the diaper bag was a battered canvas beach tote.

Heading for the closest big-box store, Jake picked up the conversation that had been left dangling earlier. "If the father hadn't been my son, I doubt if things would've gone that smoothly."

"If the father hadn't been your son," Sasha reminded him dryly, "you wouldn't have been there in the first place." She wondered if he had any idea of how many changes were in store for him over the next few days, not to mention the next few years. Granted, he'd once had a baby, but he'd been younger then. Besides, he'd had someone to share the responsibility. Whether or not he realized it, his whole life had just undergone a dramatic change.

She admitted to herself that she envied him with all her heart.

Jake switched on the radio. When static crackled noisily, he switched it off again and said something about lightning.

Lightning my hind foot, Sasha thought. His touch was enough to short out any radio. She knew from experience that there was enough voltage in that tall, muscular frame to light up a small town. Idly, she wondered what it would be like to plug into all that current.

To plug into it? Oh, for Pete's sake, quit with the visuals!

"Timmy will be so proud of you," she said as they pulled into the vast parking lot. "Why don't you try to call him while I shop?"

"You need some money." He shifted his hips and reached for his wallet, and she shook her head.

"We'll settle up later. I don't know if I can get anything but the basics here."

He looked startled. "The basics?"

She left him staring after her. Oh, honey, you have so much to learn, she thought, and I'm just the one who can teach you. That is, if I can stay ahead of the learning curve.

Maybe she'd better look for an instruction book for new parents while she was at it.

Some forty-five minutes later Sasha pushed a loaded cart to the car. She was followed by another cart pushed by a clerk. On the way to the SUV where Jake and the baby waited, she smiled, thinking about how much fun it was going to be, unloading the booty and setting up a nursery. "Thank you so much," she said to the mid-dle-aged employee who had been an enormous help. She plucked a bill from her purse and shoved it into the woman's red apron pocket.

"Oh, now, you don't have to do that—I'm just glad I could help out."

Sasha, never reticent, had told the woman the whole story when she'd asked for her assistance, leaving out only the names. When Jake, who'd been standing be-side the open back door, turned to meet them, the clerk flashed Sasha a broad smile and whispered, "Lawsa-mercy, he don't look like a grandfather to me!"

Ignoring the departing clerk, Jake stared at the two overloaded shopping carts. Before he could say a word, Sasha rushed into speech. "We'll need to get a few more things later on. I got us the same kind of formula Cheryl was using, and a complete layette with lots and lots of diapers—oh, and this funky little chest to keep every-thing in. And a bathtub. Later on we'll need a table for bathing and changing unless you already have some-thing, but the only one they had was too rickety. The bassinet came in two colors and white. I got white so it would go with whatever color you paint the nursery. They had a larger one, but since she'll be graduating to a crib pretty soon anyway, I thought..."

Jake blinked as if he suspected the two overloaded shopping carts were a mirage that had magically ap-peared in the middle of the parking lot. "Really," Sasha hurried to reassure him, "it's not as much as it looks— you know how they over-package everything. And I kept the receipts so we can return anything that doesn't work out."

For so long she'd dreamed of having a baby of her own, but that was before fate and her own bad taste in husbands had laid the dream to rest. Now, even with the perfect mate, her chances of conceiving were less than the odds of the Cubs winning the World Series again.

But even a patched-up dream with some of the parts missing was better than no dream at all, she told herself.

There was still the question of her car. Driftwinds cottage was just a few miles away, but when Jake mentioned it she told him to forget it. "You need me to help you get settled," Sasha said flatly, climbing into the back seat. "Did she wake up? Did you get too hot in here, sugar? Oh—that's probably why you left the back door open, isn't it?"

Jake growled something she couldn't quite catch, and she thought, Ah-ha! Caught you! You left it open just to look at her, to admire her—to gloat, because she's yours now, didn't you?

Aloud, she said, "She might be hungry—she's probably wet, too. I don't remember if I got any diaper-rash ointment or not, but we can stop by the nearest drugstore."

"Sasha, you don't have to come with me—with us. You've already done more than enough."

"Oh, hush up, whether or not you want to admit it, I'm already part of this whole baby deal. My name's on her adoption papers, remember?"

Jake raked his hand through his hair, looking distracted, worried, and incredibly sexy. Without giving him time to marshal his thoughts, she said, "Look, I'll just help you get everything set up and then I'll call a cab to bring me back to Kitty Hawk to pick up my car."

She knew it wouldn't be that simple. Jake probably did, too, but to her relief, he didn't argue. Poor man, he was so far out of his element he was putty in her hands.

Don't I wish, she thought longingly.

While she was shopping she'd bought herself an inexpensive tank top that was really rather nice, and changed into it in the ladies' room. Maybe she should shop the discount stores more often. Her friends had been telling her that for years, which made her do exactly the opposite.

She was supposed to have style, for Pete's sake—she was an interior designer. Who wanted a designer who bought her clothes from the same store her housekeeper did?

Jake said gruffly, "Sit up front, we need to talk."

Uh-oh, here's where I get dumped, Sasha told herself.

But they headed south toward Manteo, which meant he wasn't going to drop her off at Driftwinds. Not yet, anyway. She waited for him to speak, and when he didn't, she said, "What are we going to call her?" Neither of them particularly cared for the name on her birth certificate. "What was your mother's name?"

He pulled up at a traffic light. "Rebecca," he replied, tapping the steering wheel.

"That's nice. If she doesn't like it she can change it when she grows up. I did."

He cut her a quick glance. "Changed your name? What'd you start out with?"

"Sally June." She shrugged. "Once I grew up, it just wasn't me."

He smiled at that. It was the first smile she'd seen in hours. Evidently he was coming out of his state of shock. "Yeah, you're probably right. How'd you come by the name Sasha?"

Twisting around, she glanced at the back seat. "All's peaceful. She's just looking around and blinking. I think she's sleepy again. My name? I read it in a book. I've always been a reader, even when I had to hide my books in the barn or under my mattress."

"You read *that* kind of books?" He looked amused, which made him look younger than she'd first thought. She'd placed his age at a year or two more than her own—possibly even less, considering that he'd obviously spent most of it outdoors, probably without the benefit of sunscreen or moisturizers.

But they'd been talking about books, not the texture of his face, with those squint lines and laugh lines, and the afternoon shadow of beard that cried out to be stroked. So she said, "I read every kind of book I could get my hands on, usually at ten cents a copy from yard sales. The only trouble was, there weren't that many yard sales in our neighborhood. People tended to hang on to whatever they owned until it wore out." She made it sound like a joke. It wasn't. She'd grown up dirt-poor, which probably explained her present lifestyle.

"There's always the backs of cereal boxes." They cruised along at the speed of traffic, which was erratic at best. Jake was an excellent driver, anticipating trouble before she was even aware of it. "Or don't kids still read those?"

"Once you've read a few oatmeal boxes, you know how the story ends."

He smiled again. That was twice in the past few minutes. Sasha glanced at him, seeing the furrows between his eyebrows disappear while the ones bracketing his mouth grew deeper. This is why I knew I had to come with him, she thought. He *needs* me. He might not be ready to admit it, but he really does need me.

He could've dropped her off at her car when they'd left the restaurant. It would have taken only a few more minutes. Instead, he'd taken her with him to find Cheryl.

He could have driven her to Driftwinds and left her there after they'd seen the lawyer, or after she'd done his shopping for him. Instead, he was taking her home with him. That had to mean something.

Dream on, she mocked silently. The trouble with being a Libra was that she was heavily under the influence of Venus. Venus people weren't exactly known for their common sense.

Somewhere between the seventh and the ninth milepost, Jake's frown reappeared. Shooting her a helpless look—or at least, as helpless as a big, sexy guy in the prime of life could manage—he said, "Back to names— I thought maybe I'd let Timmy suggest one if he doesn't care for Tuesday. I talked to him while you were in the store, but we didn't get around to discussing names."

"That's fine, but what do we call her now?"

"Does it matter? I doubt if she understands the language yet."

"You'd be surprised what babies pick up on. For instance, if she gets the least idea you feel uncomfortable with her, she has ways of expressing herself that you're probably not going to like, especially in the middle of the night."

"Hey, I'm not exactly a novice. I had a baby once. I don't remember Tim being all that much trouble."

"That's because you had a wife to deal with colic and night feedings. Peaches is going to demand a lot of attention. You sure you're up to it?"

"Peaches? Is food the only thing you can think about? You should have eaten your lunch." The look he gave her was partly amusement, partly irritation.

"She has a dimple in her chin, did you notice? She probably got that from you." His was a shallow cleft, not a dimple, but connections were important. "And I guess you know her eyes might not stay the same color." Jake's were hazel. "Most babies, at least the ones in my family, are born with blue eyes. It's hard to tell about her hair, considering how little she has now, but I'll bet anything it will be curly. People with dimples in their chins often have curly hair. I read that somewhere."

Jake cut her off. In a dawn of understanding, he said slowly, "My God. You *want* her. Admit it, you want my baby!"

In the silence that followed his astonishing conclusion, Sasha couldn't come up with a single credible denial. If ever there had been a point at which she could have walked away from Jake Smith, regardless of the baggage he carried, that point had passed. Now that she was involved up to her zircon-studded ears, it was too late. Her reaction when he'd accused her of wanting his baby was a pretty good indication of just how "too-late," it was.

Darn right she wanted his baby. But logical or not, she wanted to have it the old-fashioned way, with both of them hot, naked and trembling with urgency. If they both tried long enough and hard enough, maybe a miracle would happen.

She stole a glance at his profile. Not once in their brief relationship had he given her any real indication that he was interested in her as a woman.

Oh, well…maybe once or twice. There was the way he'd looked at her while he was carrying her down several flights of stairs, and when he'd lifted her out of his SUV to take her inside the hospital. He'd caught his breath, his eyes had darkened, and then he'd caught it again. Probably her perfume. It was an old classic that was extremely hard to find, but well worth the effort.

On the other hand, he might have just pulled a muscle in his back.

At any rate, the fact that he'd driven all the way back to Muddy Landing to check on her the next day proved what a nice man he was.

Unfortunately, it wasn't his "niceness" she was interested in.

Well, it was—but that was icing on the cake. Whatever it was that set her imagination, not to mention her hormones, to spinning like a tipsy gyroscope, was more than merely physical—although the physical alone was enough to blow out a few vital circuits in her brain. She'd been in lust before, but this was different. It had nothing to do with any fancy pheromone-based cologne. Those, she had no trouble resisting.

It had nothing to do with the way he dressed. He obviously wasn't out to make a fashion statement with designer silk shirts open to show off his manly chest or Italian slacks cleverly tailored to show off the "package." His package didn't need enhancing. Regardless of what he was wearing, he was more than enough to cause a major meltdown.

And dammit, she wanted him to do more than *need* her, she wanted him to *want* her! To look at her and wonder where she'd been all his life. To know the instant she walked into a room even if it was pitch-dark and he couldn't see her. To *know.*

She wasn't a romance writer; she couldn't describe the feeling—but any woman who had ever fallen in love would know exactly what she meant.

They drove past another shopping center and Sasha tried to think of anything she might have forgotten, but she was too distracted by the hectic pace of events over the past few hours.

Why was it, she wondered as they crossed over the Washington Baum Bridge, that this particular man affected her in ways that none of the men she'd married had even come close to? Both her first and her third husbands had been more handsome. In fact, Larry had spent more than she did on salon treatments at a time when they could barely afford to pay the rent.

Frank, her fourth husband, had been richer—the jerk. At least he'd been generous…sort of. For every thousand dollars he'd spent on his own back, he'd lavished a few hundred on hers. It hadn't been enough, though—not nearly enough once she'd learned where the money had come from.

As they took a right and turned into Manteo, she was still wondering how an accidental meeting could have led to—well, to whatever this thing was that she was involved in now.

Once upon a time she used to sleep in one of her mother's old T-shirts. The thing was faded almost colorless, but the flower-entwined words Go with the Flow had still been legible across the front. When she'd asked what it meant, her mother had murmured tiredly, "Oh, honey, it don't mean anything. Just some old silliness people used to say back when I was young and foolish."

Instead of going with the flow, Sasha, who'd been Sally June back then, had insisted on swimming against the current. By the time she'd bought her house in Muddy Landing and settled down just a few miles from the beach, she knew the old mantra had nothing to do with the ocean tides. And while she didn't personally buy into the philosophy of every feel-good guru to hit the bestseller charts, she always tried to keep an open mind.

Was it too big a stretch to believe that this thing between her and Jake was one of those fate-engineered relationships? Considering all that had happened over the past few days, it definitely had the earmarks. In which case, ignoring it would be asking for trouble.

Go with the flow. If the saying had originated about the time she'd been born, she might even have been conceived at one of those love-in things her mother used to talk about back before her father had given up on farming and gotten religion. Tattered tents and VW buses with daisies and peace symbols painted all over them, guitars and penny whistles—free love and shared grass...

For all she knew she might even be a reincarnated hippie.

Probably not, though. The age was all wrong, and besides, she detested baggy, patched jeans, hairy legs and flapping boots. Especially on women.

Sasha took a deep breath as they cruised slowly down Manteo's Main Street. If this was a fate-engineered thing, then fate had better get busy fast, because once

Jake got home with his baby, she would probably never see either of them again.

Just then Jake pulled into a fast-food place. Without consulting her, he ordered bacon cheeseburgers and fries for two. Sasha inhaled the fragrance of hot grease and realized that she was starved.

Back off, fate, we've got ourselves a time-out.

"We can eat after we get home. Won't be but a few more minutes," he said, and then he frowned.

"Problem?" she asked.

"What? Oh, no. Maybe. I forgot."

"You forgot what? Whether or not you have a problem?" When he started to swear, she shushed him. "Don't imprint her innocent little mind."

"Ah, jeez… Look, Sasha, I just remembered something. It might not be so bad, but I'd better see how long it's going to take to finish."

With that cryptic remark he turned left onto Burnside, took a right and another left and pulled up in front of a duplex. A modest sign identified it as JBS Security. One of the two front doors was propped open and two shirtless men hammered on the roof. A workman with a paint-spattered beard emerged from the door on the left carrying a ladder, which he left on the front porch.

Jake said, "They were supposed to be finished today." He sounded tired. He sounded frustrated. It was all she could do not to pat his hand and say something helpful alike, "There, there."

"Can you and, uh—Peaches wait here? I'll just be a minute."

Less than five minutes later he came out again and asked if she needed a pit stop. More from curiosity than need, she said she could use one. He said, "Come on, then—I'll take the baby. I can check my messages and make a couple of calls."

So she got to meet his staff, including Miss Martha, the gray-haired secretary, and Hack, who might be an electronics genius but she would never trust him anywhere near her wheels, not on a bet.

Naturally, they had to hear the whole story. Jake sketched in the bare bones, then disappeared behind a freshly painted closed door, leaving Sasha to fill in the details. Which she did, starting with Timmy's call and ending up with the official documentation, which might or might not stand up in court if it were ever challenged.

"Well, I never," the older woman marveled. "You did the right thing. I'd like to see the judge who'd rule against one of our boys in uniform."

Hack went back to whatever he'd been working on, while Miss Martha admired the baby. "Got your grandpa's chin, haven't you, precious? It's like something you see in one of those reality shows everybody watches nowadays."

Sasha didn't watch those. She preferred her own version of reality to anything manufactured for TV. "I think her eyes are going to stay blue, don't you?"

"Our Timmy's eyes are the prettiest blue you ever saw." The two women beamed down at the infant, who seemed mesmerized, but probably wasn't. Sasha tried and failed to remember just when babies started focusing. It had been so long....

"We'll probably see plenty of her once Jake gets finished with the painting next door," Martha Blount murmured. "We did the office first. He's been sleeping in his office." She nodded toward the door behind which he'd disappeared. "There's room in there for a bassinet…or I could take her home with me and bring her to work every morning."

"We've already made arrangements," Sasha lied.

Jake emerged from his office sweating and muttering.

Miss Martha said, "Hush up, Jake. Little pitchers have big ears."

Hack glanced up from his work table and said, "Forgot to tell you, boss—I took the air-conditioning apart to see what was making that racket."

When the baby started to whimper, Miss Martha said, "If you've got a bottle ready—"

Not waiting to hear the rest, Sasha dashed out to the car and retrieved the needed supplies. If Peaches was hungry now she needed feeding now.

"Look, you've got problems," she said to Jake a few minutes later. Putting the baby to her shoulder, she said, "Why don't I just call a cab and take sweety-britches here home with me. You can bring the rest of her stuff later after you get off work. Or maybe tomorrow." Can't blame a woman for trying.

"Just sit tight, I'll be done here in a minute," Jake muttered.

Ten minutes later they were on the way north again. "Everything all right?" she asked quietly.

"Fine," he snapped.

Uh-huh. "Then what was all the fuss about back there?" she asked, half expecting him to tell her it was none of her business. It wasn't, but at this point, his business and hers were getting so intertwined that it was hard to tell where one left off and the other picked up.

"The painters can't finish my side until the end of the week. Somebody's daughter's getting married."

"That's what's got you into such a snit? A wedding?"

"The Jamisons have patched things up."

Several pieces of the puzzle came together. Jamison was the name of the couple who owned Driftwinds. Sasha didn't know anything about their personal lives, nor did she care, but evidently Jake was involved. "And that's bad?" she ventured after several minutes of silence. Fed, burped and dried, the baby slept soundly in the back seat. "If they're patching things up, where's the problem?"

It occurred to her to wonder if the peace negotiations would have any effect on her work at their cottage. Probably not, as she'd been hired by the rental agency, the only condition being that she finish the job before the holiday weekend began. It could do with a thorough airing and a couple of quarts of that spray the cleaning crew used to absorb odors, but other than that it was ready for occupancy.

"The problem," Jake said morosely, "is that I don't trust this truce. I accepted a retainer and I don't have a damn thing to show for it."

"What did you want to show for it?"

"Enough solid evidence so that he can't take her to the cleaners. Legally the place is joint property, but her money built it. All he's ever done is run for county office and lose. They keep wishy-washing around, but I'm not buying this reconciliation crap."

Sasha thought about it for several minutes. She thought briefly about her various divorces, but there was no comparison there. And then she thought about the man beside her, his muscular thighs sprawled out on the worn leather seat. *Laid-back* was the description that came to mind. Even when he was up to his ears in problems, he drove with a minimum of effort. None of this road rage you read about all the time.

She wondered if he did everything with the same minimum effort. "So what are you going to do, return the retainer?"

"I'm planning to. That's not what worries me." They were speaking quietly because of the sleeping baby in the back seat. "I have a feeling this won't be the end of it. Once we move your car away, Jamison might show up there for one last fling. I understand the place is booked solid all season after this week."

"Even if he's having an affair, why would he risk taking someone to his own cottage? That doesn't even make sense when there are all these hotels and motels around."

"It does if your face has been seen on as many campaign posters as his has. He'd be crazy to risk being seen sneaking into a motel with some bimbo."

She could think of a dozen arguments, but none worth voicing. Still, a detective had to start somewhere, and evidently Mrs. J. had reason to believe the cottage was the best bet. "Then you'll need me to baby-sit so you can take pictures." She added, "In case you get re-hired." And then tacked on, "If he's dumb enough to take some woman there, he deserves what he gets."

Jake continued to gnaw on his lower lip, obviously deep in thought. At least, she mused whimsically, he needed her for baby-sitting. She could build on that.

Build what? Woman, won't you ever learn?

Yes, but this is a two-fer.

Oh, shut up!

Granted, it didn't make a speck of sense for her to feel this bond with a baby she'd seen only hours ago—the grandchild of a man she'd known only a few days. While she might give the impression of being carefree and even somewhat superficial, by focusing on her career she had managed to ignore the ticking of her biological clock.

It had started ticking loud and clear the minute she had lifted a helpless infant into her arms.

"Look, we just passed the turn-off." Her conscience forced her to offer him an out. "If you drop me off at the cottage I can take Peaches and enough stuff to get by with home with me. Then you can hide out in the place next door and wait for something to happen. And this time," she added dryly, "you might want to be more careful about casting shadows and making noises."

He cut her a sidelong glance. "What, now you're giving me lessons in surveillance?"

"Well, I did catch you at it, remember?"

"Yeah, I remember." His mouth twisted in what was almost a smile.

She remembered, too. It was all part of that fate-engineered thing. After all these years, she had herself a baby. Albeit, a temporary one. "In case you were worried, you can take your time. On the Jamison thing, I mean—and anything else you need to do. I do a lot of my work at home, drawing up plans, ordering from suppliers." She didn't bother to mention taking in every yard sale, attic sale and estate sale within a day's drive of Muddy Landing. Those could wait. "I've got scads of stuff already on hand, so I won't need to go out anytime soon." Was she trying too hard to sell her services? Probably. She was powerfully attracted to the man, even though she'd known him less than a week—and he had a baby. And they needed her.

And maybe she needed to be needed.

"Thanks," he said dryly. Sasha tried and failed to read more into the single word. Then, without taking his eyes off the road—this close to Memorial Day weekend the midday traffic was dense and erratic—Jake laid a hand on her thigh. "How's the ankle?" he asked.

Her breath snagged in her throat. "I'd forgotten I had one." With his hand singeing a five-pointed brand on her thigh, she couldn't swear to having anything, especially a brain.

At the next stoplight, he turned to send her a wry grin. "Forgot you had an ankle? Believe me, I hadn't."

"Do I take that as a compliment?"

"Take it anyway you want." He reached across to brush the back of her neck, where her hair had long since escaped the decorative clips. "Why do you think I kept finding excuses to go back to your place? It's not exactly on the way to anywhere I need to be."

Her breath quickened. "I thought it was your guilty conscience." Not that he had any idea she'd been thinking about him when she'd tripped and fallen.

His fingers brushed her shoulder, then tucked a curl behind her ear. "Now why would I have a guilty conscience?" he teased. "I haven't done anything…yet."

Before she could come up with a halfway rational response, the car behind them honked impatiently. A stretch of several car lengths had opened up ahead of them since the light had turned green.

"Later," Jake growled, which did nothing at all to slow her heartbeat.

Was that a promise?

Or a threat?

Seven

Not until they pulled up in front of her house did either of them speak again. "Sasha, are you sure you want to do this?" Jake asked.

"I wouldn't have offered if there was the slightest doubt. If you'll just take in her bassinet and the rest of the stuff, we'll make out just fine, won't we, sugar dumpling?" Sasha unclipped her seatbelt and twisted around to check on their passenger. "Bless her heart, she's yawning—she looks just like a baby bird."

Jake took her keys and unloaded the car while Sasha counted baby toes and kissed both tiny feet. A few minutes later he returned. "You'll have to show me where you want stuff. Anything else you need, I can bring it tomorrow."

Tomorrow. Thinking of reasons to prolong the inevitable, she latched on to the promise. Sooner or later he'd come and claim his baby—the question was when? After he was done with the Jamison case, whichever way it turned out? Or maybe after his so-called interior decoration was complete? Who would she miss most, him or his baby?

Not even Solomon could answer that one, she thought ruefully.

"You sure you're up to this?" he asked, carefully unstrapping the seat and lifting seat and baby out.

Sasha led the way and held the door open. "Don't trip," she warned.

He gave her a look that defied interpretation. Placing baby, cradle and all on the coffee table, he turned to where she stood surrounded by an assortment of baby gear, plus her usual clutter. She forgot to breathe. Was it only her imagination that made her feel as if every cell in her body turned his way, like a sunflower following the sun?

Oh, Lord, she thought—all it took was the slightest encouragement and she was off on another fantasy, inventing a happy ending that wasn't going to happen.

"Sasha?" he said quietly. The house was suddenly so silent that even the quartz clock sounded loud.

"Mmm?" A complete mental and physical meltdown, that's all it was.

Jake placed his hands on her shoulders. It took only the slightest pressure to pull her into his arms. With her face against his hard, warm chest, she inhaled the scent that was pure Jake Smith. If his arms had fallen away she couldn't have moved. It was as if a giant magnet held her there.

"Fair warning. I'm about to kiss you," he said as calmly as if he were reading a public-service announcement.

In a voice that was only an octave or so higher than normal, she said, "Go ahead, I dare you."

He bit off a disbelieving laugh. She looked up, and then his face went out of focus and any hope of salvation fled from her mind.

Moist and surprisingly soft, Jake's mouth dragged against her lips, parting them. Beguiled by gentleness, she felt heat sparkle to life and flow through her veins like molten lava. Hunger was there, too, hovering in the background.

His control was maddening. Her hands fisted on the back of his shirt and she strained up onto her tiptoes. He was taller, but the three-inch soles of her sandals helped make up the difference.

And then he began to stroke her back, from shoulder to waist…and lower. When he cupped her hips to press her against his hardening groin, she wanted to tear off the layers between them.

He used his tongue. Not aggressively—not demandingly, but seductively, as if neither of them had anything better to do for the foreseeable future than to explore this thing that was happening between them.

This amazing thing that had been happening the very first time she'd ever laid eyes on him, even before she'd dialed 911, she admitted silently.

Ka-boom, ka-boom! The beat of her heart sounded like the jungle drums in those old Tarzan movies—or maybe it was his heart. The air around them was alive with electricity, she felt it all the way down to the soles of her feet.

By the time he lifted his face she was crushed in his arms so tightly she could hardly breathe. But then, who needed air? She rubbed her cheek against his shirt, in-haling his clean, sweaty scent. Please don't ever let me go, she begged silently. Let's just stay here like this for the next few years. Better yet, we could climb those stairs to where there's a queen-size bed, and—

A small sound made her catch her breath. "Peaches!" she gasped, pulling away at the thought of the small guest she had all but forgotten.

"Oh, honey—" She bent over to touch the fretful in-fant. "Let me take you out of that thing," she mur-mured.

"Wait a minute, I'll set up her bassinet." He sounded as calm as if he hadn't just kissed her senseless. "Where do you want it?"

"Oh, ah—upstairs, I guess. In my bedroom." She straightened up and glanced out the window. "Was that thunder?"

So maybe he wasn't responsible for all those special effects after all, she thought, chagrined. Only about ninety-seven percent of them.

Together they managed to get baby and bassinet up-stairs. Sasha held her while Jake settled the wicker bed on a table, after clearing it of various items, including pictures of her family.

"What about sheets? Doesn't she need something on that pad?"

"Look in the hall. There's a linen closet. A pillow-case will do just fine until I unpack everything and wash the linens."

"The hall," he muttered, remaining where he was for a few moments.

Was he having trouble concentrating, too? Served him

right for opening a door she'd thought closed for good. She knew better than to build dreams on quicksand.

"How about bringing that rocking chair up from the living room?"

He finished slipping the bassinet pad into a monogrammed Egyptian-cotton pillowcase. "You believe in rocking babies?"

She looked at him as if he'd lost his mind. "Why do you think the things were invented?"

"I remember we talked about getting one, but by the time we got around to it, Timmy was too big to be rocked." For a tough, sexy guy who could easily hold his own in almost any situation, he looked remarkably out of his element. "The one in the living room?"

"The one in the living room," she said softly, wanting to hold him and his baby for the foreseeable future.

Jake placed the rocker in the only available space. "I'll get the rest of the stuff, then I'd better head back to Manteo." Not a word about the kiss they had shared, or about how long she could keep his baby—or when he'd be back.

Sasha knew when to leave well enough alone.

Jake brought up the three-drawer chest and several parcels, his masculine presence making waves in the decidedly feminine room. Fodder, she thought ruefully, for another round of erotic dreams.

Standing beside her bed, he looked down at his granddaughter. "You think she knows where she is?"

Sasha joined him there, standing close, but not touching. "Of course she does. She's aware of color even if she can't see details. I'm positive she can feel the ambiance."

He slid his hands into his hip pockets. "The ambiance,

huh?" He glanced down at the antique Chinese rug in a faded shade of purple; at the ivory damask-patterned wallpaper and the green velvet fainting couch. Most of her furniture consisted of leftovers from various jobs or irresistibles from various estate sales. The fact that nothing went together didn't particularly bother her.

Smothering a smile, Sasha said, "You know what? I think she's far more intelligent than the average five-and-a-half-week-old." Boldly tucking her arm through his, she gazed at the solemn infant, knowing that she wouldn't be able to look at her lovely purple rug again without seeing a pair of size-twelve deck shoes planted firmly beside her queen-size bed.

What was that tacky old saying? He can park his shoes under my bed any old time?

She should be so lucky. Darn it, in spite of all her good intentions she'd gone and done it again. And now that he'd hooked and landed his baby-sitter, he was free to go about his business.

To give him credit, though, she was pretty sure that hadn't been his original intention. He'd been stunned at Timmy's call. What happened after that had simply happened, like a row of dominoes, each one tumbling the next.

"I know you have things to do," she murmured, hoping to hear him say he was in no hurry to leave.

He nodded, but made no move to go.

She tried to imprint him on her mind so that she could drag out the memory of him standing in the middle of her bedroom once he was no longer a part of her life. Probably not a good idea.

Searching for an impersonal topic to steer her away from temptation, she said, "I don't suppose the Jamison woman is your only client." According to Miss Martha, JBS Securities was seriously shorthanded. They had advertised, but so far, no one with the proper skills had applied.

"On top of that," the older woman had complained—if expressing a mild frustration could be called complaining—"Jake had to go and take on a private case."

All of which meant he was far too busy to deal with a grandchild, much less to get involved in a relationship. And while she might feel a powerful connection to him—that kiss alone had practically caused a brain meltdown—even if he was mildly interested in starting something, he didn't have time.

You buttered your bread, now lie in it, as Faylene would have said, and had on more than one occasion.

And she would. One more working mother. Working grandmother? One way or another she could do it.

The baby made a few experimental sounds and then let out a soft wail. Sasha shouldered Jake aside and said, "Here, give her to me. Come to mama, sugar pie. There, there, it's going to be all right, you wait and see." To Jake, she said, "Where did you put her bottles?"

"Come to *mama?*"

She curved a hand under the tiny body and supported her head. "Oh, hush, don't confuse her."

"Don't confuse yourself. And watch your step, will you? Those crazy shoes…" He frowned at her platform sandals.

Feeling vulnerable, Sasha promptly went on defense. "You do realize, don't you, that I've known this baby every bit as long as you have? My name is on her adoption papers, which gives me a personal interest. Be-

sides, I'm obviously more experienced than you are."
Holding the baby protectively, she glared at him.

"How do you figure that? Have you ever had a kid?"

"Twin sisters and a baby brother—I told you about
them, remember? Chief baby-sitter and bottle washer.
Not only that, next month I'm flying out to Oklahoma
to be godmother to my best friend's first baby."

Was there such a thing as a god-grandmother?

"What are you planning to do with her? I mean, with
my baby?"

"You mean right now? Tell you what—go downstairs and sit down in the living room and I'll let you
hold her while I fix her a bottle."

Frowning, he appeared to consider her words. Hadn't
he said the case he was working on was on hold? Sasha
would be the first to admit she was being a bit pre-
sumptuous, but if she'd learned one thing, it was never
to show weakness.

There was a casserole in the refrigerator that looked
Mexican. Marty must have sent it by Faylene, so at least
she wouldn't have to worry about supper. There was
more than enough for two.

By the time she got back from the kitchen with a bottle of formula, Jake was tipped back in her ergonomic
leather armchair with Peaches sprawled contentedly on
his chest, gnawing on a tiny knuckle. "I think she's
asleep," he whispered. "I'm afraid to move in case she
starts crying again."

One more memory to tuck away in her album. Sasha
stared just long enough to imprint the vision indelibly
on her mind—the tough security man in the worn jeans
and the faded black T-shirt, one big square hand cover-

ing practically the entire length of the tiny pink-clad infant.

"Things have changed a lot since I used to help Mama with the babies," she admitted as she lifted the limp form from his chest. "We actually used real diapers back then—the kind you wash and re-use. We didn't have a dryer, so in rainy weather we had drying diapers hanging all over the house. Most people were using disposables, but we couldn't afford them."

Way to go, gal! Like he really needed to know all that.

In case he'd forgotten them, she reminded him of the terrible twos, when toddlers went scouting for whatever trouble they could find—and found it. Double-trouble in the case of the twins, just about the time Buck came along. "Don't count on being able to concentrate until she's in kindergarten. By that time, if you're lucky, you should occasionally be able to get a few hours of work done."

She wondered how old Timmy had been when his mother had died, but couldn't think of a tactful way to ask. Holding the baby, she settled onto the sofa and touched her tiny lips with the nipple. When little Tuesday Smith took her cue and began suckling, she felt like crying because it felt so *right*.

Jake made no move to go. She probably should remind him of all the work he needed to be doing according to Miss Martha. Instead he was baby-sitting the baby-sitter.

Would he ever kiss her again? Could she go on living if he didn't?

Talk about going on a diet.

His long legs were crossed at the ankles, his arms

crossed over his chest. His eyes were narrowed, but not quite closed. He looked comfortable. Comfortable, tired and beautiful in the way certain men could look beautiful, that had nothing to do with any particular arrangement of features.

She thought of all the unhandsome Hollywood heroes she'd seen in movies and fallen in love with. Robert Mitchum and James Coburn. Charles Bronson and that guy who used to race around on a motorcycle—Steve McQueen. It all boiled down to chemistry. Like an elusive perfume that was impossible to describe. Either a woman reacted to it or it left her cold.

Nothing about the man seated across the room left her cold. That was something she was going to have to deal with—the sooner, the better. "What colors are you painting your house?" she asked, testing to see if he'd fallen asleep. It was drizzling outside, but not all that late, even though it seemed as if a week had passed since she'd first woken up that morning.

"Hmm?" He blinked his eyes. They widened, darkened and then narrowed as he glanced at his watch. "White."

"I mean the other side, where you live." The outside of the entire building was white. The office, which was all she'd seen, was white. She could have suggested something with a little more pizzazz if she'd been asked. For a security firm, maybe sand with caramel accents and small shots of navy and teal—something solid, reassuring and masculine.

"What about it?" he asked querulously. At least he was awake now.

"What colors are you using?"

"I told you—white." His chest rose and fell. His hands were still laced across the broad expanse. She wanted to be his hands. The plain, embarrassing truth was, she wanted to be all over him, inside and out. Maybe one desperate last fling?

Have you no pride?

Nope. Not a smidge.

From the chair, which was more comfortable than it looked, Jake watched through half-closed eyes. She was a natural. Those hips, the curve of her arms that was just right to hold a baby. Her breasts.... She probably thought she needed to lose a few pounds, but to his way of thinking she was perfect just as she was. Built just the way a woman should be built.

Cut it out, man. This is exactly the kind of thinking that got you in trouble back in high school. The same kind that landed your son in trouble ten months ago.

At least he'd married the mother of his kid. He had a feeling Tim and Cheryl were better off not going that far, but who was to say? Things were what things were.

Great. Now he was waxing philosophical. If he needed a clue that it was time to go, that was it. This baby was his responsibility, not hers, but Jake didn't kid himself that his granddaughter was the sole problem.

A large part of the problem was Sasha. It had been a long time since any woman had affected him the way she did. Hell, he'd been half aroused ever since he'd seen her sprawled out on the Jamisons' upper deck, with her shirt plastered to her breasts and her shapely legs sprawled out like an invitation. She was nothing at all like Rosemary.

Abruptly, he got to his feet. "I'd better hit the road, it's getting late."

She didn't say a word. Her eyes said everything for her, although he couldn't have interpreted the message if his life depended on it. Didn't she want him to go and leave her alone with his baby? To stay? What? Hell, he didn't even know for sure what color her eyes were.

Peaches was fed, clean, dry and sound asleep again when Marty's white van pulled up in front of the house and two women piled out. When Marty had called half an hour ago about the fund-raiser, Sasha had told her about the baby and all that had happened over the past several hours.

"Shh, y'all be quiet, I just got her down," she whispered by way of greeting.

"I can't believe it, you've got a baby!" Marty squealed. "I've got to see her. Wait'll I tell Daisy!"

The three women tiptoed upstairs to the bedroom. "Oh-h, she's so tiny," Marty whispered.

"Now you done stepped in it," was Faylene's only comment, but her voice was noticeably lacking its usual astringency.

"Come on down to the kitchen." Sasha led the way, hardly limping at all.

"I see you're getting around better. I brought you another casserole when I came by earlier on my way to the post office. Good thing I left out the jalapeños. Nursing mothers, you know." Marty snickered.

Faylene got right to the point. "We've thought up the perfect way to get Lily and this security fellow together. Things are gonna be closed up tighter'n a tick for the holiday, so he won't be working. This big do at the community center on Monday, they got the school band from over to the college in Elizabeth City comin' to play, and lemme tell you, they're *good!*"

"I'm not taking this baby around all those people," Sasha said flatly.

"Who said anything about you and her going? Lily's gonna be there helping out with the donations, so all you need to do is get this Smith fellow to carry whatever you're fixin' to donate over there for you."

"I told you, Jake lives in Manteo."

"So? He'll be coming here to see his baby, won't he?" Faylene blinked her eyes, the effect dramatic. She was the only woman in their small circle who wore more makeup than Sasha did.

"If she's still here," Sasha cautioned. "I'm only keeping her until his paint fumes are gone and the roofers finish hammering."

"You'll think of something," Marty said. "Tell him she's got the sniffles and it'll be weeks before she can be around fresh paint, then tell him you need something carried over to the center and can he come take it for you so you won't have to take her around all those crowds."

"You two are awful! That's the weakest plot I've ever heard!"

Marty picked up the book Sasha had been reading over breakfast only this morning. My God, when had her life taken such a bizarre turn? "What'd you think of her latest one?" the bookseller asked, holding up the paperback novel by one of the top romantic suspense writers.

"Speaking of weak plots?" Sasha retorted. "All right,

so maybe he'll let me keep her a few more days, but I can't ask him to take anything—and by the way, what *is* my contribution? I haven't even had time to think, I've been so busy."

"Go through all that flea-market junk you got laying around," the housekeeper said. "You got a whole herd of white elephants you need to chase outta here so I can clean this place."

Sasha had to laugh. It was true. She happened to have a weakness for used personal treasures of past generations, partly because she had nothing at all from her own family, partly because just one such item placed in the right setting could change the focus of an entire room.

"Okay, so *if* she's still here over the weekend, and *if* Jake happens to show up, and *if* he'll agree to run an errand for me, I'll send him over there with that alabaster lamp or maybe that brass sconce I haven't been able to place. He'll spot Lily, fall madly in love and swoon at her feet, is that your plan?"

Marty nibbled on a crust from the casserole she'd brought over earlier. Frowning, she murmured, "Not enough cheese."

"Next time use processed cheese slices, like I told you," said Faylene, the uncontested world's worst cook. "Look, we got her lined up to list stuff as it comes in with folks' names for them that wants something off on their taxes. Who better'n her to know the rules?"

"Monday noon's the deadline," Marty warned, "so you need to get him over there before then."

Sasha poured three glasses of sweet tea and led the way into the living room. If they stayed in the kitchen long enough, Marty would taste up every bit of the food she'd brought. Marriage seemed to have increased her appetite. "All right, let's say I can get him over here. Let's say I can prevail on him to take my donation over to the community center and say he sees Lily. What happens then? He proposes, she accepts and bingo, another match is made? Y'all are getting giddy. You know, we used to be better at this."

"And we used to have more to work with." Marty sighed. "That's the part we haven't thought out yet, but we're working on it. Lily's lost a few pounds she can't really spare, but she's still the most beautiful woman in town, present company excepted, of course."

"Of course," Sasha said dryly, and tossed today's paper at her. It was still bagged in a plastic sleeve.

Marty said, "You read the ads yet? You going to Norfolk Monday for the big sales?"

"I thought I was supposed to stay here with the baby and set up your pigeon."

"Oh, yeah. Why do they always plan everything for the same day?"

"Because it's the holiday, you goose."

They all laughed. Faylene washed the few dishes in the sink and then the two women left, offering to pick up any groceries she needed now that she wasn't quite so mobile.

Sasha closed the door and leaned against it, picturing the elegant accountant they'd been discussing. Over my dead body, she thought.

Beneath a rapidly darkening sky, a narrow band of pink sliced across the horizon as Jake drove home, his thoughts touching on his granddaughter, his son, the on-again-off-again Jamisons and the sexy, maddening woman he'd just left.

Sasha Lasiter, alias Sally June Parrish and evidently several other names. Was anything about her genuine?

Did he care?

Yeah, he cared. Not for his own sake, but for his baby's. Was he crazy to leave his granddaughter with a woman he'd known for less than a week?

The trouble was, she felt like someone he'd known all his life—and would like to know a whole lot better. So far as he knew, she hadn't tried to hide anything about her past. A superficial check of public records had pretty well corroborated what she'd told him—not that he'd expected any surprises.

Sally June Parrish, born September 28, 1967, married Lawrence Combs, married Barry Cassidy, married Russell Boone, married Frank Lasiter, with divorces spaced at suitable intervals.

She admitted freely to dyed hair, tinted contacts and fake fingernails and eyelashes. So what about her was genuine?

Admittedly, not much. Only the things that mattered, like her heart, her character—that self-deprecating sense of humor that knocked out his defenses.

One of the things he'd uncovered was the fact that she'd been doing pro bono work for years at various women's shelters and nursing homes. She was a regular speaker for various girls' groups. God knows what she taught them—how to make the most of their physical assets? How to throw together a roomful of mismatched furniture and make it come out looking pretty good? How to laugh even when you catch a heel in a crack and damn near break a leg?

None of that, he admitted as he headed home, explained the crazy way she affected him. The way she'd affected him right from the start, when he'd been shooting pictures of a lush-looking redhead sprawled out on Jamison's deck, soaking up sun while she waited for her lover to arrive.

At least that's what he'd thought at the time. Even then he'd envied Jamison without ever having met the guy. The lady would have tempted any man, married or not.

It had been a long time since Jake had looked at a woman that way. Okay, so maybe he'd looked—hell, he wasn't over the hill, far from it—but it had been a while since he'd been tempted to do anything about it. Raising a son, plus operating a business, had taken all his time and most of his energy after Rosemary had died when Timmy was seven.

Sure, he'd gone out with a few women. Dinner and a movie, that sort of thing. He'd even gone dancing at one of the nightclubs out on the beach a few times, but none of the women he'd dated turned him on. Not that they weren't attractive, but under the sleek tans, the tight jeans and the shaggy bleached hair, they'd been pretty much cut from the same pattern. Mostly they talked about movies he hadn't seen, celebrities he'd never heard of, reality shows he'd been too busy with real life to bother watching.

Sasha, on the other hand, set her own style. She definitely wasn't built to today's standards. Her clothes, even when she was supposed to be working, were neither beachy nor practical, yet he couldn't imagine her in a tailored dress or a two-piece business suit. From her crazy shoes to the top of her tousled red hair, she was the kind of woman all men dreamed of taking to bed.

Which meant she probably had men stacked up like cordwood, waiting for her to return their calls.

Reluctantly turning off the semierotic daydream, he parked in the backyard, leaving the three-car space out front available to any drop-in customers. With the holiday weekend bearing down fast—it looked to be a rainy one, too, which was never a good sign—there'd be a bunch of false alarms and screw-ups as cottages filled up with people who didn't take time to read a simple set of instructions.

He went in through the back door, frowning at the smell of paint. Work would stop for the holiday. It was a wonder they'd even got this far. Once the job was finished he could air out the rooms and bring his granddaughter home where she belonged.

Yeah? And what about the woman? Where does she belong?

He knew where he wanted her, all right. In his bed, now and for the foreseeable future, or at least until he ran out of steam and his boilers shut down.

And that made about as much sense as anything else in this cosmic comedy he called his life. Starting with that call from Timmy, his modestly rewarding, occasionally interesting, but mostly predictable life had changed beyond all recognition.

He couldn't imagine Rosemary, who'd been only twenty-six years old when she'd died, as a grandmother. She'd been a good mother—casual, but just what a boy needed, especially once he started getting interested in sports. She'd never been much for rocking or cuddling, but that was just her style.

Sasha, on the other hand…

Yeah, well…this was a whole new ball game. If there was a rule book for this kind of situation, he'd better find it and do some fast cramming, because the game had already started.

Passing through his freshly painted, semifurnished living room on his way to the shower, he wondered if tonight was too soon to drive back to Muddy Landing. Traffic died down after dark—he could make it in less than forty-five minutes.

On the other hand, if he put in a couple of hours in the office, he'd be good to go first thing tomorrow.

By the time he stepped under the needle spray, he was whistling under his breath. It wasn't a lullaby.

Eight

Was that the phone? At the shrill sound, the dream that had started out as wishful fantasy and morphed into something wildly erotic shattered and began to fade. Desperately, Sasha sought to hold on, but the bits and pieces slipped away like handfuls of fog.

She was on the upper deck of an oceanfront cottage in a canopied bed, and she was not alone—there was someone in bed with her, someone who was…

Gone.

A few glimpses lingered then disappeared. The feelings they engendered lingered longest of all, but in the end there was nothing left but a wisp of memory and a nagging sense of dissatisfaction.

Reluctantly, she opened her eyes. She was in her own living room, not on the upper deck of a half-familiar oceanfront cottage—lying on her own linen-slip-covered sofa instead of a canopied bed. Even more depressing, she was alone. She remembered putting the baby in her bassinet and coming back downstairs to turn out the lights and lock up for the night. She'd decided to read a few pages....

The shrill sound came again. It was the doorbell, not the phone. And the background noise was rain drumming down on the roof, not the ocean swishing against the shore.

"Oh, for Pete's sake, hang on, I'm coming, I'm coming," she muttered. Squinting against the glare of a reading lamp and the hall fixture, she hobbled to the door to see who on earth was calling at this hour. Middle-of-the-night visitors always meant trouble. She wished now she'd had a peephole installed in her front door, but it wouldn't have fit with her seasonal wreaths.

With her hand on the doorknob she blinked at her watch and waited for her eyes to focus. Seven minutes before *ten?* Oh, for heaven's sake, she hadn't slept more than twenty minutes at most. It only seemed longer because of that crazy dream.

She opened the door and there he stood. Her crazy dream in person. Wet hair falling over his forehead, rain glistening on the shoulders of a navy windbreaker bearing the logo of the North Carolina Aquarium on Roanoke Island.

They spoke at the same time. She said, "What do you want?"

He said, "I brought some stuff we forgot. I meant to wait until morning, but—"

Turning him away wasn't an option. Besides, he had no way of knowing she'd just been dreaming about him. Unless...

No, that was crazy.

"Come on in...I guess." He was probably worried about his baby. While he was here she could talk to him about attending the fund-raiser. "What's that?" She blinked at the red nylon bundle under his arm.

"It's, a—a backpack, I guess you'd call it. You put a baby in it and carry it on your back while you shop or run or do whatever else you need to do." He shook it out, holding it by the shoulder straps.

"While I *run?*"

"Yeah, well...some people do."

"Do I look like a runner to you?" She stepped back and led the way into the living room before she remembered that before her nap she had showered, toweled her hair and left it to air-dry, giving forty-seven cowlicks their freedom. She had slathered on moisturizer, eye cream and lip balm, and she was wearing her favorite at-home costume.

This is not about me, she told herself, it's about the baby. "Did you carry Timmy around in a sack on your back when he was barely six weeks old?" Feeling challenged always put her on the offensive. "That's scary."

He didn't react the way he was supposed to. Instead, he looked bemused. With a half smile on his face, his eyes moved slowly from her bare feet to her naked freckles, to her wild, slept-in hair.

"We had a baby carriage. Rosemary used to wheel him all over town. After supper, we both took him for carriage rides. Later on it was wagon rides, tricycle rides, bicycle rides without the training wheels."

"Yes, well, Peaches is too small for a backpack, and in case you failed to notice, sidewalks are rare in my neighborhood."

"I think you can wear it in front, too. That'd work, wouldn't it?"

Wear what—the sidewalk? With her brain out on disability, she quickly changed the subject. "You're dripping. No matter how much you water them those flowers aren't going to grow any bigger." She pointed to the stylized blossoms in her faded Oriental rug.

"You want me to leave?" He sounded plaintive, and she was pretty sure it was deliberate. A splendid specimen of prime masculinity, and he sounded *plaintive?*

I don't think so, Sasha thought, amused in spite of her irritation. Amused because he had a way of doing that to her. Irritated because he'd caught her looking her unadorned worst. The heroine of her X-rated dream hadn't been any freckled, overweight woman wearing a fright wig.

She smoothed her hair back from her face and did her instant face-lift, raising her brows, tilting her chin and sucking in her cheeks. It was one of the first things Sally June Parrish, with all her insecurities, had taught herself to do. She'd practiced for hours in front of a cracked and speckled mirror.

"Could I see her?" Jake whispered.

"She's asleep."

"I won't wake her, I just want to look at her again."

Sasha knew how he felt. How many times had she tiptoed upstairs to the bedroom just to make sure she hadn't imagined the whole thing?

"All right, but leave that thing in the foyer. I hope you saved the receipts."

"What's the difference between a foyer and a hall?"

At the foot of the stairs, she shook her head. "Don't

try to change the subject, I'm not having this conversation with you. You want to see Peaches, come on. Two minutes, that's all. Infants need all the undisturbed sleep they can get and this one has already been through enough of an upheaval."

Once more they stood side by side, close enough so that she caught a hint of soap and aftershave and something that was uniquely healthy male. Uniquely Jake.

She could feel his body heat as together they gazed down at the sleeping infant.

Jake whispered. "God, she's little, isn't she?"

"Shh. What did you expect, that she'd grown in the last few hours?"

"I think Timmy was bigger at that age, but it's been a long time."

He was standing so close his breath stirred her hair against her cheek. She did her best to ignore the tickling sensation. If he noticed her irregular breathing she could blame it on the stairs. It was no big secret that she was hardly the athletic type. "Boys are born bigger."

She knew better than that, it just popped out. Her father had called Buck the runt of the litter, among a few less-flattering things.

"Her hair looks like it's going to be curly. Tim had curls when he was born."

His warm, coffee-scented breath on her cheek raised a flurry of goose bumps along her flank. "That's not hair, it's peach fuzz."

He smiled, and then she did. As several minutes ticked past, Jake made no move to leave. Neither did Sasha. Even though the bedroom smelled of Odalisque perfume and baby powder, she was far more aware of the clean, earthy scent of his body that the rain had only accentuated. The only light in the room came from a pink-shaded lamp with a bronze Venus-on-the-halfshell body—another of her flea-market finds.

Suddenly the intimacy was smothering. Jake took a deep breath and expelled it in an uneven sigh. "Trust me, it'll grow out curly."

She didn't dare trust him, but she wasn't about to argue. The sooner he left, the less likely she'd be tempted to do something incredibly stupid. It wouldn't be the first time, but she had a feeling that this time the effects would be far more lasting.

Tucking her arm through his, she steered him out into the hall. "That's four minutes. You've used up your viewing allotment for the next two days."

"No way. Don't forget whose baby she is."

She smirked. "Don't forget who can't take care of her because he's in the middle of having his house painted in colors I wouldn't use on an outdoor privy."

"What the hell do my colors have to do with anything? Besides, last I heard white wasn't even a color."

"Shh, keep your voice down," she hissed as she flounced down the stairs. Pride was a marvelous analgesic. Her ankle didn't hurt at all.

Jake followed two steps behind, his feet thudding solidly on the carpeted stairs. At the foot of the stairs she spun around, but before she could say a word he clamped his hands on her shoulders and leaned over until his face was on a level with hers. "Listen to me. Just because I'm allowing you to keep her for a few days, you don't want to lose sight of who she belongs to."

Her gaze strayed from his narrowed eyes to his lips. Big mistake.

"The minute the work crew clears out I intend to hook up an exhaust fan and pump the place out so by the time I get her back where she belongs, you won't be able to smell a thing but good, fresh air."

"Ha!" she said weakly. With his hands gripping her shoulders and his face only inches away from hers, it was the best she could do.

"Damn right, *ha!* This has been one hell of a day, in case you hadn't noticed. I've spent most of it on the highway going back and forth between your place, my place, Cheryl's and the lawyer's, not to mention all that shopping. On the way here tonight I ran out of gas, and on top of that, the barbecue place was closed, so I haven't had anything to eat since lunch—and in case you forgot, I didn't get to finish that."

She started to interrupt but he cut her off. "Look, I'm not the sweetest guy you ever met, even when I'm in a good mood. When I'm tired, ticked off and hungry that goes double. So don't mess with me, lady, because I'm not in the mood to play games."

Somewhere during the tirade Sasha's mouth had fallen open. Her eyes had widened, while his had gone from warm hazel to cold obsidian. It was several moments before she noticed that his fingers were no longer biting into her shoulders, but had moved to the bare skin above the boat-necked caftan. "Sasha?" He sounded almost puzzled.

Unable to look away, she murmured, "Hmm?"

"I don't know what you're doing to me, but…"

And then he closed the few inches between them.

The instant before his face went out of focus, she saw his mouth soften. Then his lips brushed hers, pressed lightly and lifted before she could come to her senses enough to react.

Desperate to reclaim his touch, she took the initiative. Standing on tiptoe, she kissed him, using the tip of her tongue to lure him into responding.

By the time the kiss ended they were on the sofa with no memory of having moved. Jake's hands had found their way under her voluminous caftan. She wore panties underneath—just barely. As she wasn't wearing a bra, there was nothing to impede the way of a pair of determined hands.

He settled over her, covering half her body. There was a baby in her bedroom, otherwise she'd have led him right back upstairs.

"Talk about going from zero to sixty in ten seconds flat," he said with a short laugh.

"I know of a Lamborghini that does it in four," she replied, her voice no steadier than his.

"Sorry. Six-year-old Suburban. Ten's my best finish."

"Are we—?" Finished, she meant. Her faded caftan was up around her shoulders, her body fully revealed, flaws and all. She had managed to tug his shirt from his belt so that she could run her hands over his muscular torso. Discovering his sensitive areas, she concentrated on those, thrilling to the way he gasped when she brushed his nipples. Her fingers trailed down to his belt buckle and he sucked his breath audibly.

With a catch in his voice, Jake said, "Finished? I hope not. I don't suppose this couch of yours opens up?"

"No, but there's a downstairs bedroom."

"I can probably make it that far."

Sasha wasn't at all sure she could even stand. For the first time she regretted being a collector. There was no room to spread out where they were. He wouldn't be able to straighten his legs without kicking over a stack of something.

He stood and pulled her to her feet and into his arms. Sasha couldn't remember the last time she'd wanted a man as much as she wanted this one. The year she'd discovered sex, it had been more a matter of adolescent hormones than anything else. Comparing what she'd felt then to what she was feeling now was like comparing wading in a plastic pool to diving off the continental shelf. Both involved getting wet, but one involved testing unexplored depths.

"Which way?" he asked, his voice barely audible.

"That way," she replied without moving away. His exploring hands cupped her breasts and her knees threatened to buckle. Wrapping her arms around his waist, she held on to his belt. When her fingers slipped inside his jeans she was glad that for once she wasn't impeded by her usual array of rings. His hips felt as hard as they looked. He was hard everywhere—hard and sweet and utterly intoxicating.

With only a few more hungry kisses along the way they managed to make it to the spare room. At the moment it looked more like a warehouse than a bedroom, but at least the bed was relatively uncluttered.

Sasha swept away a stack of fabric samples and several catalogs while Jake dug his wallet out of his hip pocket, withdrew a foil packet and placed it on the bedside table.

She started to lie down, and then hesitated. Undress first? Wait to see if he wanted to undress her? Race to see who could get naked first and dive into bed together?

For a woman who'd been married four times, she suddenly felt as awkward as a virgin bride. What if he didn't like her? What if he thought she was too fat? She had a few stretch marks. She thought of them as damask, but Jake probably didn't even know what damask was.

She was still dithering when Jake lifted the caftan over her head and tossed it at the chair. Tomorrow she would tear the wretched thing into dust rags—or maybe press it in her memory book.

"Last chance to back out," he said.

As if backing out was even a faint possibility.

Quickly, he stripped off his shirt, stepped out of his shoes and shed jeans and briefs in one smooth motion, his eyes never leaving her face. She tried not to stare, but oh my, he was…

The word *glorious* came to mind, but even that didn't do him justice. Turning away, she folded back the bedspread. She hadn't even been sure there were sheets on the bed, not that it would have mattered.

He slid her yellow bikini panties down her hips, then lowered her onto the bed and came down beside her, burying his face in her throat. His tongue stroked her pulse until she wanted to scream at him. Her thighs moved restlessly. She wanted him inside her to end this exquisite torture, yet she didn't want it to end—this desperate compulsive tension that was building, aching, throbbing inside her.

The scent of arousal eddied around them as she felt him thrust involuntarily against her belly. Moisture blossomed as her eager body prepared the way. When he drew the lobe of her ear into his mouth, she groaned. When his lips moved down her throat to her breast to suckle there, she soared to a higher level, desperately near the edge.

When he moved his attentions to her other breast, circling her nipple with his tongue, her feet arched and her thighs fell apart.

This was her dream. *This* was what her dream had been all about!

Weak from all the attention lavished on long-neglected places, she caught a shuddering breath, then gasped for breath again as he took her even closer to the edge of the chasm. Her mind flickered in and out as his kisses and his clever hands wove a magic spell on her body.

If this was a dream, let it never end. Awake or asleep, he was all her fantasies come alive.

He whispered something, the words muffled against her throat. He nipped the underside of her chin with tender, ferocious kisses, then moved on to nibble her cheeks, her lips, as if he couldn't get enough of her taste. His palm stroked her belly, his fingertips tracing the creases of her groin before feathering lightly across her mound.

When his fingers slipped inside her, his thumb stroking her until she was ready to scream, she could only whimper. Torn between wanting to prolong the exquisite agony and the desperate need to end it, she cried softly, "Please..."

"Shh, sweetheart, we're getting there, give me a minute..."

When he sat up and leaned away, she thought she

would die. Don't bother with that thing, she wanted to scream at him.

So much for intelligence. So much for survival skills.

And then she stopped thinking at all as he moved over her again. In a jumble of limbs, her toes pushed against the tops of his feet, her knees bumped against his, and he knelt over her, her thighs embracing his hips. Her hands moved restlessly over the parts of him she could reach. She'd thought she was experienced? Nothing even faintly resembling this had happened to her before—this intensity that made every cell in her body quiver in anticipation.

Just then, lightning brightened the room. A moment later thunder rumbled across the sky. It seemed appropriate considering the electricity they were generating inside.

Jake took her hands and moved them slowly down his body, lingering where he wanted her attention. She gave it eagerly, testing his powers of resistance against her own power to arouse, first with feathery fingertip caresses, then with the judicious use of her fingernails.

First thing tomorrow, the acrylic goes.

Finally wrenching her hands away, he gently thrust inside her, withdrew and then thrust again. She whimpered, moving her hips restlessly. Hurry, hurry, hurry!

"What are you trying to do, woman—cripple me for life?"

"Am I succeeding?" she panted hopefully.

"Slow down, slow down—short fuse."

When she felt him withdraw she tried to grasp his shoulders, but her hands slipped off his sweat-slick skin. Then he turned, levered himself to a sitting position, and with his back braced against the padded headboard, lifted her astride his lap.

"Oh, yesss," she breathed as she wriggled against his groin. In the dim light from a small table lamp, his strained features could have been chiseled from stone.

His eyes were closed, his head back. He moved with carefully measured thrusts, his breath coming in raw gasps. "Sure you're not registered somewhere—as a— lethal agent?" he ground out.

And then there was no more room for words. Suddenly she was clinging to him, desperately trying to match the furious pace of his thrusts as fireworks began to burst around her, exploding in a brilliance of pulsating color. As if from a distance she heard a guttural cry and then her own voice cascaded over her in a series of soft, wild whimpers.

Breathless, she collapsed against his sweat-damp chest. His head was back against the headboard, his eyes still closed, his hands still gripping her hips.

Once she was able to think again, her first thought was not for herself, but for the infant upstairs. Any moment now she would need to be fed again. It had been so long since she'd cared for a baby that she'd almost forgotten what a full-time job it was. And as inevitable as it seemed, this thing that was happening between her and Jake vastly complicated an already complex situation.

They should have laid out the ground rules first.

Like what? No messing around until she's a year old? Two years old?

Where would Jake be by that time? Where would Jake's grandchild be?

Chances were, neither of them would be upstairs in her bedroom.

Nine

Sex had to be the world's best cure for insomnia, Sasha thought sometime later as she stretched luxuriantly. Parts of her body were so deliciously tender that she was half aroused just remembering. Slowly, she opened her eyes and realized it was morning, and she was still in the spare bed instead of her own upstairs bedroom.

Who had fed the baby?

There was no sign of Jake, but someone had pulled the top sheet up over her shoulders. It probably wasn't the tooth fairy.

Her first thought was Peaches. As long as she'd been delegated baby-sitter-in-chief, she intended to do a first-class job of it. Whatever happened once Jake reclaimed his granddaughter, he'd have no room for complaint on that score.

As for anything else…

Time would tell. She had the world's worst taste in picking husbands, but then, in this case, no one had mentioned marriage.

Upstairs, she looked in on the baby, marveling that anything so precious, so perfect, was sharing her bedroom, even temporarily. But then, her house didn't reek of paint and varnish. Nobody was crawling around on her roof, sounding like a cavalry brigade.

She even had a few dependable friends who would gladly take over if she had to be away for a few hours. How many available women friends did Jake have?

Well. It was a tad late to be wondering about Jake's women.

There was a half-empty bottle on the dressing table. Evidently Jake had fed her before he'd left. She collected the bottle and tiptoed away. Changing could wait. Sleep was important at this age.

What else was important? It had been so long. She remembered from back when Annie, Jeannie and Buck had been babies, when first one, and then the other two, would reach the five-alarm stage, loosely interpreted as, "I want it, and I want it *now!*"

It had taken Sasha and her mother together just to handle the twins. By the time Buck came along, Sasha knew the drill. She'd had almost complete care of the new baby while their mother tried to tame the unmanageable twins.

A few years later the three youngest members of the Parrish clan had closed ranks. She could still see them exploding from the school bus, racing up the path to the house, laughing, chattering, the girls finishing each other's sentences. Buck had been the pesky, tagalong brother, but even so, the three of them had enjoyed a closeness that had excluded her. As baby-sitter-in-chief, she'd ranked along with their parents as an authority figure—someone to be obeyed when absolutely necessary, but never included, much less confided in. At the time, she hadn't particularly resented it, but later, after she'd left home, it had made her feel sad.

Of course, Buck was gone now, but she and her sisters chatted on the phone whenever she called. They sent pictures of their families when she asked for them, which she framed and set around her house, if only to remind her that she did have a family. Their Christmas cards always included family newsletters all about promotions and camping trips and school honors, and she tried to feel a part of it all, but there was no real closeness involved. There never had been.

Maybe she should do a family newsletter. Hey, y'all, I've finally got a baby. She's only on loan, but then, I'm really too busy with all my commissions to have her full-time, anyway. Oh, and by the way, I'm in love again, and this time I have a feeling it's terminal. Ha-ha.

Ten minutes later when she tiptoed into the room again she was met by a pair of unblinking eyes in a red, tear-wet face. "Oh, honey pie, don't do that," she murmured, trying to remember the words of a lullaby she used to sing to the twins. She hummed and la-la-ed while she did the necessary cleaning and changing. Those solemn blue eyes followed her every move.

"What are you thinking, dumpling? You're not sure you like all this roadrunning you've been doing lately? You're missing your granddaddy?" She swallowed a laugh. "Oh, honey, so am I," she whispered, lifting the baby to her shoulder. "So am I."

So am I...

The first thing Jake had done on his way home was to arrange to have the Lexus picked up and driven to Muddy Landing. He dropped off the keys at a garage—the owner owed him a couple of favors—and drove the rest of way thinking about the next item on the agenda.

Next item, hell. All he wanted to do was turn back, crawl into her bed and stay there for the foreseeable future.

But if the first four guys she married couldn't satisfy her, what gave him the idea she'd be interested in an over-the-hill widower?

Maybe not over the hill—he'd pretty well proved he was still good for a few rounds—still, he was a meat-and-potatoes type and she was definitely caviar.

First stop, the office. Jake checked his phone messages while he scanned the note Miss Martha had left for him saying that she wouldn't be in until eleven or thereabouts. It was early yet for Hack. Feeling restless and vaguely unsettled, he started going through his schedule for the following week. Two installations, which he enjoyed. Three repairs, which he didn't. There was still the Jamison thing. He'd been called off, but something still didn't feel right.

In the middle of checking the addresses of the repair jobs, he paused. God, I've got a baby!

Allowing Sasha to get involved had been a mistake, but short of driving her back to Kitty Hawk and dumping her out at her car, at what point could he have excluded her? From start to finish, it had gone down like a row of dominoes.

She was right about one thing, he thought, unlocking the inside door that separated his private office from his living quarters. This was no place to bring a kid. The office was gradually airing out, but his side stunk to high heaven.

Hands on his hips, he looked around, trying to see his familiar living quarters objectively. What the devil had she meant when she'd criticized his color scheme? What was wrong with white walls, white ceilings and brown floors? Not everybody wanted to live in a lavender house with green trim, filled with the kind of furniture a guy couldn't even pronounce.

Shedding his clothes along the way, he headed for the shower, which was also painted white. What the hell had he been thinking about, getting mixed up with a woman like Sasha Lasiter?

Answer: he hadn't been thinking, at least not with his brain.

A short while later, showered, shaved and dressed in a clean version of the jeans and T-shirt he'd discarded, Jake was already outside when the office phone rang. He grabbed it on the fourth ring. "JBS Security, Jake Smith."

And then, "Mrs. Jamison?"

Several minutes later he replaced the phone. If he were inclined to be superstitious he might blame it on the phase of the moon, or some weird conjunction of planets. First Sasha, then the baby, then Sasha again—in a big way—and now this crazy on-again, off-again case he'd been working on when it had all started.

Evidently it was now on again. According to his wife, Jamison had lulled her into calling off the dogs, but the minute she lowered her guard, he'd cut the connubial cord. According to his wife, the guy had the morals of a rat snake. She wanted the goods on him, and she wanted it yesterday.

The lady didn't need a private investigator as much as she needed a sharp lawyer. Something here stunk to high heaven. Jake couldn't put his finger on it, and without evidence there wasn't a lot he could do. Trouble was, it was probably already too late.

But as long as he was back on retainer, Jake figured he might as well continue to stake out the cottage again, as Mrs. J. seemed convinced that that was where he was taking his girlfriend. During the time he'd spent watching the place, he had seen no evidence of it, other than a certain sexy redhead making herself at home on the upper deck.

Meanwhile, Hack could do the usual check, see if he could pick up another lead. Jamison was a local, his wife was from Virginia Beach. They owned properties in both places, and with the state line so close, things could get complicated.

Before he left the office, he made another attempt to reach his son. He'd tried several times in the past few hours, leaving a message each time. This time he connected on the first try.

"Hey, Dad, I was just about to call you. Jeez, I've been going crazy, wondering what was going down. Have you seen her yet? Is everything all right? Is Cheryl gonna let you have her?"

"Whoa, back up—first, everything's fine here.

Cheryl seemed relieved to let her go to family—I told her she can see the baby anytime she wants to. I've been thinking, though—did you ask Cheryl about her folks? I mean, genetically, it might be a good idea to know something about her background. I tried to get some information from her, but the way things went down, it was a pretty emotional time for all of us."

"I know her mom's dead. She and her old man don't get along. I think he drinks a lot or something. Anyway, I don't know all that much about her folks, but Cheryl's a nice girl. What do you think, is the baby okay?"

"Ah, son—she's a real beauty." Jake saw no reason to mention that she was bald and had a voice like a fire siren when she really cut loose. "All her working parts appear to be in good order, especially her lungs. I cleaned her up and gave her a bottle earlier this morning, and left her sleeping like a baby."

"You *left* her? Left her *where?*"

"Whoa, no cause for panic." So then he had to explain about Sasha and how she'd been caught up in the whole procedure, and how she'd agreed to keep the baby until the roofers were finished and he could get rid of the paint fumes. "You'd like her, son. She's good with babies—in fact, she's the one who got us in to see a lawyer so we could sew up things in record time."

"Okay…I guess. I mean, I trust your judgment, Dad, but Cheryl, is she okay with this?"

"She's fine." He could explain in more detail later. "Everything went down without a hitch, but you might want to be thinking about another name. Her birth certificate says Tuesday Smith. No middle name. It doesn't do much for me, but you'll be the one to decide. At least Cheryl gave her your last name."

They talked for a few more minutes before Corporal Timothy Burrus Smith had to leave. "Look, they're calling for me, but hey—I love you, Dad."

Jake swallowed the lump in his throat and said gruffly, "Me, too, boy. You take real good care of yourself, we'll hold down the fort here until you can take over."

"My son, the soldier," he murmured, his eyes filming over. Not too long ago, Jake mused, he'd been changing the boy's diapers and feeding him disgusting stuff like pureed spinach and squash, while Rosemary strung beach-glass beads for a Nags Head crafts shop.

Now Rosemary was gone and Timmy was headed to the Middle East with his unit, and Jake was about to start the whole routine again, this time for his granddaughter. He didn't know if that made him feel older or younger—maybe a little of both.

On his way up the beach a short while later, Jake made three stops; two to check out problematic systems and one to pick up a large coffee and a cheese, turkey and apple sandwich. Next he called Sasha, only to be told everything was just fine, and she was getting ready to put the baby down for a nap. "While she's sleeping, I'll catch up on a few things, but you do know how often she eats, don't you? Every three hours. Are you sure you're ready for that?"

He wasn't sure of anything at this point.

Well, for one thing, he was hungry. He could eat while he was on stakeout, not that he expected to catch the guy in action.

Renters had already arrived at the cottage where he

usually took up a position. Three cars filled the parking area, one carrying a kayak on top, two others with surfboard racks. Jake cruised slowly along the narrow blacktop, looking for an unobtrusive place to park.

"Well, hell," he muttered, spotting a car pulled up beside Driftwinds. He recognized it as belonging to the rental agent only because he'd had Hack run her plates the first day Jake had staked out the place. He'd seen her around, an attractive brunette, probably under thirty. "Lady, you're in my way," he muttered, wondering whether to wait for her to leave or to give up now.

On the other hand, if he was waiting for the coast to clear, maybe Jamison was waiting, too. Odds were about one in ten thousand, but what the devil, until Hack could come up with another lead—and as long as he was here with a sandwich and a cup of coffee that was growing cold—he might as well stick around a few more minutes. The agent was probably checking to make sure Sasha had finished the job. That shouldn't take long.

He bit into his sandwich as he crept along the street in search of an out-of-the-way parking place, thinking about all that had happened since he'd shot a bunch of pictures of a luscious redhead only a few days ago, under the illusion that she was Jamison's girlfriend. The setting sun had turned her hair to flame while a light breeze had blown her flimsy blouse against her breasts. And those crazy pink shoes, he thought, grinning at the memory.

Oh, hell. Those shoes….

The one he'd taken off her foot was still on his dresser. Thank God the painters had finished his bedroom first; he'd hate to get the reputation of having a foot fetish.

Spotting an empty driveway near the end of the cul-de-sac where he would have a clear view of the Jamison place, he backed in and shut off the engine. His chances of catching Custer at his last stand were about the same as his chance of winning the lottery, but it wouldn't hurt to hang around for a few more minutes while he waited for Hack to come up with another lead.

According to the facts on file, the Jamisons had a small place in Colington over on the soundside, but with neighbors on either side, he would hardly show up there with another woman.

Jake flipped down the visor to cut the sun's glare. He'd just finished his sandwich and reached for his cell phone when he saw the rental agent come outside and head toward her car. "Okay, maybe now we'll see some action," he murmured, waiting for her to get in and drive off. Chances were slim to nothing, but he needed to be doing something, and until he got another lead, this was it.

He finished his coffee and was about to punch in the quick-dial number for the office when a familiar-looking guy in Bermuda shorts and yellow T-shirt emerged from the cottage, glanced around, and hurried across the gritty pavement toward the agent's car.

Jake's memory was good, but not perfect. He'd definitely seen the guy somewhere recently…but where? From one end of the Outer Banks to the other and occasionally into lower Virginia, he covered a lot of territory.

Where was this guy's car? And what had he been doing inside the cottage? Looking the place over with an eye to booking it later in the season?

The attractive brunette was still standing beside her car when yellow-shirt joined her there. They talked for a few minutes while Jake slouched in his seat and watched through a pair of aviator sunglasses, wishing he could read lips. About half his mind was on what he was seeing, the other half on the woman he'd left sleeping a few hours ago.

He shifted uncomfortably as his body reacted to the memory. The crazy thing was that if anyone had asked him to describe his ideal woman, Sasha Lasiter wouldn't have come to mind. So why was it that after only a few days he couldn't stop thinking about her?

More to the point, why did his body react with outrageous desire toward her? Hell, he was a grandfather, not some horny kid. He had a granddaughter to think about now, not to mention a job that at the moment was stalled in its tracks. So how come he was wasting time on a stakeout that obviously wasn't going to lead anywhere, thinking about a woman who had nothing at all to do with the case he was working, other than peripherally?

But instead of clearing his mind, he kept picturing the way she tried to stare him down with her multicolored eyes. Talk about attitude, she was a regular Ms. Napoleon. And the way she bragged about all her artifices— and the way she dressed....

It didn't take any special training to know that when people went to such lengths to disguise themselves there was usually a reason for it. The trouble was, he didn't know her well enough to figure it out. He knew she was sexier than any woman he'd ever met, and that included his late wife. He knew she was flat-out gorgeous, with or without her disguise. He'd seen her with her makeup smeared and with her face scrubbed clean of all but her freckles, and it hadn't made a speck of difference. She was who she was, and it was who she was that attracted him in a way that no other woman ever had.

Jake reminded himself again that she'd had four husbands and not a one of them had suited her well enough to keep. He'd had one wife, who had suited him very well during the few years they'd been together.

Bottom line—what could a glamorous, successful woman possibly see in a dull, middle-aged businessman, a mediocre detective who couldn't even manage a simple surveillance, who didn't know a damn thing about interior decoration, much less care about it—who didn't think one way or another about fashion as long as what he had on was comfortable?

Answer? Not a whole lot.

What did he see in her? A lot more than met the eye. That was the problem. Those colored contacts did a good job of disguising the shadows, but he'd heard that wistful note in her voice when she forgot to be Sasha the Outrageous. Somewhere under all that paint and polish there was a real woman who made him want to explore more than her body.

That is, if he ever got tired of exploring her body.

"What the hell?" he muttered suddenly. Sitting up, he removed his sunglasses in time to see yellow-shirt and the agent come together in a clinch that sent heat weaves shimmering off the tarmac.

"Well, now…" he mused, stroking his jaw. Maybe he wasn't such a lousy P.I., after all. His brain might not be up to speed, but evidently his instincts were still on the job. Jamison looked older than his campaign posters, but there was no mistaking that face.

Time to find out more about the attractive brunette

who, unless he was mistaken, worked for Southern Dunes Property Management. And who better to tell him than the decorator who'd been commissioned to update one of her rentals?

"Don't be so stingy, Faylene, let me hold her," Marty reached for the baby only to have Faylene turn away with her.

"You got you a husband now. Go home and make one o' your own, this one belongs to me and Sasha, don't you, sugar dumplin'?" The housekeeper beamed at the infant in her arms. "Lawhepus, if I weren't too old, I'd have me one of these in a minute."

"That'd be one for the records," Sasha observed dryly. "Last I heard it took nine months." Her feet were propped on a cushion on the coffee table that was littered with sample books and baby paraphernalia. She had managed to squeeze in a shower between feeding and bathing the baby before her friends had showed up, but she'd spent more time rocking Peaches and trying to remember the words to the song about the looking glass and the mockingbird.

With those dark blue eyes gazing up at her so solemnly, she had choked up more than once. Watching now as her friends exclaimed over her, Sasha told herself that what she was feeling was protectiveness, not possessiveness. A few more minutes and she would put an end to it. Too much stimulation wasn't good for an infant who wasn't yet two months old.

"Did I tell you I've got us another bachelor? Kell has this carpenter friend—actually, he's more of a contractor. He's recently divorced, no kids, no noticeably bad habits." Marty leaned over the housekeeper to cup a tiny foot in her hand.

"What does he look like? Anyone a tall, gorgeous blonde with a degree in accounting might be interested in?" Sasha continued to buff her short, newly exposed fingernails. She felt naked without the acrylic versions, but long nails and babies didn't go together.

Faylene glanced up. "I thought we'd already picked out this security fellow for Lily."

"Jake has other priorities now," Sasha reminded her friends.

"So?" Marty gave up trying to steal the infant away from the housekeeper and began leafing through a catalog of accessories.

"So he has enough on his mind without getting involved in a new relationship. Besides, his son's headed overseas and Jake's in the middle of repainting his house and, like I said, now he's got this baby to think about."

"Well, pardon me, but it looks like Jake's baby has all the caregivers she needs. So why can't he take a few hours off and go to our darned fund-raiser?" Marty shot her a pointed look. "Unless you have other plans for him?"

"Don't be silly!" Sasha snapped. Feeling her face grow warm, she said, "I hardly even know the man."

Faylene glanced up from the baby on her lap. "I told you about them letters Lily's been getting, didn't I? The ones with the numbers on the front like a secret code or something? I asked her about it the other day when I saw her looking all weepy-eyed over one. She's been getting 'em, one a week, for as long as I've been working for her."

"Faye, for heaven's sake, you know better than to

gossip about things like that," Marty scolded. "What'd she say?"

"Pretended like she didn't hear me."

"It's probably a service person—someone in the military."

"I 'spect so," murmured the older woman, her attention on the infant gazing up at her so intently. "Did I tell you they're written in pencil on lined paper? First I thought it was a street number on front, but that was on the next line. A San Pedro Street—something like that."

"There's nothing like that around here," Sasha said thoughtfully. "Florida? Maybe St. Augustine?"

"Nope, California."

"Well, whatever it is, it's none of our business," Marty said self-righteously, and then spoiled the effect by suggesting it might be a tax number. "She is a CPA, after all. Maybe you misread the CA for CPA." Faylene's reading skills were on a par with her cooking.

"Not that it matters, but if you're that curious, ask her about it," Sasha said, closing the matter.

"Back to the fund-raiser, you don't mind missing it, do you, Sash? You can baby-sit for a few hours while we get your guy together with Lily, can't you?"

Sasha had an idea her friend was playing with her. She buffed harder. Before she could come up with a reason to take Jake out of the race, she heard a car pull up out in front.

Marty peered through the window. "Speak of the devil," she said, a wide grin spreading over her face.

Ten

Jake came to a full stop just inside the doorway. The expression on his face was priceless. Amused, Sasha watched his reaction to finding himself outnumbered by females.

Faylene looked up and broke into a broad smile, re-arranging scores of wrinkles on her heavily made-up face. "Hey there. I gotcha baby here. She don't look much like you, I'll say that for her."

Marty said, "Well, hi there."

"Uh…ladies," he murmured cautiously.

Sasha said, "Now I know what Daniel must have looked like standing in the door of the lion's den. Come on in, Jake, we were just talking about you. You've met my friends, haven't you?"

He nodded and then his gaze returned to the baby in Faylene's lap. Waving tiny pink fists, Tuesday Smith, aka

Peaches, was making noises that Sasha recognized as meaning, "Enough with this hands-on stuff, I need a nap."

Evidently, Jake had forgotten how to interpret baby language. "Is she—?"

"Hurting? Don't think so. Starving? No way, she was fed less than half an hour ago. Wet? Probably. Mostly, she's just ready for a nap, aren't you, sugar? We're still working on a mutually convenient schedule."

Sasha scooped the baby from Faylene's lap and moved closer so that Jake could see her tiny face. Inhaling the warm soap-and-outdoorsy scent of his skin, she told herself with a sense of mystic certainty that blindfolded, and with nothing more than that, she could have picked him out of any lineup. It had to be pheromones, she thought wistfully. She couldn't afford for it to be anything more complicated than chemistry. Even that was almost more than she could handle. "Thank you for sending my car home," she murmured.

Jake nodded. "No problem."

While he concentrated on the baby, Sasha happened to glance at Marty, who was looking him over with undisguised interest.

The bookseller caught her eye, winked and blushed. "We were just talking about the fund-raiser planned for tomorrow night, Jake. Did Sasha tell you about it?"

"What fund-raiser?"

"It's just a local project," Sasha dismissed. "I doubt if you'd be interested." Turning away, she sank down onto the sofa and lifted the baby to her shoulder, patting her on the back.

As the two most comfortable chairs were taken, Jake settled beside her, his weight tilting the cushion so that she found herself leaning on his shoulder. "What kind of local project?" he asked.

Their voices overlapping, Marty and Faylene described the summer camp that featured fishing, kayaking, camping and even fly-tying. "It costs two hundred bucks for a two-week session," said Marty.

"I got a good friend, Bob Ed Cutrell, down at the marina," Faylene said. "You might know him—he outfits 'em so the gear don't cost nothing extra, but—"

Marty picked up. "But a lot of them still can't afford it. This is not exactly a high-income district, in case you hadn't noticed. Commercial fishing barely makes expenses these days, and the storm flooded so many fields, it'll take at least another year to recover."

To Sasha, seated beside him on the sofa, it seemed the most natural thing in the world to lean against Jake Smith while holding his baby in her arms. Gazing down at the small bundle sleeping so peacefully on her shoulder, she murmured, "What about it, sweety pie, you want to go to summer camp?"

Marty looked from Sasha to Jake, as if trying to measure the degree of involvement. "So what about it, Jake—shall we count you in?"

If Jake felt pressured, he was tactful enough not to show it. "Can I get back to you?" When he reached for the infant, his hands brushed against Sasha's breast. "Here you go, baby, come to Granddad."

As if his touch weren't enough to melt any residual resistance she might feel, his voice finished her off. Fighting against the urge to trade places with the baby in his arms, Sasha tugged the pink flannel square from her shoulder and spread it over his.

"I'd forgotten about that part," Jake said, obviously not really bothered by the risk of a damp shoulder. They traded lingering smiles until the other two women stood and collected their purses.

"Guess we'd better be going," said Marty, a gleam of amusement in her eyes. "I brought you a few more books. Since you're temporarily house-bound, you might even get caught up on your reading." She indicated the stack of paperbacks on the floor beside the cluttered escritoire.

Faylene said, "I turned the fridge back on after I wiped it out, so don't open the door till it has a chance to catch up."

"Don't bother to see us out," Marty said dryly as the two women exchanged unmistakable smirks.

"Did I miss something?" Jake asked when the front door closed behind them.

"I hope so. They mean well, but—" Sasha shook her head. She wasn't about to tell him about the match-making she and her friends occasionally did—especially after the way Marty had looked at the two of them together, as if measuring them for a double harness.

"Here, I'll take her now—she's yawning."

How could any man be so darned tempting with a baby in his arms, spit-up on his shirt and a goofy grin on his face? All she had to do was look at him to remember last night and what had probably been the biggest mistake of her life.

Which, considering her track record, was saying a lot.

"Give me another few minutes. Look, the reason I came by—we need to talk."

Uh-oh. Crunch time. She'd known it was coming, she

just hadn't wanted to think about it. Once he took the baby home with him, he'd have no reason to return to Muddy Landing.

Feeling as if she were dragging an anchor, she stood and reached for the baby to take her upstairs. Jake sighed and reluctantly handed her over.

When she came downstairs a few minutes later, he said, "Without breaking any confidences, what can you tell me about the agent handling the Jamison rental?"

"Katie McIver?" Puzzled, Sasha wondered what the rental agent had to do with their baby. "I've known her several years, but only in a business capacity. I did their offices—Southern Dunes Property Management? Since then she's called me several times for makeovers and quick patch-up jobs. Mostly the owners take care of that sort of thing themselves, but now and then they leave it to the agency." She settled down, this time in the armchair instead of the sofa. "I know she's well respected. I know she handles several of their top rentals. Other than that, I don't really know much about her."

Jake nodded silently, as if he were processing the information. "Do you know if she's married?"

"We've never really discussed much besides budgets and timetables. Once we had coffee together at Southern Bean, but I don't remember anything we talked about except the damage Hurricane Isabel did to her cottages." Increasingly puzzled, she asked, "Why do you need to know all this?"

Absently, Jake stroked his jaw. "Then you wouldn't happen to know if she's, um—involved in a relationship?"

"I told you, we've never discussed anything like that. Is there a reason why you need to know?" She forced herself to stamp down a twinge of jealousy. Katie had to be on the sunny side of thirty. She'd probably end up managing the agency one of these days, because she was every bit as smart as she was attractive. "Why don't you just ask her? I don't like talking about people behind their back."

The vertical lines between his dark eyebrows deepened. "Sorry. I shouldn't have asked. Something unexpected came up on my way here and I wanted to get a feel for it before I went any further."

"I read enough suspense novels to know about questioning witnesses. I couldn't help you even if I wanted to. Why don't you ask Katie whatever it is you want to know? I've got her cell phone number if I can remember where I put it."

"This case I was working on when you and I met?"

"When you invaded my privacy, you mean," she corrected. Arms crossed over her bosom, she tried a chilly look, but she was in too deep. She gave up trying. "But then you came to my rescue after I hurt my ankle, so I suppose we're even," she admitted grudgingly.

"Yeah, well…things got sort of crazy there for a while. I don't know how much I told you before, but the owners of the cottage where you were, ah—"

"Working, but taking a tiny, well-earned break," she supplied before he could accuse her of goofing off on the job.

"Right. Anyway, they're getting a divorce and the wife hired me to check out her suspicions concerning her husband and another woman. She got the idea he was using their cottage as a—a—"

"Love nest?" Sasha thought about the scent of cigarette smoke and the rumpled cushions. And there was the cork she'd found in an otherwise empty trash can.

"I don't know how much love was involved, but yeah—I guess you could call it that."

"Did she have any evidence? The wife, I mean?"

"A friend told her she'd heard rumors that Jamison might be using the place as his private playground." Jake settled into the green leather-covered chair. "Evidence is what I'm supposed to get."

Indignation built swiftly. "You took all those pictures of me thinking I was waiting to meet a lover? I don't know whether to be amused, flattered or insulted." She settled on amusement as the least problematic.

"Hey, I never claimed to be one of those super sleuths you read about or watch on TV. Every now and then I like to try my hand at something besides security systems just to prove I'm not—"

"Over the hill," she finished for him, and stopped just short of saying, take it from me, you're not.

Judging from his expression, the same thought occurred to Jake. Sasha settled on the sofa, putting the coffee table between them.

Over the hill?

Uh-uh, no way. She'd had lovers both older and younger. Jake was in a class by himself.

He smiled. "I was going to say rusty, but back to what we were talking about." The smile faded. "My client called a few days ago to say they'd gotten back together and my services were no longer needed. She called again just as I was about to leave this morning."

"To say what, sic him?"

Jake nodded. "Words to that effect."

"And—?" Sasha prompted.

"And I just came across evidence possibly involving your rental agent."

"What evidence? Circumstantial? Gossip?"

"Nothing circumstantial about a lip-lock that timed out at just under two minutes."

"You're kidding," she said slowly. "Katie and Mr. Jamison? How can you be sure? I've never even seen the man, much less met him. I've never met either of the owners."

"His face is plastered on campaign posters every time we have another election. One of the reasons why he can't just book a room for a few hours." Jake described the frustrating, off-again, on-again case he'd been working on for the past several days.

"Hmm...you know what it sounds like to me?" Rising, Sasha went to the bottom of the stairs and listened for sounds from the baby. A moment later, she settled back into the chair. "All's quiet. Bless her heart, she'll probably sleep for another hour, at least." Taking a deep breath, she said, "You know what I think? I think he patched things up just long enough to throw his wife off guard and get her signature on a few documents." The soft contours of her face hardened imperceptibly. "Any woman who signs anything at all under those circumstances—anything but a restraining order—is asking for trouble."

When he continued to watch her, she averted her face. "Have you ever had to sign one of those?" He sounded grim.

"We're not talking about me. Besides, the kind of man who needs a restraining order usually ignores it."

"Sasha?"

He waited.

Finally, she said, "One of my husbands was…physical. When he drank too much, or when I didn't do things just fast enough or high enough to suit him."

Jake closed his eyes momentarily, as if ignoring it could change the past.

She shrugged. "At least by the time I was old enough to marry, I'd learned how to handle—that sort of thing. I only had to get a restraining order once."

Jake leaned forward as if to rise, but she shook her head. "Honey, let me tell you something, if shedding husbands was an Olympic sport, I'd win gold every single time." She laughed, but with her eyes glittering, the effect was hardly amusing. "You want me to advise your client on the proper way to get rid of unwanted rodents?"

He couldn't think of a single thing to say—nothing that made sense under the circumstances. He'd known her for less than a week, yet he'd instinctively trusted her with his granddaughter. He'd seen her all dressed up in her fancy outfits, her makeup and her gaudy jewelry—he'd seen her barefoot, wearing a shapeless, colorless tent with her makeup smeared over half her face.

Either way, the effect she had on him was the same. The thought of any man mistreating her made his blood boil. She might pretend to be tough, but it didn't take a security expert to see through her defenses.

With a Sashalike toss of the head, she said, "Peaches is probably going to sleep for a while, so why don't I make us something for lunch? Or have you already eaten?"

* * *

Over Marty's leftover casserole Sasha asked about the progress on his house. She had tiptoed upstairs to check on the sleeping baby.

Jake said, "Another few days and the work will be finished. I can use a window fan to pump the place out." He asked about any commitments she had that might take her out of town over the next several days, and she told him that wouldn't be a problem.

"This close to the season, I've already done most of the hands-on work." She wouldn't allow it to be a problem. She happened to be in the middle of doing a new suite of offices and was angling to get a bid on another one, but Marty or Faye could baby-sit if she had to run over to the beach. At least she had her car back now, even if her ankle wasn't quite a hundred percent.

Sasha watched his throat move as he finished off his iced tea. In all her experience with the opposite sex it had never even occurred to her that the throat was a major erogenous zone.

On the other hand, just thinking about the way he had flicked his tongue in the hollow at the base of her throat was enough to steal the air right out of her lungs.

Jake caught her staring and lifted one eyebrow. He looked delicious, but then, when had he ever looked any other way? The man was no clotheshorse, which suited her just fine, having been married to a couple of *GQ* types.

"About Katie and Jamison—are you sure?" she asked. "Maybe it was just an air kiss. I mean, if she's been managing his cottage all these years, chances are they're friends."

"You want a demonstration?" Shoving his chair back from the table, Jake took her hand and pulled her to her feet. "They were standing about like this."

He was no more than five inches away, close enough to feel the heat, to smell his soap and aftershave. Sasha breathed deeply, as if to fill herself with his essence. Her pulse was pounding, her lips parted and waited.

"She was facing me—his back was to me, but once he moved closer, like this—" Jake closed the distance until her breasts were pressed against his chest "—I couldn't see all that much, but I seriously doubt if they were discussing the weather." His voice was starting to sound thick, almost strangled.

Sasha couldn't have spoken if her life depended on it.

"Actually, I think it was more like this," he whispered, his breath stirring tendrils of hair against her face.

Just as it had before, his kiss began slowly with a soft, moist touch—a gentle, teasing brush of lips that quickly escalated into a major event. Was there a Richter scale for kisses?

If so, his registered at least a twelve.

Standing on her tiptoes, Sasha lifted her arms around his neck and pressed against him. Through two layers of clothing, she couldn't get close enough. While his teasing tongue explored her mouth, driving her mad with need, his hands cupped her hips, moving her back and forth against his erection until her trembling legs were barely able to support her. She could feel the moisture gathering, preparing her for what was to come.

Lifting his mouth from hers, he whispered, "Is that bed still available?"

His hands cupped her breasts, his thumbs stroking her taut nipples. She managed to nod. At this point, speech was beyond her. This is crazy, she thought. She was already in over her head. If he took her to bed one more time, she might sink without a trace.

Exactly what are your intentions, Mr. Smith?

Great sex, what else?

Exactly! Great sex and what else?

But if ever there was a time for that old T-shirt philosophy to kick in, it was now. She shut up and went with the flow.

Jake closed the bedroom door and turned to her, his eyes glittering with an intensity that was purely electric. "You're sure?"

Reading her answer in her eyes—there were some things no amount of artifice could hide—he pulled off his shirt and unbuckled his belt. Then, with his jeans unfastened, they came together for another bone-melting kiss, and any lingering uncertainty she might have harbored about the way she felt melted right along with her bones.

Using both hands, she slid his jeans and briefs down over his hips, then laughed shakily when he nearly stumbled trying to kick them off over his shoes.

"Oh, no," he taunted, "you're not getting me naked while you're still wrapped up in that circus tent. I know all about power plays."

"This circus tent, as you call it, just happens to be the most comfortable thing I own," she informed him, her voice muffled as she pulled the caftan over her head. At least it was one of her newer ones. Besides, it was a little late to dash upstairs and change into something from Victoria's Secret.

The moment she was undressed, Jake lowered her to the bed and came down beside her. "You're incredibly beautiful," he murmured.

She was so far gone she actually believed him. "So are you," she whispered. "Your nose—"

"Broken twice."

"Your eyes..."

"Reading glasses."

"Me, too," she admitted, but then all thought of minor flaws disappeared. When she trailed her fingers through the narrow pelt of flat curls that arrowed down from his chest, past his hard middle to his groin, Jake sucked his breath audibly.

He was hard *everywhere*.

He kissed her eyes, her nose, and then he found her mouth again, hurling her into another dimension. The only reality was the aching, pulsating sweetness that left her helpless and needy, from the top of her Spice Tea hair to her Rhinestone Pink toenails. She shivered as his hands skimmed down her sides to cup her hips. When his fingers spanned the exquisitely sensitive skin of her groin, tracing the line and teasing her with quick forays into her moist center, her hips moved involuntarily.

She gasped, "Please—I need—"

"Hold on while I—"

"Now," she begged.

"First I need to—"

She could feel him hot and hard and heavy, pulsing against her. When he leaned on one elbow to reach the bedside table, she knew what he was doing. She'd seen him remove the foil package from his wallet and place it there. By her own standards, at least, she'd been safe and sensible all her life, and look where it had got her.

He covered her hand with his and began moving it toward ground zero. When her hand closed around him she forgot to breathe.

He groaned. Moving against her palm, he whispered, "No—no, wait a minute—"

As if waiting were even a faint possibility. He was like molten steel, and she wanted him desperately, wildly, far beyond the reach of common sense. She wanted him any way she could have him, but most of all she wanted him inside her where a five-alarm need was blazing out of control.

Using her thumb to caress, she squeezed and stroked, slowly at first and then faster. Curled around his naked back, her hips moved in unison with her hand until he gripped her wrist, lifting her hand away.

Moments later he moved over her again. "Now," he whispered roughly as he plunged inside her hot, tight center. The sweetest pleasure pulsated around them as they raced toward the finish line. All too soon her climax triggered his and Jake shouted hoarsely, collapsing on top of her.

Eventually, with both their bodies slick with sweat, he rolled onto his back, pulling her on top of him. Later, when she could gather enough energy to speak, Sasha said, "I'm too heavy for you."

He barely opened his eyes. "You move and I'll…"

"Take your toys and go home?" she teased lazily.

"Yeah, something like that." He grinned without opening his eyes. A few minutes later, when both their pulse rates slowed to something approximating normal, he said, "What toys are we talking about, hmm?"

She chuckled. "The one I'm playing with at the moment?"

There went the old pulse rate again, like one of those test-your-strength gizmos at the county fair. "It takes two to play that game."

"I know," she purred. "Interested in a rematch?"

"You talked me into it."

"Best two out of three?"

"You're on," he drawled, and rolled over onto his side, facing her.

This time they made love at almost a leisurely pace. Sated, they took the time to explore, to discover and exploit newly sensitized areas that had been neglected in their earlier rush.

One tiny spot between her thigh and her belly. Attention there drove her wild.

The thin skin behind Jake's knees and the arches of his feet, where a single stroke could render him helpless. Sasha tickled him there, then took advantage of his helplessness to kiss every inch of his torso, lingering in places that made him close his eyes and groan. When it was her turn, he returned the favor. She twisted and whimpered under his sweet assault until neither of them could wait another second.

This time she straddled him, clasping him with her thighs. Panting, she matched him stroke for stroke, her head flung back, her eyes tightly closed. She felt herself tightening around him, heard him cry out her name, and then she collapsed, her sweat-damp body melting into his.

Eventually, Jake said, "That's it. Write me off as a casualty."

Sliding off him onto her side, Sasha curled up in a fetal position—as if that might postpone facing reality. Either she'd forgotten everything she'd ever known about men—about sex—or she'd just entered an alternate reality.

She thought, I hardly even know this man, but I don't know if I can live without him. Oh, God, what have I done?

I'm not ready for this, Jake thought. He pretended to be asleep because he wasn't ready to answer any questions. In case she asked any questions.

In case she asked what? About his intentions?

Who had "intentions" in these days of instant gratification? You parked your brain, unleashed your libido, a good time was had by all, and that was the end of it, right?

Wrong. He knew better than that. He'd always known better than that, even in his wildest oat-sowing days. The trouble was, this woman had somehow managed to infiltrate his dull, orderly life until now she was as necessary to him as the air he breathed. He had no idea how it had happened, he only knew it had.

While she'd been watching him undress, he'd been thanking his lucky stars he'd been a swimmer all his life. He could still run five miles, although not with any great speed. There might be a few gray hairs on his head, but the hair on his body was still dark.

She stirred beside him and murmured, "Jake?"

"Hmm?" A smart man would get up, get dressed and get going before he got in any deeper. But then, he'd never been known for his intellect.

"You 'wake?"

"Umm-hmm."

When she rolled over toward him, his hand brushed against her. The gentle swell of her belly was far sexier than anything revealed by all those rail-thin, near-naked beach bunnies that flocked to the area each season. If ever a woman was made for love...

"Who won?" she murmured. He could tell by the sound of her voice that she was smiling.

So he smiled, too. "Who's keeping score? Call it a draw."

When they heard a familiar wail, he sat up. "I'll get her, honey, you stay here."

Still without opening her eyes, Sasha smiled. "You don't have to do that."

"You change her while I get a bottle ready."

Recovering from a state of boneless lethargy, Sasha managed to sit up just as Jake scooped up his clothes and disappeared into the bathroom, his pale buttocks in stark contrast to his lightly tanned thighs and darkly tanned back. Shoving her hair from her face, she glanced around for her clothes, pulled on the minimum and hurried upstairs.

By the time she reached the bedroom, it had occurred to her that a little later on, the guestroom might make a fine nursery. She could clear out the flea market and estate-sale finds she'd been storing there, maybe roll on a water-based paint—something in pink, with a border of Disney characters dancing across the top....

Just outside the door she stopped and closed her eyes. You idiot! Won't you ever learn? Never invest what you

can't afford to lose. Her second husband, who hadn't
bothered to practice what he preached, had taught her that.
Obviously, the lesson had been wasted.

Eleven

Jake left while Sasha was giving the baby a bottle. Fled the scene might be a better description. He felt like a deserter, but there was no way he was going to be able to get his mind back on track while she was tipped back in the big leather armchair, her bare feet on the coffee table, with his tiny granddaughter cradled in her arms. How any woman could manage to look sexy and maternal at the same time was a mystery to him. One he couldn't afford to dwell on, not when a single whiff of her hand lotion and he was rarin' to ride again.

He'd tried telling himself it was only sex, but there was no "only" about it. Nothing about Sasha Lasiter could ever be called "only." That's what made it so damn scary. He had known—all right, he had sensed— that there was something special about her right from the first. Why else would he have been snapping pictures of her even though they were evidence of nothing except that here was a beautiful woman.

And now things had gone too far to turn back, even if he'd wanted to turn back.

But before he could deal with any new beginnings, he had some old business to finish.

Hearing him drive off, Sasha felt like throwing something at him. "See you later," he'd called out as soon as she'd settled down with the baby. The coward!

Oh, he'd be back, she wasn't worried about that, but for what? Her or his baby? And what about after he took his baby home to his drab white-on-white house? What then? Would she ever see him again?

Setting the bottle on the coffee table, she eased the baby onto her shoulder. "Well, you've gone and done it now, haven't you, Sally June?"

Talk about jumping out of the frying pan into the fire.

Jake wasn't like all the others. That didn't mean he was perfect, it just meant that she had a whole new set of rules to learn. Unfortunately, despite all her experience, she'd jumped headfirst into the game without knowing where the boundaries were, what the stakes were.

No point in blaming it on Fate—not unless Fate had a terrific sense of humor. If anything, she'd have to blame it on a pink, spike-heeled, ankle-strap shoe. That's what had started it all.

She sighed, inhaling the sweet baby smell, taking comfort from the tiny warm bundle that fit so perfectly in the curve of her bosom. As much as she wanted his baby, she wanted the man even more. It was more than sex, although that had been unbelievably good. The chemistry between them was...explosive was the only word she could think of to describe it.

But it was far more than that. Right from the beginning there'd been something about the man that had fit into a hollow she didn't even know she possessed. Like two halves of a whole. Like two lovers reunited after lifetimes of being apart.

"Heaven help me," she whispered as she headed upstairs with the sleeping infant, "I've gone and done it again—fallen in love."

The next time the phone rang she was rinsing out a few tiny garments. Wiping her hands on her skirt, she grabbed the receiver. "Lasiter residence."

"How come you're answering like that?" Marty asked.

"Oh, hi. Because if it's a client, I'm not in, not until I can work out a baby-sitting schedule. Are you calling to sign up for a time slot?"

"Dream on. I've got my own business to run, remember?"

Sasha sighed. "I know that, I was only joking."

"Tired of playing mama so soon?"

"No way, but I've got an appointment at the beach tomorrow at three that I'd really like to keep. It shouldn't take but a couple of hours. How about it, can you spare Faylene that long? Tomorrow's your day, isn't it?"

"With Kell building our new addition on to the back and customers in and out the front, cleaning's hardly worth the effort, anyway, so Faye's free. Speaking of big events, did you get Jake lined up for Monday? I called earlier, but I guess you were out."

"Sorry, it didn't come up again after y'all left."

There was a long silence, and then Marty said softly, "Aw, honey…. You want him for yourself, don't you?"

Avoiding a direct answer, Sasha said, "You know what? I don't think Lily's all that interested in meeting anyone new. You know those letters Faye says she gets every week? Maybe she's already involved."

"And maybe they're from her maiden aunt. Anyway, it won't hurt to expose her to a few candidates."

"Go ahead and expose all you want to, just—"

Marty, whose intuition had a way of clicking on just when it was most inconvenient, finished the sentence. "Just not your guy, huh? Gotcha, hon. But at this rate we might as well give up matchmaking. We're running out of bachelors."

"There's still Gus and Egbert."

"You jest. Lily and Gus don't even speak the same language, and she's taller and smarter than Egbert."

"Well, what about that guy at the license bureau, the one with the dimples? I heard he's single."

"Ever seen him out from behind that desk? Major spare tire."

"So? Bob Ed's spare tire doesn't seem to bother Faylene," Sasha reminded her friend.

"Look, Kell's calling—l gotta go, but you just concentrate on reeling Jake in, y'hear? This time you've got yourself a keeper."

"I have?" Sasha murmured softly after replacing the

phone. Then why did she feel like she'd just jumped off a high building without so much as an umbrella to slow the fall?

To say Jake was frustrated was an understatement. Sasha's landline was busy, she wasn't answering her cell phone; he had those two installations to do before the weekend, and he finally had a solid lead in the Jamison case. Now all he had to do was prove it.

The trouble was, he couldn't seem to focus on anything but racing back to Muddy Landing. Back to Sasha and his grandbaby.

Probably a good thing he couldn't reach her by phone. If he told her he was on the way and she said not to bother, then what? When it came to this crazy business of falling in love, he was years out of practice. Some things got easier the second time around. Some things didn't.

In the meantime, he had a job to do. Pulling in at Southern Dunes Property Management, he looked around for a white Durango with a personalized license plate. Now that most rentals, including Driftwinds, were booked solid for the season, Jamison and his playmate would have to make other arrangements. Rather than risk his vehicle being spotted where he had no business being, a smart man would park elsewhere and hitch a ride with someone else.

In this case, his lover—who might have a legitimate reason for parking outside an empty cottage.

McIver's car was missing from her designated parking place. He spotted Jamison's Durango half hidden by a giant oleander bush. Unless the gentleman was inside the office, three guesses where he could be found.

Make that with whom he could be found. Jake didn't have to catch them in bed together; all he had to do was catch the two of them together in a place where Jamison had no business being. A smart lawyer should be able to use circumstantial evidence and a guilty conscience as leverage.

When he walked inside he was carrying a conspicuous envelope that happened to contain his truck registration and maintenance record. The reception area was empty except for a middle-aged woman behind a small desk.

"May I help you, sir?"

"I'm looking for Katie—Katie McIver?"

"I'm sorry, you just missed her." She looked at the envelope. "If you'd like to leave that here, I could give it to her when she comes in."

"You wouldn't know where I could find her, would you? I won't take up but a minute of her time, but it's important."

It was midafternoon when Sasha heard the slam of a car door out in the driveway. Her heart skipped a beat and began to pound as she glanced through the window. She was furious with Jake for staying away so long. He could have called to see how Peaches was doing, if nothing else.

She touched her hair. Determined not to take extra pains, she'd shoved it up and anchored it with a clip, trusting nature and gravity to do the rest. Wearing layered tank tops in pink and orange and a sheer flowered skirt—casual, but flattering—she took her time going down the stairs. No shoes, but a toe ring on each foot.

By the time he rang the doorbell, she was cool and composed. As for the flush on her face, she had no control over that. Taking a deep, steadying breath, she arranged a polite smile. "Well, hi, Jake."

Polite. Friendly. Palpitations don't count.

"I thought I'd stop by to see if you needed anything," he said.

She stepped back, affecting an offhand manner. "Since you just happened to be in the neighborhood?"

They both knew he had no real business in Muddy Landing. He'd already admitted as much. "Should I have made an appointment?"

Sasha shook her head. Maybe she needed a dose of that allergy medication they advertised so much. Not only palpitations, but hoarseness and watery eyes. "You want to see her?" she asked when she could trust her voice not to give her away. "She's upstairs. I just put her down. She stayed awake a long time after her last bottle."

Jake cleared his throat. If she didn't know better she'd think he was as self-conscious as she was. "I, uh—could we talk first?"

Oh, God, he had something to say that she wasn't going to like hearing. He was taking his baby and leaving for good. "You know, she's much better off here. Changes can't be good for her—she's already had too many."

"Yeah, I'm with you there." Jake swallowed hard. She could see his throat working, see the tension in his eyes. "Look, I'm about as far out in left field as I've ever been in my life, but Sasha—have I been taking too much for granted? I mean, this is crazy, right? We've known each other less than a week."

Closing her eyes Sasha held her breath and uttered a silent prayer. This was not about the baby, this was about—

"Would you like to come in?" she asked.

Leading the way into the living room, she lowered herself carefully at one end of the sofa. Jake took the other end. Her face still felt hot. His was about as pale as someone with a perennial tan could be.

She waited for him to get to the point.

"Look, you don't have to take it if you don't like it. I mean, you've already got so many. Or we can exchange it. It might not even fit, I wasn't sure of what size you wore."

"You bought me a pair of *shoes?*"

Wordlessly, he shook his head. He turned toward her, one knee hitched up onto the cushion so that the other one was practically on the floor. A shaft of late-morning sunshine slanted through the window to highlight the salt-and-pepper gray at his temples.

He looked gorgeous and sexy and totally out of his depth.

Her heart kicked into overdrive. "Jake, what are you trying to say?" She didn't dare try to guess. If she guessed wrong, she'd be devastated.

He opened his left hand, and there on his palm was a small jeweler's box. "I'm doing this all wrong, aren't I? I should have said something first."

"Say something *now*," she exclaimed.

"Hoo-boy, this is kind of hard to put into words, but

here it goes." He took a deep breath. "You know about me—about Rosemary, I mean. We were young, but I loved her with all my heart. There hasn't been anyone—not serious, I mean—since then."

His self-deprecating smile hurt her heart. She closed her eyes until he whispered, "Until now."

Only then did she dare allow herself to hope, having learned caution in a hard school.

"Sasha, ever since we got together, things have been screwed up. Normally, these things—I mean, you and me—well, it usually takes longer. You know what I mean."

Slowly, she shook her head. "I haven't a clue."

"Okay, let me say this. For the past dozen years or so since I lost Rosemary, I've managed pretty well. We'd just started the business, so I could concentrate on that, but mostly I concentrated on Timmy. He was too young to understand why his mother wasn't there, but as he got older, things got better. You lost a brother, so you know how it is. You don't forget, but after a while you move on. You know what I'm saying?"

She hadn't a clue. Yes, she knew what grief felt like. So did he. But that was years ago, and this was now. He was still clutching the ring box. She didn't even glance at it. Instead she stared him in the eye through her turquoise contacts. If he thought he could just pay her off for services rendered—baby-sitting and otherwise—with a piece of jewelry, she would kill him. Flat-out kill him!

His shoulders fell. He closed his eyes briefly and then said, "I think maybe I'm all alone out here, so how about knocking me in the head and calling Hack to come pick up the body."

"Jake, what is it you're trying to say?"

Ignoring her, he continued speaking, as if he had to get it all out before he ran out of breath. "But if you happen to feel anything like the same way I do, then maybe you could wear my ring and we could sort of explore this thing as we go along. Please?"

Oh, yes, oh, yes, oh, yes!

Some men were glib, others needed help. Sasha was nothing if not helpful. "Jake, if you're trying to ask if I want to have an—an affair, then—"

He shook his head. Her hopes took a sharp dip, then recovered.

"Or I guess we could start out that way if you want to. Sort of take things gradually, get to know each other better. Then maybe in a few days—that is, a few weeks…"

To heck with caution. She reached for his hand. Ignoring the ring box, she pulled him into her arms, knowing she was taking the chance of a lifetime. "I thought you'd never ask," she whispered.

A few hours later, barefoot and shirtless with his jeans unsnapped at the waist, Jake brought her coffee in bed. "Two sugars and a dash of diet cream, right?"

Sasha sat up and gave him a smug, lazy smile. "This is so decadent, but then I've always adored decadence." Other than her new ring, designed and made by a Nags Head goldsmith, of yellow gold and white, with three small diamonds, she wore only a sated look.

"Is it teachable?"

"What, decadence?" She held open the bedcovers, scented with sex and Odalisque and essence of Jake. "With me as your tutor, you'll master the art in no time."

"Hey, let's not be in too big a hurry," he said, his voice huskier than usual. "Let's give it a few decades, shall we?"

* * * * *

THE LAST REILLY
STANDING

by
Maureen Child

MAUREEN CHILD

is a California native who loves to travel. Every chance they get, she and her husband are taking off on another research trip. The author of more than sixty books, Maureen loves a happy ending and still swears that she has the best job in the world. She lives in Southern California with her husband, two children and a golden retriever with delusions of grandeur.

Visit her website at www.maureenchild.com

One

Aidan Reilly was so close to winning, he could almost taste the celebratory champagne. Okay, beer.

The longest three months of his *life* were coming to an end. Only three more weeks to go and he'd be the winner of the bet he and his brothers had entered into so grudgingly at the beginning of the summer.

He shuddered thinking about it, even now. Ninety days of no sex and the winner received the whole ten thousand dollars left to the Reilly triplets by their great-uncle. It was all their older brother, Father Liam Reilly's fault. He'd waved the red flag of challenge at them, insisting that priests were *way* tougher than Marines—since he'd had to give up sex for *life*. Well, no self-respecting Reilly ever turned down a challenge. Though this one had been tougher to survive than any of them had thought.

Brian and Connor had already folded—which left Aidan alone to hold up the family honor—and make sure their older brother, Father Liam, couldn't laugh his ass off at all of them.

It wasn't even about the money anymore, Aidan thought, staring across their table at the Lighthouse restaurant at Liam. Their older brother wanted them all to lose the bet so *he* could use the money for a new roof on his church. Well, Aidan wasn't about to tell him yet, but once he won this bet and had all of his brothers admitting that *he* was the strongest of the bunch then he planned on giving the money to Liam anyway.

He didn't need it. Being a single Marine, he made enough money to support himself and that was all he cared about. He'd never entered the bet for the *money*.

What he wanted was to *win*.

He leaned back on the bench seat and avoided letting his gaze drift around the crowded restaurant. The Lighthouse was a spot favored by families, so he was pretty safe. The only women he had to worry about in here were the waitresses—and they looked too damn good for his well-being. And at that thought, he shifted his gaze back to the surface of his drink.

"Worried?" Brian muttered, lifting his glass to take a sip of beer.

"Hell no—I'm closing in on the finish line."

"Yeah, well. You haven't won yet."

"Only a matter of time." Aidan smiled, while keeping his gaze fixed on his glass of beer.

"Gotta say," Connor admitted, leaning forward to brace his forearms on the table. "I'm impressed. Didn't think you'd last this long."

"I did," Liam said, taking a drink of his own beer.

"Yeah?" Aidan lifted his gaze and grinned at his older brother, ignoring the other two—identical replicas of himself. "Because I'm the strongest, right?" he spared a quick look at his fellow triplets and sneered. "Hah."

"Actually," Liam said smiling, "it's because you've always been the most stubborn."

Beside him, Connor laughed and Aidan gave him a quick elbow jab. "I'll take what I can get," he said.

"You've still got three weeks to go," Brian reminded him from his seat beside Liam. "And while Connor and I are getting regular sex from our lovely wives, you're a man *alone*."

There was that. Aidan scowled as he took a sip of his beer and made a point of keeping his gaze locked on the three men sitting with him. One glimpse of some gorgeous blonde or a curvy redhead or God help him, a pretty brunette and he'd have to go home and take yet another cold shower. Hell, he'd spent so much time in icy water lately between the showers and his work as a USMC rescue diver, he felt like a damn penguin.

"I can make it," he said tightly.

"Three weeks is a long time," Connor pointed out.

"I've already made it through *nine* weeks," Aidan reminded them. Nine long, miserable weeks. But the worst was over now. He was on the downhill slide. He'd make it. Damned if he wouldn't.

"Yeah," Liam said with a knowing smile, "but everyone knows the *last* mile of the race is always the most difficult."

"Thanks a lot."

"Twenty-one whole days," Liam said, making the three weeks sound even longer.

"How many *hours* is that?" Brian wondered.

"Man, you guys are cruel."

"What're brothers for?" Connor asked.

Aidan shook his head and kicked back on the bench seat. Ignoring Liam and smirking at his identical brothers, he said, "Do I have to remind you two what wusses you both were? How you both caved so easily?"

Brian grimaced and Connor shifted in his seat.

"Nope," Aidan muttered, smiling to himself, "guess not."

Bright and early the next morning, Terry Evans took a long look around the Frog House bookstore and told herself this would be a snap. A good change of pace. An interesting bump in the long, straight highway of her life.

Then a five-year-old boy grabbed a book away from a three-year-old girl, resulting in a howl rarely heard outside of the nature channel on TV during a documentary on coyotes.

Terry winced and smiled at the harried moms as they raced to snatch up their respective children. Oh, yeah, she thought, suddenly rethinking her generous offer to help out a friend. A snap.

There were kids all over the bookstore. No big surprise there, since the shop catered to those ten and under. Not to mention their moms.

Frog House was filled with pillow-stuffed nooks and crannies, where kids could curl up with a book while their mothers sat at the small round tables, sipping fresh coffee. The kids had a great time, exploring a place where everything was "hands on" and the moms could relax, knowing that their children couldn't possibly get into trouble here.

Donna had wanted a kid-friendly store and she'd built a child's fantasy. Murals of fairy tales covered the walls, and bookshelves were low enough that even the top shelf was within reach of tiny hands. There was a coloring corner, with child-size tables littered with coloring books and every color crayon imaginable. During story hour, every day at four o'clock, at least twenty kids sat on the bright rugs, listening with rapt attention to the designated reader.

Terry sighed a little and smiled as the squabbling kids settled down again, each with their own book this time. If her gaze lingered on the five-year-old boy a moment or two longer, she told herself no one but she would notice.

Her heart ached, but it was an old pain now, more familiar than startling. She'd learned to live with it. Learned that it would never really go away.

And if truth were told, she didn't want to lose that pain. Because if she did, she would have to lose the memories that caused it and she would never allow herself to do *that*.

"Excuse me?"

She turned her gaze from the kids at the "play time" table that was littered with discarded coloring books and half-eaten crayons, to face…*A MAN*.

At first sight of him, she immediately thought of him in Capital Letters. As her temperature climbed, she took a second or two to check him out completely. Tall, easily over six feet, he wore a black T-shirt with USMC stamped on the left side of his impressive chest.

Not surprising to find a Marine standing in the shop. After all, Baywater, South Carolina, was just a short drive down the road from Parris Island, the Marine Corps Recruit Depot—not to mention the Marine Corps Air Station in Beaufort.

But *this* Marine had her complete attention.

The Man's muscles rippled beneath the soft, worn fabric of his shirt and when he folded his arms across his chest, she nearly applauded the move. His waist was narrow, hips nonexistent and his long legs were hugged by worn, threadbare jeans. The hem of those jeans stacked up on the top of his battered cowboy boots.

Oh, my.

She lifted her gaze to his face and felt her internal temperature spike another ten points. Black hair, unfortunately militarily short, ice-blue eyes, a squared off jaw and a straight nose that could have come off a Roman coin. Then he smiled and she saw gorgeous white teeth and a dimple, God help her, in his right cheek.

Did it suddenly get hot in there?

"Hello?" He lifted one hand and snapped his fingers in front of her face. "You okay?"

Minor meltdown, she wanted to say, but for a change, Terry wisely kept her mouth shut. For a second. "Sorry. What can I do for you?"

He gave her a slow smile that notched up the heat in her southern regions and she groaned inwardly. She'd walked into that one. Figured he was a man who could take a simple statement and make it sound like an invitation to sweaty sheets.

"Can I help you?" She shook her head. This wasn't getting any better.

Finally, though, he quit smiling, stepped up closer to her and looked around the bookstore as if searching for something in particular. "Can you tell me where Donna Fletcher is?" he asked, shifting his gaze back to hers.

Terry checked her wristwatch, then looked up at him again. "Right now, she's about halfway to Hawaii."

"Already?" He looked stunned. "She didn't tell me she was leaving early."

One of Terry's perfectly arched, dark blond eyebrows lifted. "Was there some special reason she *should?"*

He scraped one hand across his square jaw. "Suppose not," he admitted, then blew out a breath. "It's just that I'm supposed to be doing a project for her and—"

Realization dawned. Actually, Terry felt as if she were in a cartoon and someone had just penciled in a lightbulb over her head. "You're Aidan Reilly."

His gaze snapped to hers. "How'd you know that?"

She smiled, shook her hair back and told herself that she was going to have to have a long conversation with Donna one of these days.

Her very best friend had told her all about the bet that Aidan had entered into with his brothers—and that she, Donna, had offered Aidan the bookstore as a safe place to hide out from women. In exchange, of course, for Aidan agreeing to build a "reading castle" for the kids. But, she'd never mentioned that Aidan Reilly looked like a walking billboard for good sex.

Actually, *exceptional* sex.

Maybe even *amazing, incredible, earthshaking* sex.

Terry was beginning to suspect a setup.

Donna, a romantic at heart, had decided that what

Terry needed was a permanent man. Someone to love. Someone to love *her*. The fact that Terry wasn't interested in anything more permanent than a long weekend, didn't really enter into Donna's plans.

Aidan Reilly, it seemed, was the latest salvo fired in an ongoing battle.

And though Terry still wasn't interested, she had to admit that Donna was using some first-class ammunition.

He was snapping his fingers in her face again. She reached up and swatted his hand away. "You keep doing that. It's annoying."

"You keep zoning out," he said. "Even more annoying."

Good point. "Sorry. I'm a little tired. Got in late last night and had to open the shop first thing this morning."

"Fascinating," Aidan replied. "Still doesn't tell me how you know my name and why Donna didn't tell me she was leaving three days early."

"Donna told me your name, and by the way, I'm Terry Evans," she said and smiled at a woman who walked up and handed her a book ready for purchase. Walking around behind the counter, Terry rang up the sale, bagged the book and handled the credit card transaction. When she'd finished, she wished the woman a good day, turned back to face Mr. Tall, Dark and Gorgeous and picked up right where she left off. "And I'm guessing she didn't tell you she was leaving early because she didn't think it was any of your business."

He scowled at her and strangely enough, she found *that* expression even more intriguing than the flash of dimple when he smiled.

"I told her I'd take her and the kids to the airport," he muttered. "But she wasn't supposed to leave until Friday."

"She got an earlier flight and grabbed it," Terry explained with a shrug. "I took her and the kids to the airport," she added, remembering the warm little hugs and the sticky kisses she'd received last night as the Fletcher family set off for their vacation.

He blew out a breath. "Probably good. She could use the break."

"Yes," Terry said. "She really can. Her folks live on Maui, you know and they're dying to see the kids and with—"

"—Tony deployed overseas," Aidan finished for her, "she needed to get away."

"Yeah. Worry takes a lot out of you." Heck, Terry wasn't even married to Tony Fletcher and she worried about his safety. She couldn't imagine what it was like for a Marine wife. Having to run the house, keep sane, deal with kids, all while keeping one corner of your brain saying a constant stream of prayers for your husband.

"So I'm told."

"But," Terry said, waggling her index finger in a

"follow me" signal, "Donna told me all about your 'problem' before she left."

"Is that right?"

She nodded as she stepped behind the glass case containing fresh muffins, brownies and cookies. Grabbing a tall paper cup from the stack near the espresso machine, she added, "And she told me how you like your coffee."

He smiled again, and Terry told herself to ignore the wildly fluctuating heat barometer inside her. Seriously, though, the man was like a lightning rod. He channeled hormones and turned them into heat that simmered just under a woman's skin. Pretty potent stuff.

"The day's looking a little better already."

She smiled, glanced at him, then looked away quickly—watching Aidan Reilly was *not* conducive to concentration. And running the complicated machine with dials and steamers and nozzles and whatchamacallits required concentration. While the steamer hissed, she risked another quick glance at him and noted that he was now leaning on the glass countertop, watching her closely.

His eyes were blue enough to swim in, she thought idly and wondered just how many women had taken that particular plunge.

"So what did Donna say, exactly?" he asked.

Clearing her throat noisily, she said, "She told me about the silly bet you and your brothers made."

"Silly?"

"Completely." She pulled the stainless steel pitcher of frothing milk free of the heating bars, then wiped them down with a damp towel. As she poured the hot milk into the cup, she kept talking. "She told me that she'd offered you the use of the bookstore as a sort of demilitarized zone and in return, you're going to build a castle for the kids."

That was how Donna had put it, anyway. She remembered the brief explanation she'd gotten only the night before.

Aidan's a sweetie, Donna told her, *packing up the last of the kids' stuff. But he's determined to win this stupid bet. So I told him he could hang out at the bookstore when he's off base. It's pretty safe there since not many single women come to the shop. And in return, he's promised to build a "reading castle" for my littlest customers.*

And I'm supposed to protect him from women? Terry asked.

Please, honey, Donna said laughing. He doesn't need protecting. He just needs a safe zone to wait out the rest of the bet.

And you're being so accommodating, why?

Donna closed the suitcase, then spotted a ragged blanket with more holes than fabric, sighed and opened the suitcase again to stuff Mr. Blankie inside. When she was finished, she sat on the bed and looked up at Terry. Because he's been a good friend while Tony's been deployed. He comes over here if I need

*the sink fixed or if the car takes a dump. He and Tony
went through boot camp together. They're like best
friends and Aidan's...family.*

Which was why, Terry told herself, she was standing here staring into a pair of blue eyes that shone
with all kinds of exciting sparks.

"Demilitarized zone, huh?" he asked. "Well, that's
one way of putting it."

She smiled and spooned on a layer of foam before
snapping a plastic lid on the coffee cup and handing
it over. "Donna says you spend your time off from
the base here, hiding out because most of her customers are young married moms—and therefore *safe*."

He took a sip of coffee, lifted both eyebrows and
nodded. "Not bad."

"Thank you."

"And I don't consider it hiding out."

"Really? What do you call it?"

"Strategic maneuvering."

Terry smiled. "Whatever helps. So, you've got to
last three more weeks without sex to win the bet."

"That's about the size of it."

Now it was her turn to lift her brows and smile
at him.

Took Aidan a minute, to catch the joke playing out
in her eyes, but finally he grinned in appreciation.
Not only was she gorgeous, but she had a quick,
wicked mind. Normally he liked that in a woman.

But this wasn't "normal." This was a time when

he had to stay stronger than he ever had before. And having Terry around for the next few weeks wasn't going to make life easier.

She was still watching him, a playful smirk on her mouth. "This isn't about size."

"It's *always* about size," she retorted and stepped out from behind the espresso machine. "This time, it's just about the size of your ego."

He followed her as she walked to the kids play table and idly straightened up the mess. He tried not to notice the fall of her pale blond hair against her porcelain cheek. Just like he tried to ignore the curve of her hip or the way the hem of her skirt lifted in back as she bent over the scattered books. And he *really* tried not to notice her legs.

What the hell had Donna been thinking? Bringing in Terry Evans to help him stay away from sex was like lighting a fire to prevent heat.

Oh, yeah.

This was gonna work out just fine.

Scowling slightly, he said, "You don't know me well enough to know I have an ego."

"Please." She gave a short laugh and looked at him over her shoulder. "Look at you. Of course you do."

"I think that was a compliment."

"See?" she pointed out. "Ego."

"Touché."

She gave him a brief, elegant nod.

He watched while she wiped up a crayon mess and

when she straightened and tossed her hair back from her face, he said, "So you're going to help me win the bet, huh?"

"You got it."

"How?"

She smiled and he felt the powerful slam of it hit him like a sledgehammer.

"Why, First Sergeant Reilly, if some gorgeous woman shows up, I'll just throw myself on you like you were a live grenade."

He looked her up and down slowly, completely. Then he shook his head. "Terry Evans...*that* kind of help and I'm a dead man."

Two

Summer in South Carolina could bring a grown man—even a *Marine*—to his knees weeping.

And September, though technically the beginning of fall, was actually summer's last chance to drum every citizen of the South into the dirt. Today, summer was doing a hell of a job of it.

Aidan paused, tipped his head back and stared up at the sweeping expanse of blue sky, looking for a cloud. *Any* cloud. But there was nothing to blot the heat of the sun and no shade nearby in the alley behind the bookstore.

He could have worked inside, but being out in the heat, away from Terry Evans made him feel just a little *safer*. Not that he was generally a man who ran for cover. Actually he was just the opposite. He liked the thrill of a risk. The punch of adrenaline when it raced through him. The sensation of balancing on the fine edge between life and death.

And he was smart enough to know that it wasn't adrenaline he felt when he looked at Donna's friend Terry. It was heat, pure and simple. The kind of heat he had to avoid for three more long, agonizing weeks.

"Donna," he muttered, "what in the hell were you thinking?"

He got no answer, of course, so he focused instead on the pile of wooden planks in front of him. "Just do the job, idiot."

Aidan had learned early the importance of focusing on the task at hand, despite the distractions around him. In the Corps, that focus could mean the difference between life and death.

And God knew, Terry Evans was a distraction.

The woman's laugh rang out a little too often. And her voice, when she spoke to the kids streaming in and out of the specialty bookstore, was soft and dreamy. Just the kind of voice a man liked to hear coming from the pillow beside his.

"Yeah. Concentrating." Aidan muttered the words as he slammed a hammer down onto a nail head. The solid slam against the wood jolted up his arm and hopefully, would shake thoughts of Terry out of his mind.

He couldn't believe his miserable luck. He'd

thought riding out the last three weeks of this bet would be easy, as long as he was here, in the bookstore. Actually he'd thought for sure that Donna would be closing the place while she was gone. Giving him a peaceful place to work and keep his head down until the bet was over.

But, no. Instead of peace and quiet, he got a Dolly Parton lookalike. Good thing he preferred brunettes—or he'd be a dead man already.

"How's it going?"

Her voice, from too close by, startled him, and Aidan slammed the hammer down onto his thumb. Pain streaked through him and stars danced in front of his closed eyes as he grabbed his injured thumb and squeezed. He clenched his jaw, trapping every cuss word he'd ever learned—and there were *many* of them—locked inside him.

Shifting a look at her, he nearly groaned again. Not from pain, this time. But from the absolute misery of having to look at a gorgeous woman and realize that he couldn't do what he'd normally do. Which was, offer to buy her a drink. Turn on the Reilly charm. Work his magic until he had her right where he wanted her.

In the dark.

In his bed.

Naked.

Oh, yeah, Aidan thought, his gaze locking on her sharp green eyes. The next three weeks were going to be a nightmare.

His thumb throbbed in time with the steady thud of his heart. While he stared at her, she cocked her hip, folded her arms beneath her truly impressive breasts and watched him with a benign look that told him she knew exactly what he'd been thinking.

"You know," she said finally, shaking her hair back from her face as a soft sea wind darted down the alley. "If you keep looking at women like that, you'll never last another three weeks."

He grinned and the pain in his thumb eased up a little. "Yeah? Irresistible, am I?"

She moved to the next step down from the porch, then sat down, her skirt hiking up, giving Aidan a better glimpse of her legs.

"Oh, I think I'll be able to restrain myself."

"Good to know."

"Besides," she pointed out, "you're not really interested in me."

"I'm not?" Intrigued, he forgot about his aching thumb. Hooking the claw tip of his hammer through a belt loop on his jeans, he planted one hand on the back wall of the bookstore, crossed one foot over the other and looked down at her.

"Nope." She smoothed her palms over her dark green skirt and demurely slid both legs to the side, crossing her feet neatly at the ankles.

A *demure* Dolly Parton.

Great.

"Face it, Aidan—I can call you Aidan, right?"

"That's my name."

"Well, face it, Aidan, you're a starving man and I'm a hamburger."

He snorted, looked her up and down thoroughly, then lifted his gaze back to hers. "Darlin', you're no hamburger. You're a steak."

She smiled. "Well, thanks. But like I said, you're a starving man. A man like you? No sex for nine weeks?" She shook her head slowly, still smiling. "I'm thinking that even hamburger would start looking like filet mignon."

"You have looked into a mirror lately, right?"

"Every day."

"And you see hamburger."

"I see eyes that are too big, a mouth that's too wide, a nose that turns up at the end, a scar on my eyebrow and a chin that has a stupid dent in it."

Amazing, Aidan thought. He'd been with enough women to know when one of them was fishing for compliments. And to be honest, most of them never had to fish around him. He was always the first to compliment a woman on her hair, her shoes, her smile…but this woman wasn't fishing.

"You know what I see?" He pushed away from the wall, hooked his thumbs into the back pockets of his jeans and looked down at her with a critical eye.

"Steak?"

"Grass-green eyes, a wide, luscious mouth, a pixie nose, an intriguing little blip in a perfectly curved eyebrow and a lickable dimple in a softly rounded chin."

She tipped her head to one side, studied him for a long moment, then blew out a breath. "Oh, you're very good."

"Yeah. And you're quite the filet yourself."

She held out one hand to him and Aidan took it. His fingers closed around hers and he could have sworn he felt the zing of something hot and lusty shoot straight from her fingertips to the area of his body most neglected lately.

When she was standing, Terry let go of his hand and rubbed her fingers together to dissipate the lingering heat she felt on her skin. "You know, it's a wonder you've lasted nine weeks," she said.

"Is that right?"

Forcing a laugh she didn't quite feel, she pointed out, "Hello? You just made a move on the woman who's supposed to be helping you *win* the stupid bet."

He scowled a bit.

"Seriously. You just can't help yourself, can you?"

"Excuse me?"

"Flirting." She absently brushed off the seat of her skirt with both hands, then stepped up onto the porch again. Grabbing hold of the doorknob, she gave it a twist, then turned to look at Aidan Reilly again. "Flirting is like breathing to you. You do it without even thinking about it."

"I wasn't flirting," he argued, grabbing the hammer off his belt loop.

"Please. 'Grass-green eyes? Lickable dimple?'"

"I was just—"

"Making a move," she finished for him and shook her head slowly. "And really? It was *so* blatant. Not subtle at all."

"Is that right?"

"Oh, yeah," Terry said and opened the door. "Does that kind of thing usually work for you? I mean, are women really that gullible? That easy to maneuver?"

He frowned up at her and Terry smiled inwardly. The man had more than enough confidence. She hadn't shattered him any. Maybe a couple of dings in a healthy ego, but she was pretty sure he could take it. Besides, if he ever found out how his words had hit her—about the fires still licking at her insides—well, let's just say, he wouldn't be winning any bets.

And Terry wasn't here for the scenery.

She wasn't here to get lucky with a Marine, either.

She was here to help out her dearest friend.

Then she'd be going back home.

"I don't 'maneuver' women," he said tightly.

"Sure you do," Terry quipped. "You just don't usually get caught doing it."

"You're not an easy woman, are you?"

"Depends on what you mean by *easy*."

"Not what you think I mean," he countered.

"I guess we'll see, won't we? In the next few weeks, that is."

He inhaled sharply, deeply and his scowl went just a little darker. "Exactly why did you come out here, anyway? Just to get a few digs in?"

"Actually," she said, pushing the door open, "I came to see if you wanted some iced tea."

"Oh." He balanced the hammer in one palm and slapped it rhythmically against his hand. "Well then, that'd be great. Thanks."

"It's in the fridge. Help yourself whenever you want it." She took a step inside, then stopped when he spoke up again.

"You're not going to bring it out here?"

Shaking her head again, Terry smiled. "Apparently you're used to women who fetch and carry. Sorry to disappoint you."

He gave her a slow smile. "I'll let you know when I'm disappointed, darlin'."

Terry sucked in a gulp of air, squared her shoulders and stepped into the air-conditioned haven of the small kitchen at the back of the store. She closed the door behind her, leaned against it and stared up at the ceiling. "Damn it, Donna. What have you gotten me into?"

The next couple of days were...*interesting*. If Terry could have looked at them objectively, she might have considered them an excellent exercise in self-control.

Instead she was just a little on edge and wondering how she was going to get through the next three weeks. Not only was Aidan Reilly an incredibly sexy man, but he was also a sexually starved man. As for Terry…she couldn't remember her last orgasm.

She'd done her share of dating—God, she hated that word—in the last few years. But being willing to go to dinner and a play with a man was a far cry from wanting him in her bed. She was picky, and she was the first to admit it. She didn't do one-night stands, and she couldn't bring herself to invest in a long-term relationship, so that pretty much left her out of the bedroom Olympics.

Which didn't really bother her most of the time. She kept busy. She was on more charitable boards than she could count, her fund-raising abilities were legendary and because of her gift with numbers, she'd been handed the reins of her family's financial empire three years ago.

This was the first "vacation" she'd had in years. Most people wouldn't consider working in a small-town bookstore a holiday. But for Terry, it was a treat.

Well, except for Aidan Reilly.

This whole situation just went to prove that Fate had a sense of humor. Putting a woman who'd been too long without sex in the position of keeping the world's sexiest man from *having* sex, had to be a cosmic joke.

Aidan cringed as he stepped into the blissfully

cool store and stopped in the open doorway leading from the kitchen to the main shop. Kids cried and shouted and laughed. Their mothers chitchatted, oblivious to the racket and he stood there, silently wishing he were out at sea.

He'd never really understood the draw of having children. To him, they looked like tiny anchors on long, heavy chains, designed to drag a man down. Besides, they were too damn loud.

He'd only come inside because he had the main structure of the reading castle finished and needed Terry to take a look at it. He laughed inwardly. Hell, he didn't really need her opinion. He'd gone over the plans and the basic idea with Donna, who'd already approved the whole thing.

What he really wanted was another look at the woman whose face had been invading his dreams for the last couple of nights. Self-preservation instincts told him to keep his distance—but the instinct that continuously prodded him to volunteer for dangerous missions was stronger. Which explained why he was now knee-deep in kids, waiting for a glimpse of Terry Evans.

Then there she was, moving through the sea of children like a sleek sailboat through choppy seas. Dipping and swaying with an instinctive elegance, she had a smile for each of the noisy kids and seemed completely unflustered by the racket.

She took a seat in a splash of afternoon sunlight,

as the children gathered on the floor in front of her. They quieted down slowly, giggles and grumbles fading into silence as Terry picked up a book and began to read. Her voice lifted and fell with the rhythm of the story, and Aidan, like the kids, couldn't take his gaze off her.

Terry held the colorful book up every now and then, to show the pictures and the kids laughed along with her as she acted out the different voices of the characters.

She was really something, Aidan thought. Even while a part of him really appreciated the picture she made—a larger part of him was shouting out *warning!*

If he had any sense he'd leave. He'd made it through nine long weeks of temptation and he wasn't about to lose the bet now, just because of a curvy blonde with hypnotic eyes.

He snorted. *"Hypnotic?"*

Man. He was in bad shape.

The kids laughed at something in the story and with an effort, he shook himself out of the stupor he'd slipped into. Screw having her check over his work. Screw hanging around this magnet for kiddies. He'd just go back outside, move the skeleton of the castle into the storage shed and get the hell outta Dodge.

He'd no sooner planned his escape than the cell phone he kept jammed in his jeans pocket let out a muffled ring. Digging for it, he checked the number, flipped the phone open and answered it while he headed for the back door.

"Get your butt back here, boy. We gotta move." J.T., the chopper pilot Aidan worked with, spoke fast. "Sport boat capsized about five miles out."

"On my way." Instantly, every thought but work raced out of his mind.

Aidan snapped the phone closed, jammed it into his pocket and headed out. He glanced back over his shoulder as he hit the doorway leading to the kitchen and the back door beyond. Terry's gaze slammed into his and he read a question in her eyes.

Just one more good reason to keep his distance, he told himself as he turned and stalked out. He wasn't a man who liked having to explain himself.

Having no one but himself to answer to kept life simple.

If he was lonely sometimes, that could be solved with friends or with a willing woman who knew not to expect any tomorrows out of him.

Terry Evans was not that kind of woman.

She had *tomorrows* written all over her.

Which should be enough to keep Aidan the hell away from her.

Three

The sea swallowed him.

In that one instant, when his head slipped below the cold water, Aidan wondered, as he always did, with just a small corner of his mind, if this might be the time the sea would keep him. Hold him, drag him down to the darkest water, where sunlight never touched. Where fish never swam. Where the cold was as deep as the darkness.

And just as quickly as it came, that thought disappeared, pushed aside so that he could do the job he'd trained for. He gave a couple of hard, powerful kicks, tipped his head back and breached the surface of the water. Cloud-dappled sunlight welcomed him, and he took a moment to find his bearings. Glancing to his left, he spotted the capsized sport boat about ten feet away, then shifted his gaze to the helicopter, hovering loudly about ten feet over head. The blades whipped the air, churning the already choppy water into a white foamed froth. The noise was tremendous. He lifted one arm, waved to Monk, hanging out the side of the chopper, then struck out swimming toward the boat and the two men perched on top of the upended hull.

"Man," the older one of the two shouted as he got nearer, "are we glad to see you guys."

Aidan grinned. Grabbing hold of the boat, he looked up at the men. They looked like father and son. The younger of the two couldn't have been more than seventeen. He looked scared and cold. Couldn't hardly blame him. Couldn't be easy to have your boat flip over on you.

He slapped the side of the boat. "You two need a ride?"

The helicopter came closer, dragging the orange steel cage basket through the water, skimming the surface, splashing through the whitecaps.

"Hell, yes," the older man shouted and slapped his son on the back. "Take Danny first."

Aidan shook his head as the basket came closer. Grabbing hold of it, he kept kicking, keeping his head above water and spitting out mouthfuls of it as it slapped him in the face. "No need. Basket's big enough. We all go."

The kid looked a little dubious and who could blame him? But to give him his due, he bit back on his own fears and slid down the side of the hull into the water. Aidan was ready for him, grabbing one arm with his free hand and tugging him closer. Over his radio, he heard Monk muttering.

"Move it along, will you, Reilly?"

"I'm getting there. Hold your horses."

"Who you talking to?" The kid shouted as he scrambled, with Aidan's help, into the basket and then inched to one side of it, with a two fisted, white knuckle grip on the rail.

"Them!" Aidan shouted and pointed skyward toward the hovering chopper. Then turning his gaze on the older man, he yelled, "Let's go!"

The man slid down and got into the basket with less trouble than his son had had. Then Aidan climbed in, and shouted, "Take us home, J.T."

While the chopper pilot moved off, the basket swung lazily into the air, like some amusement park ride. Monk operated the winch, raising the basket to the open door of the chopper, then when it was close enough, he grabbed hold and pulled it aboard.

"Everybody okay?" he shouted to be heard over the roar of the helicopter's engine.

"Fine." The older man climbed out, then reached

a hand to his son, to help him into the belly of the chopper. "Thanks for dropping by."

Monk draped the two guys in blankets while Aidan grinned and clambered out of the basket wiping water out of his face. "Always a pleasure," he yelled, feeling the adrenaline still pumping inside. "What happened to your boat?"

The man shook his head and leaned back against the shell of the chopper. "Damn thing started taking on water. Almost before we'd finished radioing for help, she got bottom heavy and did a roll, pitching us into the drink."

"Don't like boats," Monk shouted to no one in particular as he grabbed hold of one of the straps hanging from the roof of the chopper. "If God wanted us in the water, he would have given us gills."

Aidan laughed at his friend's solemn voice. The man hated water. Strange that he'd ended up in Search and Rescue. "But flying's okay?" he prodded, knowing the answer even before he asked the question.

"Hell, yes. It's *safer.* You ever see a tidal wave in the sky?"

While the man and his son relaxed to enjoy the ride, Aidan laughed at Monk and told himself he was a lucky man—jumping out of helicopters for a living—did it get any better than that?

By the next afternoon, Terry was ready for a break. She'd spent the last several days either in the bookstore, or tucked away in Donna's tiny, cottage-style house. She didn't know anyone in town—except for Aidan Reilly—and she hadn't seen him since he'd rushed out of the bookstore the previous afternoon.

Not that she *wanted* to see him, of course.

But spending too much time on her own only gave her too much time to think. Not necessarily a good thing.

Still, just because she was alone in a strange city, didn't mean she couldn't get out and mingle. Which was why she was spending her lunch hour walking along a crowded boardwalk, disinterestedly peering into the shop windows as she passed.

Although now, she was rethinking the whole, "get out and see some of Baywater" idea. The September sun beamed down from a brassy sky and simmered on the sidewalk before radiating back up to snarl at the pedestrians.

Even in a tank top and linen shorts, she felt the heat sizzling around her and realized that South Carolina muggy was *way* different than Manhattan muggy. She lifted her hair off her neck and let the soft ocean wind kiss her sweat dampened skin. One brief moment of coolness was her reward, but it was over almost before she could enjoy it.

All around her, families laughed and talked together. Kids with zinc oxide on their noses bounced in their tennies, eager to hit the beach. Young couples snuggled and held hands and the sound of cameras clicking was almost musical.

She came to the corner and stood on the sidewalk, watching the cars stream past along Main street. Well, "stream" was subjective. They were moving faster than she could walk, but traffic was pretty impressive for such a small town. When the light changed, she jumped off the curb and hurried across the street, unerringly headed for the dock and the ocean beyond. The nearer she got to the water, the brisker the wind felt and the ocean spray on her face was cool and welcome.

Boats lined the dock. Everything from small skiffs and dinky rowboats to huge pleasure crafts and mini yachts, bumped alongside each other like close friends at a cocktail party. Fishermen littered the pier, their poles and lines dangling over the weather beaten railings. A couple of skateboarders whizzed through the crowds, weaving in and out of the mob of people like dancers exhibiting precision steps. A balloon slipped free of a little girl's grasp and while her mother consoled her, the wind carried the bright splotch of red high into the sky.

Terry smiled to herself and kept walking. The scent of hot dogs and suntan lotion filled the air and as she passed a vendor, she stopped, giving in to hunger. She bought a hot dog and a soda, then carried them down a steep set of stairs to the rocks and the narrow beach below. Close enough to the pier that she heard the crowd, but far enough away that she felt just a touch of solitude.

Perching on a rock, she brought her knees up, took a bite of her hot dog and only half listened to the sounds around her as she focused her gaze on a couple of surfers, riding a low wave toward shore. Close to the sea, the temperature was easier to take.

"Still, strange to be sitting on a beach in the middle of the day," she murmured, then glanced around quickly. Talking to yourself was the first sign of a wandering mind. She sure as heck didn't want witnesses.

If she were back home right now, she'd be rushing down Fifth Avenue, clutching her purse to her side and walking fast enough to keep up with the incredible pulse and rhythm of New York City. She'd be racing from one meeting to the next, lining up volunteers and donations for whichever charitable organization she was working for at the time. There would be luncheons and brunches and coffee-fueled meetings at trendy restaurants.

Busy days and empty nights.

She shivered, took another bite of the hot dog and told herself that her life was full. She did good work—important work. In the grand scheme of things did it really matter that at some point in the last five years, she'd actually stopped *living* her life?

"Great," she muttered, rolling up her napkin and taking a swallow of her soda. "Self-pity party at the pier. Bring your own *whine*."

She pushed off the rock and started for the shoreline where the water edged in across the sand, staining it dark and shining. Terry smiled, kicked off her sandals and let the cool, wet sand slide around her feet. The ocean rippled close and lapped over her skin and she kicked at it idly, sending spray into the air.

When her cell phone rang, she almost ignored it. Then sighing, she reached into her shorts pocket, pulled out her phone and glanced at the number before answering.

"Donna. How's Hawaii?"

"God, it's good to be home for a while," her friend said with a sigh of contentment. Then she added quickly, "Jamie, don't hit your brother with the sand shovel."

Terry chuckled and started walking slowly along the edge of the ocean. The tide rolled in and out again with comforting regularity and the shouts of the children on the beach played a nice counterpoint.

"How's it going there?" Donna asked as soon as the Jamie situation was settled.

"Fine. Business is good."

"And Aidan?"

Terry pulled the phone away from her ear and smirked at it. "You are completely shameless."

"Gee, don't know what you mean."

"Right." Terry laughed. "You're impossible."

"I'm a romantic."

"Who's wasting her time."

"Come on," Donna wheedled. "You've got to admit he's gorgeous."

"He is," Terry admitted with a sigh as an image of Aidan Reilly rose in her mind. "I give you that. But the man swore off sex, remember?"

"Uh-huh. And trust me," Donna said. "He's a man on the edge. Wouldn't take much effort to push him over."

"I thought you were supposed to be *helping* him."

"I'm *trying* to help both of you."

"And it seems so much like interfering."

"To the suspicious mind…"

"Not interested," Terry said firmly and half wondered if she was trying to convince Donna or herself. Then she said it again, just for good measure. "Seriously. Not interested."

"Fine, fine," Donna agreed. "I can see you're going to be stubborn, so forget I said anything."

"Already working on it," Terry assured her and swished one foot through a rush of cold seawater.

From a distance, a shout floated to her and she looked up in time to see a man jump off the pier and drop, feet first, into the ocean below. "What an idiot."

"What? Who are you talking about?"

Shaking her head, Terry said, "Some moron just jumped off the pier."

"That's nuts," Donna screeched. "That close to shore, there are rocks and sandbars and—"

"Now he's swimming to shore, so apparently he survived."

"You know what they say," Donna said, "God protects fools and drunks—Jamie, don't hit your brother with the sand pail, either!"

"Whether he's a fool or drunk is still a mystery," Terry murmured, only half listening to her friend as she kept her gaze locked on the idiot swimming through the waves. "But he's a good swimmer."

When he finally hit shore, he stood up and turned toward her. His dark T-shirt clung to his muscular chest and his sodden cutoff jeans shorts hung from his narrow hips. As she watched, he came closer, grinning now and Terry's stomach fluttered weirdly as she whispered, "I don't believe it."

"What?"

"It's him. Aidan."

"The moron who jumped off the pier?"

"The very one and he's headed this way," Terry said, trying to ignore the stutter of her heart and the jolt in the pit of her stomach.

"Well, well, well," Donna said, laughing, "isn't this fascinating?"

"Go save Danny from Jamie," Terry muttered and hung up while Donna was still laughing.

Stuffing the phone back into her pocket, she gripped her sandals tightly in one fist and waited as Aidan came closer. If she had any sense at all, she'd turn around and head back the way she'd come. Take the stairs up to Main Street and get back to the bookstore.

But simple pride kept her in place.

No way was she going to run away from him. Give him the satisfaction of knowing that he could get to her without even an effort.

"Come here often?" Aidan asked.

"Are you insane?"

His grin widened and her heart did a fast two-step. Ridiculous how this man could jitter her equilibrium.

"Not legally," he said and swiped the water from his face with one tanned, long fingered hand.

His soaking wet shorts hung low across his narrow hips. His legs were long and tan and his feet were bare. He looked athletic, rugged and way too good.

"You jumped off the pier."

"Yeah." He half turned and waved one arm over his head.

Two men on the pier waved back.

"Your keepers?" she asked.

Aidan laughed and turned back to look at her. "My brothers. Well, two of 'em."

Staring at Terry, he could see she was annoyed and damned if she still wasn't an amazing looking woman. Her green eyes flashed at him and disapproval radiated off of her. But there was something else, too…something like excitement. And that made the jump off the pier and the swim to shore more than worthwhile.

He could still hear Connor's and Brian's hoots of glee when he'd spotted Terry and told them to take his fishing gear home for him. No doubt they were already planning to make room for him in the convertible they'd be riding around base come Battle Color Day. But hell with that, Aidan told himself. No way was he going to be seen in public wearing a grass skirt and a coconut bra like his bet-losing brothers.

Nope.

Instead he planned on having a front row seat for the spectacle—cheering them on while basking in the glow of their envy—for him having won the bet.

"The other two thirds of your set of triplets?"

One of his eyebrows lifted. "Donna tell you lots about me or what?"

"Just the basics," Terry said and walked a little further into the ankle deep water. "She never mentioned your death wish."

He threw his head back and laughed. "Death wish? From jumping off that short pier? Babe, that little jump was like rolling off the couch to me."

"What about the rocks? Sandbars?"

He waved her points away and joined her in the froth of water sluicing up over the sand. "From the fourth pylon to the sixth, there's a trench, deeper water. We've been jumping off that stupid pier since we were kids."

"So you've always been crazy."

"Pretty much."

"You grew up here?"

"Ah, so Donna did leave out a few details."

Terry chuckled, glanced at him and gave him a half shrug. "There's that ego again. Contrary to what you may believe, Donna and I didn't really discuss you in great depth."

He laughed again. Something about the way she could quickly go from fury to prickly to laughing really got to him. Nothing like a woman whose moods you couldn't predict to keep a man on his toes.

Not to mention her lushly packed body. It hadn't been hard to spot her from the pier. Her profile was tough to miss. She had more dangerous curves than the Indy 500 and her shoulder-length blond hair flew out around her in the sea wind like a starting flag. Probably every male within miles had already started their engines.

God knew *his* was up and running.

He brushed that thought aside, though. He wasn't some hormone driven teenager with his first case of lust. He could control himself. He could talk to her without drooling all over her. And he'd damn well prove that to both himself and the brothers he *knew* were still watching from the pier.

"Well then," he said and walked closer to her, dragging his feet through the icy froth of water, "let me regale you with tales of the Reilly brothers."

She smiled and shook her head. "So this is a comedy?"

"With us? Damn straight." He shifted his gaze from hers to the endless stretch of ocean laid out in front of them.

The sunlight glittered on the surface of the water, like a spotlight on diamonds. A few sailboats skimmed close to shore, their sails bellied in the wind. Surfers lazily rode the minor swells in toward shore and overhead, seagulls danced and screeched. A couple of kids with swim floats raced in and out of the water while their parents watched from a blanket and from not too far away, came the tinny sound of country music sliding from a radio.

"We moved to Baywater when we were thirteen. Liam was fifteen. Our dad was a Marine, so up until then, we'd traveled all over the damn place." He smiled when he said it, remembering all the moves with a lot more fondness than his mother felt for them. "We were stationed in Germany, Okinawa, California and even a quick stint in Hawaii."

"All before you were thirteen?"

"Yep." The water was cold, the sun was hot and a gorgeous woman was standing beside him. Days just didn't get any better than this. "Anyway, when he was assigned to MCAS Beaufort—"

"MCAS?"

He grinned. "Sorry. Marines tend to talk in acronyms. MCAS. Marine Corps Air Station."

"Ah…" She nodded.

"When he was assigned there, we followed just like always. He made every move seem like an adventure. New town, new friends, new school."

She was quiet for a minute or two, then looked up at him with eyes that looked deep. "Must have been hard."

"Could have been," he admitted, caught for a moment or two by the empathy in her eyes. But he didn't need her sympathy. "Probably was for other Marine brats. But we always had each other. So we'd go into a new school with built-in friends."

"Handy."

More than handy, he thought. The Reilly brothers had stuck together through thick and thin. Even when they were battling—which was pretty damn often— there was a bond between the four of them that had been stronger than any outside pressure.

"Hey, there's a lot to be said for having a big family. Always someone to hang with."

"Or fight with?"

"Oh, yeah. We had some great ones. Still do on occasion. You have brothers and sisters?"

"One," she said. "Brother. Older. We're not close."

There was a story there that she wasn't telling. He could see it in the way she shifted slightly away from him. Her body language said a hell of a lot more than she was. "Why not?"

She stiffened a little further, lifted her chin as if

preparing for a battle that she was used to fighting. Then she said, "Lots of reasons. But we weren't talking about me, remember?"

Shut down. Neatly. Politely. Completely. Okay. He'd let it go, he thought. Come back to it another time. He wanted to know why her green eyes looked shadowed. Why her brow furrowed at mention of her family. And yet…he really didn't want to explore *why* he wanted to know.

So he was happy enough to turn the talk back to him and his family.

For now.

"Right." He blew out a breath, focused on the sea again and started talking. "Anyway, Mom handled everything, as usual. Dad made it an adventure, Mom made it all work. She handled the packing, the bills, the requisitions, the dealing with the movers…everything. Basically all us guys had to do was show up."

"Your mother's crazy, too," she said, though her words were filled with more than a little admiration.

He laughed shortly. "She'd be the first to agree with that." He shrugged and stared hard at the horizon, where sea met sky and both blended, becoming a part of each other. "But, everything changed when we moved here. Mom loved it. Said she felt a 'connection' to this place. She loved everything about Beaufort, the south, the people. When she found Baywater on a shopping trip, she told my dad that here is where they'd be staying."

"Could he do that? Just opt to stop being deployed?"

"Not easy, but, yeah. Ask for an assignment to a company that doesn't deploy and you're pretty safe. But Mom wouldn't let him do that. She knew how much he enjoyed the deployments."

"But what about when he was reassigned to live somewhere else for a year or two? That happens, doesn't it?"

"You bet. Mom just told him 'happy trails' and that she'd be right here, letting us go to school and have some stability." He shoved both hands into his jeans pockets and winced as he realized he'd dived into the water still carrying his wallet. Damn it. But he hadn't been thinking. He'd taken one look at Terry and jumped off the pier.

He shook his head. "Mom wanted us to be able to finish out high school in the same place."

"So she stayed here with you guys and let him go?"

"Yep." He smiled to himself. "Dad would head off for six months and Mom would be right here, running the show until he got back. She told him this was home and she wasn't leaving it again."

"Strong woman."

"You have *no* idea." He laughed, remembering how his mother had managed to ride herd on four teenage sons and make it all look easy. "Dad lasted another year or two, then wangled an assignment back to MCAS and they've been here ever since. He retired not long after that—"

"Now?"

Aidan sighed. "He died a few years back."

"I'm sorry."

He looked at her. "Thanks. Mom's still in their house here in Baywater and loving the fact that all three of her sons are stationed close enough for her to irritate whenever she wants to."

"And you're all nuts about her."

He shrugged. "Hard not to be."

"And your other brother?"

"Ah, Liam. *Father* Liam." Aidan looked down at her, then lifted one hand to tuck a long strand of silky blond hair behind her ear. "Every Irish woman's dream is to be able to say, 'my son the priest.' Liam's church, St. Sebastian's, is here in town, too, so Mom lucked out. For a while anyway. Until one of us is transferred out."

"Even apart, though, you'll still have each other."

He studied her and noticed the shadows were back, haunting her eyes. Something inside him wanted to reassure her. To wipe away the shadows and make her smile.

And that worried the hell out of him.

Four

By late afternoon, the wind had picked up, the sky was crowded with clouds and Terry was still trying to convince herself that Aidan wasn't getting to her.

But he was.

"Damn it."

She closed the shop, locked the door behind her and stepped out onto the sidewalk. Tilting her head back, she watched the slate-gray clouds colliding into each other like bumper cars gone amuck.

"Storm coming." A soft voice, female, with just a touch of humor in it.

Terry turned, smiling, to face Selma Wyatt. At least seventy years old, Selma's blue eyes sparkled with a kind of vitality that Terry envied. The woman's long, silver hair hung in one thick, neat braid, across the shoulder of her gauzy, pale yellow, ankle skimming dress. The toes of her purple sneakers peeked from beneath the hem.

"Yeah," Terry said with another quick look skyward. "Sure looks like it."

Selma shook her head until that thick braid swung out like a pendulum. "Not the storm I'm talking about, honey."

"Ah…" Terry nodded sagely and didn't bother to hide her smile. "See something interesting in your cards?"

The older woman ran the spirit shop/palm reader emporium next door. And though Terry had never been one to believe in the whole "mystic" thing, she figured Selma must be good at what she did, because there was an almost constant stream of customers coming and going from the Spirit Shop all day long.

In the few days Terry had been in town, Selma had pretty much adopted her. She'd taken her out to lunch, introduced her to the noontime crowd at Delilah's diner and pretty much elected herself friend and watchdog. She'd even offered to give Terry a "reading," but she'd declined, since, if her future was anything like her past…Terry really didn't want to know.

"Heck no, honey," Selma said. "Didn't need the cards for this one. It's in the air. Can't you feel it?"

A slight chill danced up Terry's spine before she shook it off, telling herself that Selma'd been staring into her crystal ball too long. "The only storm I feel is the one blowing in off the ocean."

Selma smiled patiently—the same kind of smile an adult gave a two-year-old who insists on tying his own shoe even though he can't quite manage it. "Of course, dear. Pay no attention to me." Then she paused, cocked her head and said, "Oh. There it is. Wait for it."

A little impatient now and feeling just a bit uneasy, Terry inhaled sharply and asked, "Wait for what?"

Then she heard it.

A low rumble of sound.

Like distant thunder, it growled and roared as it came closer. The fine hairs at the back of Terry's neck lifted and she turned her head toward the sound.

Overhead, lightning shimmered behind the clouds, just a warning. A hint of bigger things to come.

But she forgot all about the storm as she watched a huge motorcycle slink to the curb and stop. In the dim light of dusk, the spotless chrome sparkled and shone and the black paint gleamed like fresh sin.

And speaking of sin…

Aidan Reilly sat astride the motorcycle and dropped both booted feet to the ground to steady the bike while he looked at her.

"Now *that's* a storm, honey," Selma murmured. "A big one."

Terry hardly heard her. Her breath came fast and short. Her heartbeat jittered unsteadily and every cell in her body caught fire at once.

He wore faded jeans and the battered cowboy boots he'd had on the first day she met him. His black T-shirt was strained across his chest, looking about two sizes too small—not that she was complaining. He wore dark glasses that hid his eyes from her, but no helmet and he looked...*dangerous*.

Her stomach fisted and she swallowed hard against the gigantic knot of something hot and needy lodged in her throat.

Then he smiled and Terry felt her toes curl.

Oh, this couldn't be good.

"Evening, Ms. Wyatt," he said, his voice as low and rumbly as the engine of the machine vibrating beneath him.

"Aidan," Selma said with a nod and a smile. "Come to have your fortune read?"

He grinned. "Now, Ms. Wyatt, you know I like surprises."

"Then I'll leave you to them," she said and headed off down the sidewalk.

Terry barely registered the fact that the woman was gone. All she could think was, it just wasn't fair for a man to look that good.

And why did he have to have a motorcycle?

"Terry!"

She blinked her way out of a very interesting daydream and realized that he must have been calling her name for a couple of minutes. How embarrassing was *that?*

Burying her own jittery reaction to him under a snarl of much more comfortable indignation, she snapped, "What're you doing here, Aidan?"

He glanced at the sky just as a grumble of thunder rolled out, long and low, and filled with the promise of coming rain. Then he glanced back at her. "Just thought maybe you could use a ride back to Donna's house."

"I can walk," she said, turning to put action to the words. The faster she got some distance between she and Aidan, the better, all the way around. "Thanks anyway."

He kept pace with her, rolling the bike and walking it down the side of the street with his long legs. "Gonna rain any time now," he pointed out.

"Then I'd better hurry," she countered, telling herself to put one foot in front of the other. To keep moving. To for heaven's sake, don't *look* at him.

He chuckled. "You're so stubborn you'd rather get wet than accept a ride from me?"

She chanced a quick glance at him. "Hello? On a motorcycle, I'd get wet anyway."

"Yeah," he pointed out with a quick grin that showed off the dimple she'd been spending too much time thinking about, "but you'd be moving faster. Having more fun."

"Slow can be fun, too," she said tightly and wondered why she suddenly sounded like a ninety-year-old librarian.

"I grant you. In some things, slow is *way* better."

She stumbled when the images *that* remark blossomed in full, glorious color in her brain. Oh, God. Did his voice just drop another notch, or was she simply going deaf from the pounding of her own heartbeat? Swallowing hard, she demanded, "Don't you have to be somewhere?"

"I'm right where I want to be."

"And what about the bet?" she asked hotly, stopping short to face him.

He lifted one eyebrow, took off his dark glasses and hooked them in the collar of his shirt. "Babe. I asked you to ride the motorcycle—didn't ask you to ride *me*."

A quick rush of heat swamped Terry and she wondered if everyone was seeing those little black dots now fluttering in her vision—or if it was just her. Probably just her. Which couldn't be a good sign.

Taking a deep breath, she got a good tight hold on suddenly rampaging hormones and told herself to get over it. She wasn't looking for a fling and if she were, she wouldn't be looking at Aidan Reilly. The man had sworn off the very thing she was suddenly hungry for. So what point was there in getting herself whipped up into a frenzy?

None.

So okay, she could do this. She could be a grown-up. And besides…a fat, solitary raindrop splattered on top of her head. He had a point. If he took her home on that rolling sex machine, then she'd be in out of the rain a lot faster than she would be if she was stubborn and insisted on walking.

This was purely an act of necessity.

Nothing out of the ordinary to accept a ride from a friend of a friend.

He was just doing her a favor.

Not the favor she secretly *wanted*, but he didn't have to know that.

"Okay," she said, trying to shut up the internal argument she was having with herself. "I'll take the ride. Thanks."

He gave her a slow smile that set fire to the soles of her feet, but she refused to feel the flames. As the rain spattered around her, she walked to the bike. He reached back and unstrapped a shiny black helmet from the tall, chrome backrest bar.

"Good," he said, handing it to her. "Put this on."

"Why do I have to wear a helmet and you don't?" she asked, taking the darn thing.

"Because my head's a lot harder than yours."

"Don't bet on it," she muttered, but yanked the helmet on and fixed the strap under her chin.

"Looks good on you."

"Oh, I'm sure," she said and swung her left leg over the seat as she climbed aboard. Good thing she'd worn linen shorts to work today instead of a skirt.

He half turned to look at her. "Grab hold of my waist and hang on."

Oh, boy.

Beneath her, the powerful engine throbbed and purred as he gunned the motor. The resulting vibrations of the bike set up a series of trembling quivers inside her that took her to the brink of something really interesting.

And she hadn't even touched him yet.

"Are you going to hang on or what?"

She gritted her teeth and grabbed hold of his waist. She didn't have to wrap her arms around him or anything. A simple handhold would be enough, she told herself and fought the rush of something hot and dark and sweet as he revved the engine again and eased the bike onto the street.

The stoplight at the corner was red, so they didn't go far.

She heard the smile in his voice as he glanced back over his shoulder and said, "You're gonna have to get a better grip on me than *that*."

"I'm fine," she insisted, trying not to think about her thighs aligned along his or the powerful engine vibrating beneath her.

"What's wrong, babe? I *worry* you?"

"Not at all. Why don't you just take care of driving and I'll take care of me."

"Your call." He shrugged, turned his face forward again and when the light blinked to green, he took off like the hounds of hell were right behind them.

"Hey!" She shrieked and instinctively wrapped both arms around his middle.

He chuckled and she felt his body shake with silent laughter.

Let him laugh, she thought. She was more interested in keeping her perch on the bike than she was in pretending to be aloof.

He steered the bike down Main street, threading between the cars chugging lazily along the road. As they picked up speed, the wind slapped at her, raindrops pelted her like tiny bullets of ice and Terry relaxed enough to smile, enjoying the rush of air, the sense of freedom and the small, tingling sensation of danger.

It had been so long.

Before her life had become one charitable function after another, she had sought out things like this. Motorcycles, paragliding, deep sea dives, rock climbing.

She hadn't always been adventurous—but when her world collapsed, Terry had stopped caring. She'd gone out of her way to *live* every moment. She'd sought out the most exciting, the most heart pounding, risky activities she could find and then lost herself—and her pain—in the adrenaline rush.

Until five years ago.

When she'd awakened in a hospital one morning, to find herself lying there with a broken arm and leg. And she'd finally realized that chasing death wasn't living. That burying her pain didn't make it disappear. And that the only way to make that pain livable was to help people however she could.

Since that morning, she'd become a champion of causes. Terry Evans became the "go to" girl for most charitable foundations in and around Manhattan. She arranged flashy fund-raisers, was able to browbeat bazillionaires into contributions they'd never had any intention of making and could turn a celebrity auction into the event of the year. And she did it all with a calm, cool smile that managed to hide the *real* Terry from almost everyone.

She had legions of acquaintances, but very few *friends.* And the friends she *did* have, were more her family than those she was related to by blood.

Which was how she'd ended up in Baywater, South Carolina, sitting behind a hunk in jeans, riding a motorcycle in the rain.

Because of Donna.

Since that awful moment twelve years ago, when Terry's world dropped out from under her, Donna had been there for her. She'd cried with her, hugged her and supported her when Terry had taken her stand against her family. Donna Fletcher was the one link to her past that Terry treasured.

"How you doin' back there?"

Aidan's shout cut into her thoughts and Terry inhaled sharply, reminding herself that the past was long gone. "I'm fine," she called back, to be heard over the roar of the engine.

Rain still spattered, as if the storm just couldn't work up the energy to get serious. As they roared along the road, streetlights winked into life and the few raindrops falling were spotlighted in the glow.

A car whizzed past, its radio blaring, tires spitting up water in its wake. Terry ducked her head behind Aidan's shoulder and stared out to one side as the storefronts gave way to houses and those to trees lining the coast road.

The throb of the engine beneath her, the rush of wind all around her, her arms around Aidan's hard middle and the cool splat of rain against her skin, was mesmerizing. Which was why it took her an extra minute or two to notice something.

"Hey!" she shouted, lifting her head. "You missed the turn to Donna's street."

"No, I didn't."

"You passed it."

"Yes, but I didn't *miss* it."

She squeezed her arms tight around him and he grunted. "What're you up to?"

"Can't you just enjoy the ride?" he asked.

"Not until you tell me what's going on." Damn it. She'd relaxed her guard. She never should have taken this ride from him. She'd known it was a mistake the minute she climbed onto the bike. But what red-blooded woman would have been able to say "no" to a Marine cowboy biker?

"Aidan…"

"Relax, babe—"

"Stop calling me *babe.*"

He laughed. She felt it shake through him and it made her grit her teeth even harder. The minute he stopped this bike, she was jumping off and *walking* if she had to, back to Donna's house.

The magic of the ride was gone as she simmered quietly in a temper that flashed and flared inside her. By the time he finally *did* stop the bike, Terry didn't even pause to see where they were before she leapt off her perch, snatched off her helmet and glared at him.

"You really *are* nuts, aren't you?"

He grinned at her and she realized that sexy or not, that smile could get really irritating.

"Thought you might like to take a little sightseeing tour."

"In the *rain?*"

He held out one hand palm up and shrugged. "We drove out of the rain a few minutes ago."

Frowning, Terry lifted her face to the sky and saw that he was right. They'd driven far enough out of Baywater that they'd left the brief summer storm behind them. Now, she took a minute and glanced around. She stood on a cliff road, the ocean far below them. The road behind them was nearly deserted and lined by towering trees that dipped and swayed in the wind as if dancing to a tune only they could hear.

When she finally turned to look at Aidan again, she found him standing beside her, staring out over the black water. Moonlight peeked out from behind the clouds, darting in and out of shadows, like a child playing hide-and-seek.

"Worth the ride?" he asked.

She shifted her gaze to the view and had to admit, it was gorgeous. Moonlight danced on the water, then winked out of existence when the clouds scudded across the surface of the moon. Whitecaps dazzled with phosphorescence that looked ghostly in the darkness.

"It's beautiful."

"One of my favorite spots," he said, walking closer to the edge of the cliff, until he could curl his hands around the top bar of the iron guard rail. "I come up here when I need to get away from people for a while."

She joined him, taking slow, almost reluctant steps. "Then you really shouldn't bring *people* with you."

He glanced at her and shrugged. "Usually don't."

Idly she swung the helmet in her left hand, slapping it gently against her thigh. "So why me?"

"Interesting question."

"That's not an answer."

He turned his back on the view and faced her, leaning against the railing and crossing his arms over his chest. "Don't have one," he admitted after a long moment.

His blue eyes fixed on her, Terry had to force herself to stand still beneath his steady regard. She didn't want to think about the subtle licks of warmth invading the pit of her stomach. She *did* want to hold onto her temper, but it was already fading.

"I just wanted to see you again."

"Why?"

He laughed shortly. "Beats the hell outta me."

"Aidan," she said on a sigh, "this isn't a good idea."

"Which idea is that?"

"This," she said, waving one arm even as she gripped the helmet in one tight fist. *"Us.* You. Me."

"Well that about covers everything," he said, still smiling, "except for what I feel when I'm around you."

"Aidan…"

"You feel it, too."

Oh, boy howdy.

But that wasn't the point.

"Doesn't really matter what we feel, does it?" She tipped her chin up and stared at him, unwilling to let him know just how close she was to losing control.

"Why not?"

"Because whatever it is, it's based on hormones."

"And your problem with that is…?"

"For heaven's sake, Aidan, we're not high school kids."

"What's that got to do with anything?"

Think, she told herself. But all the urging in the world wasn't quite enough to kick-start her brain when her body was obviously in charge, here.

Shaking his head, Aidan spoke again. "There's something here, Terry. Between us."

"There can't be," she said.

He laughed and the low, throaty sound rolled over her with a warmth that dispelled the chill wind. "Why the hell not?"

"Your stupid *bet,* for one thing."

He blew that off with a wave of his hand. "I'm not talking about sex."

That stopped her.

"You're not?"

"Was that disappointment I heard in your voice?" he asked.

"Of course not," she covered quickly. "Just…confusion."

His eyebrows wiggled. "Well, let me clear things up for you. I haven't forgotten about the bet. A little less than three weeks to go and I'm the champion Reilly."

"And that's important to you?"

"Damn straight. I want to be able to lord it over my brothers forever."

"That's mature."

He shrugged and smiled. "*Anyway,* I wasn't talking about sex before, Terry. Though it appears I am now, and can I just say, I'm happy to hear you bring it up?"

"Cut it out," she said and tossed the helmet to him. He caught it neatly. "You don't want to lose a bet and I'm not looking for a summer fling."

"Oh, I'm not going to lose the bet," he said and

pushed away from the rail to walk toward her. "And I'm not looking to be your 'fling,' either."

"Good."

"But…"

"No buts…"

"But…" He repeated as he walked closer, keeping pace even as she inched back warily. "There's lots of things two people can do without actually having sex."

"This is *so* not a conversation I want to have."

"Then we're on the same page after all."

"What?" The wind raced past her, tossing her hair across her eyes and Terry frantically reached up to push it away. Wouldn't pay to take her gaze off him. He was just too smooth to *not* keep an eye on.

He tossed the helmet toward the bike and watched it roll until it came to a stop on the ground beside the front wheel. Then he shifted his gaze back to her, stepped up close and grabbed her hips in a hard, two-fisted grip.

"Aidan…"

"Terry…" He bent his head, smiled and whispered, "Shut up," just before he kissed her.

Five

He groaned as his mouth came down over hers.

Aidan hadn't planned to kiss her.

Hell, if it came to that, he hadn't planned to *see* her tonight. When he left the base, he'd headed straight for the Off Duty, a local bar that catered to Marines. He'd had a beer, and shot a game of pool with a First Sergeant who had more money than pool playing ability. He'd joked around with a few of his friends, bought a round of drinks for a gunnery sergeant about to be deployed—and then he left. Hadn't been able to sit there talking shop with the guys because his mind was somewhere else.

With Terry Evans.

The damn woman had been in his brain all day. Her face had haunted him. Her smile had tempted him. Her temper intrigued him. Since earlier that afternoon, when he'd jumped off the pier to see her— she'd been with him. And he hadn't been able to shake her, despite his efforts.

Now, with his mouth on hers, Aidan felt her slip even deeper inside him.

The taste of her, the feel of her against him, swamped him with more sensations than he'd ever experienced before.

And he wanted more.

He held her tighter to him, wrapping his arms around her middle, sliding his hands up and down her back, following the line of her spine, cupping the curve of her behind.

Her mouth opened under his and his tongue swept within, exploring, defining, discovering her secrets, reveling in the rush of sensations rippling through him.

She sighed into his mouth and her breath filled him. He swallowed it and demanded more. His arms tightened around her further, squeezing until she moaned against him and he could have sworn he felt the imprint of her body on his.

And still it wasn't enough.

Too many weeks of celibacy, he thought wildly, while he tore his mouth from hers to run his lips and tongue along the column of her throat. Too long without the taste of a woman, without the feel of her heat. That's all this was. A reaction to deprivation.

"No," he murmured, running the tip of his tongue across her skin until she shivered and grabbed at his shoulders. That wasn't all. He'd been horny before. He'd been needy before. And he'd never known such an all encompassing hunger. He didn't just *want*.

He wanted *her.*

"Aidan…"

He barely heard her whisper over the roaring in his ears. His heartbeat thundered in his chest and his blood pumped with a blinding passion that left him breathless.

"Aidan…"

Groggily, like a man waking up from a three-day drunk, Aidan lifted his head and stared down at her. "Terry—" He touched her face, running his fingertips down her cheek. She closed her eyes and shuddered in an unsteady breath.

"This is *not* good," she finally said, in a voice so soft, a freshening wind nearly carried it away.

He forced a short laugh. "I don't know. I thought it was *damn* good."

"That's not what I meant," she said and stepped back, away from him.

His hand fell to his side and he fisted it, as if to capture the feel of her skin on his fingertips. Already, he wanted to be touching her again. Already, he missed the taste of her. Warning bells clanged in the back of his brain, but Aidan ignored them. His heartbeat was still racing and his breathing way less than steady.

From below them, came the thunderous, pulsing roar of the ocean as breakers smashed into the rocks. Out on the highway, a solitary car streamed by, its engine whining briefly before disappearing into the darkness. And here on the cliff's edge, an icy wind swept past them, around them,

Drawing them together and at the same time, holding them apart.

"Look, Aidan," she said, lifting both hands to shove her wind-tousled hair back from her face, "I just think that this is…*dangerous*."

He gave her a quick grin. "Nothing wrong with a little danger. It spices things up."

A quick, harsh laugh shot from her throat. "Oh, man," she said, turning away from him to stare out over the ocean, "it's probably a good thing we didn't meet five years ago."

Intrigued, he stepped up beside her and tried not to notice when she inched away from him. "Why five years ago?"

She glanced at him and in the pale wash of moonlight, her blue eyes shone. "Back then," she said softly, "I'd have given you a run for your money, dangerwise."

"Yeah?" He smiled down at her, even as her features shuttered and her own smile faded.

She shifted her gaze back to the water and took the step or two that brought her close to the iron guardrail. She closed her hands over the top rung, lifted her face into the wind and said, "Yeah. Parasailing, deep sea dives, mountain climbing…"

"You? Danger girl?" He grinned as he stared at her, trying to imagine her racing through life looking for an adrenaline rush. Nope. He just couldn't picture it.

"It was a long time ago."

"Sounds like fun."

"It was. For a while."

Aidan leaned one hip against the top railing, folded his arms over his chest and watched her, thoughtfully now. "What changed?"

She leaned forward, straining toward the ocean as if trying to escape the conversation. "*I* changed."

"A shame."

Glancing at him, she smiled briefly. "You *would* think so."

He shrugged. "Nothing wrong with chasing life at high speed."

"I suppose," she said softly. "Unless it's not about chasing as much as it is about running."

"From what?"

He wanted to know, even though a part of him wondered how this conversation had taken such a turn. A minute ago, he'd held her in his arms, tasted her breath, captured her sighs, felt her tremble in his grasp. Now, she was standing just inches from him and yet, it felt as though she were miles away.

"Life?" One word, more of a question than a statement.

Misery etched itself onto her features and even in the dim light of a nearly cloud covered moon, Aidan saw the shadows crouched in her eyes. He wanted to reach for her, but something told him she wouldn't welcome the contact.

Not now.

"You want to talk about it?"

She looked at him again, seemed to consider it, then said, "No. I don't."

Disappointment rose up inside him and surprised the hell out of Aidan. He'd wanted to know what put the shadows in her eyes. What it was that had such power over her that years later, just the memory of it could bring pain strong enough to make her shudder with it.

Always before, he'd kept his relationships on a superficial level. It was, he'd always assured himself, where he felt most comfortable. He wasn't looking to find a happily ever after. He wasn't looking for Ms. Right—more like Ms. Right *Now*.

He'd never really bought into the whole concept of being married to one person for*ever.* There were just too many women and not enough time as far as Aidan was concerned. He liked his action hot and his women temporary. And that outlook on life had served him well so far.

Didn't matter that his brothers—fellow triplets—had just lately fallen into the cozy clutches of two great women. Hell, he didn't mind being the last Reilly standing. He'd go through life proudly carrying the Bachelor banner.

So why then, did he suddenly want to know Terry Evans's secrets? Why did he *care* about whatever it was making her sad? It wasn't any of his business. Shouldn't affect him.

And yet…

"I really think you should take me home, now," she said, splintering his thoughts with the effectiveness of a hand grenade.

Probably best, he thought, but heard himself ask, "Still running?"

She stiffened and narrowed her eyes.

Well, great. Way to go, Aidan. Nice job.

He held up both hands and gave her a smile. "Never mind. Stupid thing to say."

"Fine. Can we go now?"

"Sure." He pushed away from the railing, took her elbow in a firm grip and steered her the few steps toward the bike. Bending down, he scooped up the helmet, then handed it to her.

She took it in both hands, and staring at it as if she'd never seen it before, she said, "Look, Aidan, about that kiss…"

He swung his left leg over the bike and settled onto the seat. Looking up at her, he gave her a smile he figured she needed about now. "Just a kiss, babe. Not a world ender."

"Right," she said and pulled the helmet on. She buckled the strap, then climbed onto the bike behind him.

"Just a kiss."

Her thighs aligned along his.

Her arms came around his waist.

Her breasts pressed into his back.

Aidan fired up the engine and revved it hard, gritting his teeth as he steered the bike out onto the road and back toward the storm hovering over Baywater.

Oh, yeah.

Just a kiss.

No problem.

"So what's the problem?"

Aidan glared at his older brother, then threw the basketball at him. "Haven't you been listening?"

Liam laughed, took the ball and bounced it idly, keeping one eye on the ball and one eye on his brother. "You mean to the rambling story you've been telling me for the last hour and a half? Yes. I was listening."

Aidan muttered a curse, bent down and snatched up a water bottle from the side of the driveway behind St. Sebastian's church. Uncapping it, he took a long drink, hoping the still cold water would put out some of the fires that had been with him since he dropped Terry off at Donna's house the night before.

It didn't.

And the weather wasn't helping any, either. Hot. Hot and humid, with the air so damn thick, it felt as though you should chew it before inhaling. Roiling gray clouds moved sluggishly across the sky and a hot wind occasionally kicked up out of nowhere. Hurricane season in the south.

Aidan exhaled sharply and narrowed his eyes on the sky. He had a feeling in his bones that the hurricane even now building up in the ocean would be headed their way all too soon. Which meant that the Search and Rescue unit would be on high alert twenty-four hours a day—not just for sea rescues, but working with the local police as well. In times of emergency, people didn't care *who* saved them—as long as they got saved.

Ordinarily the Coast Guard would take up a lot of the slack when it came to disaster time. But here, just outside Beaufort, the closest Coast Guard unit was stationed in Savannah and no one was going to sit around and wait for help. He squinted as the sun briefly peeped out from behind a bank of clouds and thought about the last hurricane that had blown through just a month ago.

Baywater was lucky that time around. Got plenty of rain and enough wind to snatch off shutters and toss old trees. But nothing as devastating as the outer banks had seen. He hoped their luck would hold.

"Worried about the storm?" Liam asked, drawing Aidan out of his thoughts.

"A little," he said, shrugging. "Weather report says it's going to skip us this time, hit in North Carolina. But my bones tell me different."

Liam nodded and glanced skyward. "I hate hoping for disaster to visit someone else."

"You're not. You're just doing what everyone else is doing and hoping it skips *us.*"

Aidan recapped the water bottle, tossed it onto the grass under the shade of an oak tree and snapped another look at Liam. "So back to the point...where's the advice, *Father?* You're a priest, for God's sake. Say something meaningful."

Liam chuckled, turned on one heel and jumped, firing the basketball at the hoop tacked up over the garage behind the rectory. *Swish.* The ball swept through the net without ever touching the rim of the basket. Grinning, he trotted up to retrieve the ball, then tossed it back to his brother. "What kind of advice did you have in mind, Aidan?"

"Something *comforting,* damn it."

Liam laughed again. "Since when do you need comfort on the subject of women?"

This couldn't get much more humiliating, so he spilled his guts. "Since a few days ago, all right?" Hadn't he just spent the last hour or so explaining all of this?

"Donna's friend Terry is getting to you."

"I didn't say that."

"Sure you did."

No. He deliberately had *not* said that. In fact, he'd talked circles around himself in an effort to stay far away from such a statement. Apparently, though, Liam was good enough at reading his brothers that he didn't need a flat out admission.

"What do you want me to say, Aidan?"

"I don't know. You're the priest. Come up with something."

Liam laughed, bounced the basketball a couple of times, then shot it at his brother. Aidan snatched it and held on to it with a viselike grip.

All night, he'd thought about Terry. About that kiss. About the way she'd looked up at him in the moonlight. About those damn shadows in her eyes. And all night, he'd kicked himself for not staying with her. For not digging out what it was she didn't want to talk about.

Which was just so unusual for him, he'd shown up at the church at the crack of dawn for a little sympathy from the family priest. So far, he hadn't gotten much more than his butt kicked in a game of Horse.

Liam walked to where he'd dropped his own bottle of cold water, grabbed it and glugged down half of it before speaking again. "Aidan, you're just shook up because you've never been interested in a woman beyond getting her into your bed before."

Aidan stared at him. "That's it? That's the best you've got? They teach you that at priest school?"

"You're not mad at me, you know," Liam said, capping the bottle again and tossing it to the lawn.

"Really? Cause I think I am."

"You're mad at *you*."

"That's brilliant. For this I got up early and came over here." Nodding, he tossed the ball back to Liam, then bent to snatch up his T-shirt. Dragging it over his head, he shoved his arms through the sleeves and glared at his older brother again.

"Don't you want to know *why* you're mad at yourself?"

"Enlighten me."

"Because you care about her. And you don't want to."

That was a little close to home, but he wasn't going to give Liam the satisfaction of admitting it. "Don't build this up into some hearts-and-flowers deal. I've only known her a few days."

Liam shrugged and used the hem of his sleeveless jersey to wipe sweat off his forehead. "There's a time limit?"

He snorted. "You're way off base here."

"Sure."

"Seriously." Aidan bounced the basketball again, listening to the solid slap of the ball against the pavement, concentrating on the smack of the ball against his palms. "There's nothing going on between us."

Beyond some amazing sexual chemistry and some curiosity on his part.

"So why're you here?"

"Believe me, I'm kicking myself for coming."

Liam grinned. "You want to know what I think as long as its what you *want* me to think."

"You know," Aidan snarled with a shake of his head, "why we come to you for advice on women is beyond me, anyway. You haven't had a date in fifteen years."

"And you've never been a priest, yet you always feel free to complain about the church."

"Good point."

"But, whether you want this advice or not, I'm going to give it to you." Liam came closer, took the ball from Aidan and bounced it a couple of times while he gathered his thoughts.

Finally he looked at his brother and said, "You've got an opportunity here, Aidan."

"And what's that?"

"You've got the chance to get to know a woman *outside* your bed. Who knows? Maybe you'll like her."

"I do like her." He scowled slightly as those words shot from him before he could keep them bottled up inside where they belonged.

Liam smiled. "Maybe there's hope for you yet, Aidan."

"Yeah, yeah," he muttered and grabbed the ball back from his brother, bouncing it idly a few times while he tried to figure out just when he'd started *liking* Terry Evans.

"So. You gonna last the rest of the bet?"

He snapped his gaze up to meet Liam's. "Damn straight I am."

"Uh-huh." Liam caught the ball on a bounce and backed up, still dribbling. "But just so you know, I picked up Connor's and Brian's grass skirts and co-conut bras the other day."

Well that cheered him right up. Aidan laughed, picturing his brothers, mortified, driving around in a convertible while every Marine in the south was free to laugh their asses off at the Reilly brothers. "Excellent."

"And just in case," Liam said, taking a shot for the hoop, "I picked up a set for *you,* too."

He stiffened. "Not a chance, Liam. No way is that going to happen."

"We'll see about that, won't we? Still have a couple of weeks to go…"

Before Aidan could argue, thunder rolled, grimly, determinedly and the leaves on the trees rattled as a sharp wind blasted through. Aidan glanced up at the sky, watched the gray clouds gathering.

"What do you think?"

"I think we might not get lucky this time."

"Could be days yet before we know."

"Yeah."

"You on call?" Liam asked, teasing forgotten.

"Hurricane season? Always." Hopefully the hur-ricane would burn itself out before reaching them, but even if the full brunt of the storm didn't hit Bay-water, the accompanying winds and drenching rain could do plenty of damage.

"Hard to believe anyone would want to take a boat out in weather like this," Liam was saying.

But Aidan knew differently. Folks never figured that bad things would happen to *them*. It was always the "other" guy who ended up with his picture in the paper.

"Oh, there's always some idiot who thinks a storm warning is for everybody *else* in the city." He grabbed the ball back from Liam and ran three long strides before leaping at the hoop and dunking the ball.

Liam caught the rebound and made a jump of his own as Aidan said, "I guarantee you, right now, there's some guy out on the ocean who never should have left his house."

Six

She should never have left the house.

"Damn it!" Terry turned the ignition key again and listened with disgust to the pitiful whinewhinewhine of an engine trying to start—and failing.

She slammed one fist onto the dash, then gripped the wheel with both hands, squeezing it tightly instead of tearing her own hair out. "I don't believe this," she muttered, lifting her gaze to stare out over the wind-whipped ocean.

She scooped her hair back out of her eyes and stared off in the direction of Baywater. She couldn't see land. A sinking sensation opened up in the pit of her stomach—and she only hoped the boat wouldn't start feeling the same thing. The stupid boat *had* managed to get a few miles out to sea before the engine gave up and sputtered an ugly death. Now she could only pray that the hull of the damn thing was in better shape than its motor.

"What were you thinking?" Good question, but she didn't have a good answer.

She'd been up all night, trying to sleep but unable to close her eyes without being sucked back into the vortex of emotions that Aidan Reilly had stirred inside her. It had all started with the roar and grumble of that damned motorcycle. And sitting behind him, pressed close to his hard, warm body hadn't helped anything.

It had been so long since she'd experienced that flash of awareness, that spark of…*adventure.* She'd believed herself past the need or the desire for those feelings, but once awakened, she hadn't been able to put them to rest again.

She wanted to curse him for it.

But a part of her was grateful.

And then there was that *kiss.* She closed her eyes now and let herself feel it again. That amazing, soul-stirring, heart-crashing, bone-melting kiss. Every inch of her body had jumped to attention and clamored for more. He'd stirred something within her even more intriguing than that quest for adventure. Aidan Reilly had made her remember just how long it had been since she'd felt…*anything.*

She opened her eyes again and sighed as she scanned the ocean, unsuccessfully, for a hint of another boat. Someone she could wave down for assistance. She was, however, *alone.*

And it was all Aidan Reilly's fault.

Just before dawn, Terry had given up on sleep and surrendered to the urge driving her to get up and do something. She'd made her way down to the harbor, found a boat rental place and slapped down enough cash to allow her to steer her own course for a few hours.

That's all she'd wanted. To get out onto the ocean. To feel the wind in her face, the salt spray against her skin. To feel...*free.*

"Of course, it would have helped if the stupid boat would run." Muttering curses, she flipped the radio on, picked up the handset and said, "Mayday, mayday." She let up on the button and listened. Nothing. Not even static. She switched channels, spinning the dial as if it were a wheel of fortune.

Still nothing.

Why she was surprised, she couldn't say. If the engine didn't run, why should the radio work?

Oh, she really was an idiot. She hadn't thought this through. Hadn't checked the boat over before setting out. Hadn't done a damn thing to help herself.

Then she remembered her cell phone. Giving up on the radio, she rummaged in her brown leather shoulder bag and came up with a tiny, flip-top phone.

Sighing, she did the only thing she could do and dialed nine-one-one.

"911, what's the nature of your emergency?"

God, it felt good to hear a voice that wasn't her own. "Hi. This is Terry Evans. I'm stranded in the ocean, a few miles outside Baywater. I'm stalled. Engine won't turn over and the sea—" she glanced out over the frothing waves and blistering wind "—is getting bad."

"Name of the boat?"

"*Wet Noodle*," Terry said, cringing at the ridiculous name for the rusting pile of flotsam. "If you could just call the Coast Guard for me—"

"No Coast Guard around here, ma'am," the operator said, a low country accent drawing out her words until they were a soothing lullaby of sound. Comforting, soothing. "But we'll get someone right out to help you. You just hang on a bit, all right?"

Lowering to admit, but she did need help. Soon. She should have checked the weather before setting out this morning. Should have checked out the boat, but that would have been too smart. Too logical. And she hadn't been feeling logical this morning.

She'd been feeling…*restless*.

"That's good. Thanks." She nodded, as if the operator could see her. "Could you get them to hurry, though?"

Then the voice was gone and Terry was alone again. She dumped the phone back into her purse and braced her feet wide apart, to help keep her balance as the choppy waves crashed against the rusted hull of the boat from hell.

Hang on?

What else could she do but hang on?

"One of Bucky's boats," Monk shouted, despite the mic he wore on his helmet. "The poor fool that rented it, couldn't even use the radio to call for help—didn't work—had to do it on a cell phone."

Disgusted, Aidan said, "I'm surprised any of Bucky's boats are still floating. The man's a menace."

Monk nodded. "Someone should put that old coot out of business."

"Yeah, but without Bucky renting out those rust buckets of his, who the hell would we have to rescue?"

Monk shook his head somberly. A bear of a man at six-four and about two hundred fifty pounds, Monk took up a lot of space and always managed to look as though he'd just lost his best friend. He leaned out and stared down at the ocean as it whizzed past beneath them, he said, "Things're getting ugly down there, Reilly."

Monk's voice came through the earpiece he wore, despite the thunderous noise of the Marine helicopter as it sliced through the air about twenty feet above the surface of the water.

Aidan looked out for himself and noticed the froth of whitecaps and the choppy sea. Storm was brewing out in the Atlantic and it was getting closer. Hell, he could feel the chopper pushing hard against a headwind. Another couple of days, that hurricane just might hit landfall and then they were in for a hell of a ride.

"Looks bad, man," Monk said, still shaking his head.

"Relax, Monk. You don't have to dive in, remember?"

"Damn right I remember," the big man said, glancing at him. "No way in hell do I go swimming in a fish's dining room. You divers are nuts."

"You know most people are afraid of flying."

"There's no figuring people," Monk said and pulled a stick of gum out of the pocket of his flight suit. Unwrapping it, he added, "They'll go swimming with sharks, or sit out on a puny little boat to wave to whales, but they're afraid of a plane—precision aeronautics." Shaking his head, he popped the gum into his mouth and chewed. "Makes no sense."

"Almost on 'em," J.T. said over the mic from the pilot's seat. "E.T.A. two minutes."

Monk grabbed hold of one of the chicken straps and leaned far out of the chopper, more at home in the air than most people were on land. "Yep. There it is. Hell, whoever's on it's lucky it hasn't sunk yet. Damn that Bucky to hell and back. Prob'ly a couple hungry sharks down there right now."

"Jeez, Monk," J.T. complained. "Let it go, will ya?"

Aidan laughed as he geared up, checking his dive

suit and adjusting his mask. "Just be ready with the basket. We'll bring up the passengers and leave the boat. Let Bucky worry about hauling it back in."

"Now that's justice," Monk muttered, "send the old bastard out in one of his own boats."

Aidan smiled and stepped to the open hatchway. J.T. brought the chopper in low and hovered steadily, despite the wind trying to push them back toward shore. Glancing down into the boiling surf, Aidan shot a quick look at the small boat rocking wildly with the waves, then lifted a hand to Monk, held on to his face mask and jumped.

That first second out of the chopper was the biggest rush he knew. For that one moment, he was flying. Free and easy, the wind whipping around him, tethered to neither land nor ship, and Aidan felt...*alive* in a way he never could if he were stuck in a nine to five job.

Then he hit the water and the icy slap of it jolted him just like always. Darkness grabbed at him with cold hands and held him briefly in the shadowy quiet. Then he was kicking for the surface again and breaching, just ten feet or so from the boat that looked as if it was going to rock itself to pieces any second.

Being one of Bucky's Bombs, it probably would.

He struck out with strong strokes and in a few seconds was grabbing hold of the side of the boat. Someone on board grabbed his hands and when he tipped his face up to say hello, his grin died.

"Terry?"

"For God's sake," she complained. *"You?"*

"Just what I was thinking, damn it."

Aidan shook his head, then waved to Monk, still hanging out of the chopper. In another second, the man had the rescue basket swung out into the wind and was winching it down carefully, one hand on the cable.

Turning his gaze back on Terry, Aidan hooked his arms over the side of the boat and said, "What the hell were you thinking coming out now?"

She pushed windblown hair out of her eyes and glared at him. Not much of a welcome for the guy who'd come to save her.

Her lips pinched together as if she really didn't want to answer. But she did. "I just wanted to go out on the water for a couple of hours."

"Been watching any news lately?"

"No."

"Guess not. Ever heard of Hurricane Igor?"

"Hurricane?" She shouted to be heard over the wake of the chopper.

Torn between amazement and fury at the astonishment on her features, Aidan snapped, "Get your stuff, we're taking you out of here."

"What about the boat?"

"We'll radio it in. Bucky can come get his own damn boat this time."

She stared at him. "How'd you know I rented it—"

His back teeth ground together. "It's rusty as hell

and it's dead as Moses. Has to be one of Bucky's. Now let's get going, huh?"

Terry had already turned away, though, gathering up her purse and a small thermos.

"You ready?" he shouted as the rescue basket dragged through the water toward him.

"As ready as I'll ever be."

"Swing your legs over the side." He called out and reached to steady her as she did what she was told. With one hand, he grabbed the basket, hauling it closer, then looked up at her. "You're gonna get wet."

For the first time since he'd arrived, she smiled and threw her head back, tossing her hair out of her face again. "Not as wet as I *thought* I was going to get."

Admiration roared through him like an F-18. Amazing woman. No hysterics. No whining about the situation. No fear. Just calm acceptance and simple obedience to his orders.

Aidan laughed while he held the basket steady for her. She slipped off the edge of the boat and landed inelegantly in the basket. Ocean water sloshed over the edges and surged up through the iron grillwork to soak her pale green shorts and halfway up her T-shirt. "Whoa!" she shouted as the cold gave her a solid jolt.

She held her purse aloft to keep it dry and clutched the iron railing with her free hand. Once she was in, Aidan climbed aboard, too, then waved to Monk. The winch cranked and the basket left the water, swinging wildly in the wind, turning, spinning, while Terry's grip on the rail tightened until her knuckles were white.

Aidan watched her, noted the excitement in her eyes, dusted with a healthy dose of fear, and he felt…*something.* His heart hadn't been steady since the moment he'd looked up into her green eyes. Finding her out here, in rough weather, all alone, had, for one moment, scared the tar out of him. But now, watching her take the wild ride with the enthusiasm of a kid at an amusement park, he felt something completely different.

Something deeper.

Something warmer.

Something dangerous.

By the time they reached the base, she was shivering despite the blanket Monk had provided. She didn't argue when Aidan told her he'd drive her home and she was damn quiet on the trip.

But then, so was he. Too busy trying to figure out just what he was feeling to speak, he concentrated on driving—though he indulged himself more than once with quick, sidelong glances at his passenger.

They were more than halfway home when the storm jumped into high gear. Lightning sliced the gray clouds open like a knife puncturing a water balloon and rain poured out in a blinding slash.

"Glad I'm not still on the boat," she muttered, clutching the blanket a little more tightly around her.

Her voice, quiet, was almost lost in the pounding of the rain on the roof of Aidan's SUV. He gripped the steering wheel with both fists and asked, "Why the hell were you out there at all?"

She sighed and let her head drop to the seat back. "I just wanted to be out on the ocean for a while. To just...*be*."

"And you decided to wait for hurricane weather for this outing?"

"I didn't know about the hurricane."

"Most people check the weather before they head out in a boat."

"Well, I'm not most people, I guess then, am I?"

"Already knew that," he muttered, remembering that stab of shock he'd felt when he'd seen her, sitting in that damn rust bucket. "And why the hell did you rent a boat from Bucky of all damn people?"

"He was the only one open."

He slapped one hand against the wheel and squinted into the driving rain. It was like trying to drive through a carwash. "Well, that should have told you something right there. Nobody in their right mind is renting out boats with a hurricane coming in."

"I didn't know about the hurricane. I already told you."

He blew out a breath and took one hand off the wheel long enough to scrape it across his face. "Fine. Fine. Not going to argue that one again."

"Gee, thanks." She turned her head on the seat

back to look at him. "Not that I don't appreciate the rescue, but I could do without the lecture."

"Yeah, probably." But damn it, if they hadn't been able to get to her, then what? She'd have been stranded in the middle of the damn ocean with a hurricane headed her way. In one of Bucky's boats, for God's sake. Which was about as safe as taking a cruise in a colander.

"Shook me a little, seeing you out there," he admitted finally.

"Shook me, too," she said. "Been awhile since I've been in a situation like that."

"You've done this before?" he asked, and made a left off the main highway into a subdivision of tidy homes and narrow streets. The trees lining Elmwood Drive were dancing and swaying with the punch of the wind and experience told him that if Igor didn't change directions mighty damn soon, most of those trees were going to be pulled up by the roots and tossed like sticks.

"Last time," she said, capturing his attention again, "it was on the Gulf Coast. Took a hired boat out and a friend of mine ran it across a sand bar. Ripped the bottom out and we were treading water for what felt like days."

He shook his head. Sounded like something he and his buddies would get into. Why it bothered him to think of *Terry* being in that situation, he didn't want to acknowledge.

"It's your fault anyway," she said suddenly, her tone shifting from memory to fury.

"Yeah?" He snorted an astonished laugh as he pulled into Donna's driveway. Throwing the gearshift into Park, he yanked up on the brake hard enough to spring the damn thing, then turned to face the woman beside him. "How d'you figure?"

"Last night." She waved one hand at him accusingly. "That motorcycle ride. That—" She snapped her mouth shut, shook her head, and opened the car door to a blast of wind and rain that swamped her the moment she stepped out. She slammed the door hard enough to rock the car, then stalked around the front end and headed for the porch.

Aidan was just a heartbeat behind her. Damned if he'd let her say something halfway and then stop. He joined her on the narrow porch and was grateful for the slight overhang that kept most of the punishing rain from slamming their heads. The wind pushed at them though and slanted the rain in at them sideways. Her hands were shaking. So Aidan took the key from her and opened the door.

She stepped into the foyer of Donna Fletcher's bungalow and Aidan stepped in after her, before she could close the door on him. He swung the door closed behind him, then turned to face her.

"Thanks for the ride home," she said tightly, lifting her chin in an age old gesture of defiance. "Bye."

Terry's insides were jumping. She'd been stranded

on a storm-tossed ocean, picked up in an iron basket and helicoptered to a Marine base. She'd had rain and wind and noise all before she'd had two cups of coffee.

But none of that accounted for what she was feeling at the moment. She felt as though she were balanced on the very edge of a cliff, with rocks below and no guardrail above. And it wasn't the rescue at sea doing it to her, damn it.

It was *Aidan.*

She swallowed hard, pushed past him and marched through the small, neat living room to the kitchen beyond. She hit the light switch on the wall and kept walking, straight through the bright yellow room to the service porch.

Aidan was right behind her.

She heard his heavy steps, but would have *felt* his presence even if she couldn't hear him.

She hadn't really expected him to leave, but oh, how she'd hoped he would. At the moment, her emotions were as tangled as her wind-tossed hair and spending more time with Aidan wasn't going to help any.

For heaven's sake, he'd jumped out of a helicopter to ride to her rescue. She leaned on the gleaming white washing machine, closed her eyes and she could still see him, jumping out of that chopper, hitting the water and disappearing beneath the surface. Even before she'd known it was Aidan, she'd been caught up in the…*heroics* of the diver.

Then, when she'd seen him grinning up at her, her heart had jumped in her chest. The man affected her in ways no one else ever had.

And, damn it, she didn't know what to do about that.

"Finish," Aidan said, taking hold of her arm and turning her around to face him.

She ignored the blistering sensation of heat that snaked up her arm from where his skin met hers. "Finish what?"

"What you were saying. The motorcycle—and the—" he prompted.

She inhaled sharply, blew it out and tapped the toe of her soaking wet shoe against the floor. Glancing up at him, she demanded, "You're not going to let this go, are you?"

"Nope."

Another breath. Another stall. She shifted her gaze from his to the window over the back door. Rain pelted against the glass. Though it was barely noon, it looked like dusk outside. Wind rattled the window glass and howled under the eaves of the house, sounding like lost souls looking for a way out.

Well hell. She knew just how they felt.

She needed a way out of this situation and she didn't think she was going to get one. Aidan's hand tightened on her arm.

Finally she turned to meet his gaze again. "Fine. The *kiss,* all right? Happy now?"

"Delirious."

"Good. Now go away."

"Not likely."

"Seriously, Aidan." She kept her voice steady, which was no small task, considering the way her heart was thumping in her chest, "I think you should leave."

"Probably should," he admitted, sliding his hand up her arm. "But not about to."

"This is so not a good idea," she muttered, already leaning toward him, lifting her face.

"I hear that."

"But we're going to anyway," she said and ended with a hopeful, "aren't we?"

"Oh, yeah."

Seven

Terry sighed into him as Aidan pulled her close. His arms came around her and Terry lost herself in his eyes. Blue. Deeper than the sky, wilder than the sea.

Then his mouth took hers, her own eyes closed and stars exploded behind her shuttered lids. Every square inch of her body lit up and flashed like a neon sign at midnight. Tingles of awareness skittered through her and she forgot to breathe.

But then, air was overrated anyway.

He parted her lips and her tongue tangled with his in a frenzied, twisting dance of rocketing desire. Her heartbeat ratcheted into a fierce pounding that nearly deafened her. Her blood raced, her mind went blissfully blank and she gave herself up to the incredible sensation of taking and being taken.

His hands swept up and down her back and finally settled on her behind. She felt the imprint of each of his fingers against the cold, damp fabric of her shorts and he heated her so that she wouldn't have been surprised to see steam rising up around them.

She reached for him, linking her arms around his neck and pulling him closer, tighter, to her. Mouths meshed, breath mingling, sighs humming in the air, she felt him surround her with the kind of heat she'd never known before.

This was new.

This was amazing.

This was terrifying.

One small corner of her brain remained oddly rational despite the rush of hunger leaving her dazzled and breathless. And when he pulled his mouth from hers to run his tongue down the length of her throat, Terry tipped her head back, stared at the ceiling and tried to listen to that rationality.

She knew this was a mistake. Knew that there could be nothing between her and this man. And *knew,* without a doubt, that if he stopped touching her, she'd simply dissolve into a sticky, gooey puddle of unresolved want.

A low, deep tingle started just south of the pit of her stomach. She twisted against him, rocking her hips instinctively against his, pressing close, needing…needing…

"You're killing me," Aidan whispered, his breath brushing her skin until goose bumps raced gleefully up and down her spine.

"Trust me," she managed to say, "I don't want you *dead*."

He chuckled and she felt the low vibration of his laughter move through his body. Her hands swept across his back, tracing muscles barely hidden beneath the soft fabric of his T-shirt. And oh, she wanted his skin beneath her hands. She wanted to define every inch of his sculpted chest and back with her fingertips. She wanted to trail her hands down his body slowly, watching his eyes flash and spark as she took his length in her hands.

"Oh, boy," she whispered brokenly as her own thoughts fired her need to a fever pitch that left her nearly breathless.

"Yeah," he murmured, nibbling at the base of her throat, "just what I was thinking. Need to touch you."

"Oh, yeah. Now. Please now," she said, shutting down that small rational voice in her head. She didn't want reason. She didn't want to think.

She wanted an orgasm, damn it.

His hands moved, sliding between their bodies to the waistband of her shorts. Her breath came fast and furious as she felt him fumble with the button and zipper. Silently she cried, *Now, now, now. Hurry, hurry, hurry.*

She was so close.

It had been so long.

Too long since she'd felt a man's hands on her.

And even then, it hadn't been like this.

It had *never* been like this.

Terry fought for air. Fought to stand still. Fought to not knock his hands out of the way and undo her shorts herself.

Finally, *finally,* she felt the button give and the zipper slide down and she groaned as he slid one hand across her abdomen. "Aidan…"

"Have to touch you, Terry. Have to feel your heat. Now. Now."

"Now," she agreed and kept a tight grip on his shoulders as his hand slipped beneath the elastic band of her silk and lace panties and down, further, further until his fingertips touched her core and she jolted in his arms. "Aidan!"

He bit her neck gently, lightly, then stroked her skin with his tongue as his fingers worked their magic. He dipped first one finger and then two into her depths and she rocked against him, wanting more, wanting to feel him deeper, wanting to feel a *different* part of him, full and deep within her body.

She shifted her position, widening her stance, welcoming him higher, closer, and still it wasn't enough.

"Oh…my…*Aidan…*"

"More," he murmured and before she knew what was happening, he'd pulled his hand free, then tugged her shorts and panties down and off. Grabbing her at the waist, he lifted her, then plopped her down onto the washing machine.

The cold metal bit into her skin, but nothing could stop the flames consuming her. Terry didn't think about what they were doing. Didn't stop to care that he was still dressed while she was mostly naked on her friend's service porch.

The rain hammered at the roof and windows. The wind shrieked and slammed into the house. It was as if even nature had been pushed farther than it could take and had been forced to surrender itself to the moment.

Terry ran her hands over his face, smoothing her thumbs over his mouth, his cheekbones. Her vision was blurred with want. Her breathing staggered in and out of her lungs.

He leaned in and kissed her hungrily, desperately, grinding his mouth against hers in a fierce assault that left her trembling and starving for more. But he pulled away, despite her clinging hands, despite her soft moans of protest.

His big, strong hands grabbed her hips and pulled her close to the edge of the steel machine and then he parted her thighs, pushing her legs apart with gentle determination.

"Aidan…" she whispered and heard the plea in her

own voice and couldn't be embarrassed by it. She was too far gone. Too far along the road of no return. She knew only need. Knew only the hunger that had her in its grasp and wouldn't let go. "Touch me."

He cupped her cheek in the palm of one hand, bent to kiss her briefly, then moved back to stare into her eyes while he dipped his fingers into her heat again. In and out, his fingers built a rhythm that she felt right down to her bones.

"I've never wanted *anyone* the way I want you. Never."

She laughed. Shortly, harshly, desperately. "Then take me, already."

He grinned and that dimple of his shot a flame of something sweet and sharp into her heart. Grabbing her hips with both hands again, he dropped to one knee in front of her and Terry's breath stopped. She knew what he was going to do. Knew it, felt it and wanted it with a passion more fierce than anything she'd ever felt before.

His strong hands gripped her hips, holding her in place. Her heart stopped—hell, the *world* stopped— as she watched him lean in to take her in the most intimate way possible.

His mouth covered her and she groaned aloud, rocking into him. Leaning back, she braced her hands on the washing machine, searching for purchase in a suddenly spinning universe. But Aidan's hands on her hips kept her centered even when she felt herself falling, falling, into a chasm filled with spikes of pleasure and whirlpools of almost delirious need.

He tasted her, his tongue stroking, licking, tasting. His breath dusted her heat, pumping her even higher, faster. Again and again, he dipped into her center, his tongue defining every line, every curve, every inner most secret.

And Terry watched him, unable to look away. Unable to take her gaze from him. Her body rocked in his grasp as she rode the crest of a wave that had been too long banked inside her. She felt herself spiraling, flying faster. A blissful sort of tension gripped her and tightened almost painfully. Her goal was close, and getting closer with every passing second.

She lifted one hand and cupped the back of his head. His short, black hair felt soft beneath her palm. His tongue stroked her core again, in a long, stroking caress that sent her rushing forward toward the fireworks she knew were waiting.

"Aidan!" She shouted his name as the first spasm shattered what was left of her control. Holding him tightly to her, she concentrated solely on the feel of him so intimately joined to her. Her body trembled, her heart ached.

And when the fireworks finally exploded within, she called his name again.

This time in a broken whisper.

When the last of her climax had passed, Aidan stood up and pulled her into the circle of his arms.

She melted into him, locking her legs around his middle and drawing him in close.

She staggered him.

His own heart pounded in tandem with hers. He'd felt her release in every cell of his body. He'd felt the joy, experienced the pleasure and shared the hunger.

And now he wanted more.

Sweeping his hands up, he bracketed her face in his palms and stared into eyes gone glassy with unleashed passion.

"Aidan," she said, struggling to catch her breath, "that was…"

"…just a warm-up," he finished for her and kissed her, swallowing her sigh. Her arms came around him and she scooted closer to him on the stupid washing machine. "I want you," he said when he could manage to tear himself off her mouth. "I want you really bad."

"I'm so glad," she said, giving him a quick smile that shattered something inside him. She leaned in to kiss him again, then stopped, holding him at arm's length as she looked deeply into his eyes. "But what about the bet?"

The bet.

Aidan's already fogged over brain started clicking. If he gave in to what he wanted, he'd lose that stupid bet and end up in a grass skirt and a coconut bra. And what was worse, he'd have to listen to his brothers ragging on him the way he'd been hassling *them* for the last few weeks.

He looked at Terry. Felt the slim strength of her legs locked around his hips. Noted the full, luscious lips just a breath away from his.

Didn't take long to make up his mind.

"Screw the bet."

"I was so hoping you'd say that," Terry whispered, and dropped her hands to the waistband of his jeans.

The backs of her fingers brushed against his abdomen and Aidan's body tightened even further. If he didn't have her soon, he was a dead man. And he wouldn't be dying happy.

"Right there with you, babe," he muttered, dropping a kiss on the top of her head, the curve of her shoulder.

"This is crazy."

"Oh, yeah, no doubt.

"And *so* necessary," she whispered on a choked off laugh.

"Right again. Love a woman who's right so often."

"Unusual man," she murmured as she finally worked the last button of his fly free.

"I like to think so," he managed to say through clenched teeth.

"No underwear," she whispered, sliding her hand down, down, *bingo*.

"Too confining." He hissed in another breath as she stroked him.

"So are your jeans."

"Good point." He let go of her long enough to shove at his jeans—and his cell phone rang. "Damn it."

"Don't answer it," she urged, scraping her palms up now, under his shirt, across his chest.

"Have to. I'm on call," he muttered grimly, already digging for the damn thing out of his jeans pocket. He flipped it open, checked the number and cursed again, viciously. He glanced at her. "It's the base."

Stepping away from her reluctantly, he answered it. "What?"

"Hey, boy, we got another call. Get your ass back here."

J.T.'s voice sounded almost cheerful—for that alone, Aidan wanted to wring his neck. Shoving one hand through his hair, he muttered, "What's up?"

"Some guy fell off a charter fishing boat. Nobody noticed till they got back to the dock." J.T. snorted. "Apparently the guy was a real idiot and people were so grateful that he was 'quiet,' they never questioned it."

"Who the hell would go fishing in this weather?"

"Got enough money to convince the captain, a charter boat's gonna give it a go. You coming or what?"

"Yeah. Be there in fifteen." Aidan flipped the phone closed, heaved a sigh and buttoned up his jeans. Then bending down, he grabbed Terry's shorts and tossed them to her.

"You're leaving."

"Have to."

"So," she said, giving him a smile he knew she wasn't feeling. "I'm not the only idiot out on the water today."

"Looks that way." He watched her and everything in him wanted to ignore the call to duty. For the first time…*ever,* he wanted to blow it all off. To stay here. To lose himself in a woman he'd known less than a week.

That shocked the hell out of him.

He scraped one hand across his face, shoved the phone back into his pocket and stepped up close to her, still perched on the edge of the washing machine. A buzz of passion, excitement, still coursed through him. He reached out and took her face between his palms. Kissing her once, twice, he pulled back and looked into her eyes for a long minute before speaking again.

"Do me a favor?"

She licked her lips and sent a white-hot blast of need shooting right through him.

"What?"

Aidan inhaled slowly, deeply, and let the air slide from his lungs. "Stay home today. Keep the shop closed."

"Aidan, I—"

"Trust me," he interrupted neatly. "Nobody's going to be out shopping today. They'll all be hunkering down, waiting for the hurricane."

She sighed. "If the hurricane *is* coming, then I need to go to the shop. Board up the windows. Donna told me where everything is and—"

"I'll do it."

She bristled. "I'm not helpless, Aidan. I can do it."

"Didn't say you were helpless," he muttered, wondering where the soft buzz of sexual electricity had gone. "Just—*wait* for me, all right? I'll help when I'm off-duty. You want to start boarding up here, okay by me. Just watch yourself."

For a second or two, he thought she might argue. Then she nodded.

"I will."

He kissed her again, one last, lingering kiss filled with promise and disappointment and regret. Then he took a step back and turned for the doorway to the kitchen. "Gotta go."

"Aidan?"

He stopped to look at her.

"Be careful out there."

A slow, wicked smile curved his mouth. "I'm *always* careful, babe."

And then he was gone.

Eight

The neighbors helped.

It seemed when hurricane season rolled around, there were *no* strangers.

Rain slashed at Baywater, coming in so fast and so furiously that it was hard to see as far as across the street. The wind whipped through the trees and tore loose shingles off houses that shuddered with the force of the pre-hurricane gusts.

Donna had been prepared, Terry gave her friend points for that. All of the wood used for boarding up the windows and glass topped doors was stacked neatly in the garage and clearly labeled, telling Terry exactly where each piece went. With the help of a couple of neighbors, Donna's house was as protected as it was going to get in just a couple of hours.

Then there was nothing to do but wait.

Making herself a cup of coffee, Terry winced as she listened to the slam of hammering rain crashing against the house. She kept the TV on, as one of Donna's neighbors had warned her to listen for evacuation notices.

Her stomach churned and her nerves were stretched to the breaking point. She cradled the coffee cup between her palms and tried not to notice the howl and shriek of the wind as it whipped past the house.

"Okay, adventure is one thing," she muttered, glancing at the ceiling as though she would be able to look through it to the storm-tossed sky above. "This is nuts."

And Aidan was out in it.

It had been hours since he'd left her to go on another rescue mission. Hours since she'd taken an easy breath. She shouldn't be worried. This was what he did. The man was trained. And good at his job. She'd seen that for herself only that morning. Though listening to the weather now, she still couldn't believe she'd been dumb enough to go out on a boat today.

But it didn't seem to matter that she knew Aidan was well trained and very capable. She felt a cold, tight fist close around her heart as her mind drew images of him leaping out of that helicopter into the churning mass of the sea. She pictured him swimming toward that lost fisherman and getting swallowed by an ocean that was determined to not give up its prize.

As those images and more raced through her brain, Terry shivered, set the coffee cup down on the kitchen counter and walked out of the room. She crossed the living room, dark now, despite the lamps turned on to keep the shadows at bay. With the boarded up windows, she felt as though she were in a coffin.

Alone.

Afraid.

Shaking her head, she grabbed the doorknob, gave it a turn and opened the door. Instantly wind whipped rain slashed at her, sweeping through the screen door into the foyer as if it had been perched on the porch, just waiting for its chance.

The world was wild.

Trees bobbed and swayed, like desperate sinners, pleading for forgiveness. Rain sluiced out of a gunmetal-gray sky. Houses were boarded up. No one was on the street. People were locked up, shut in and praying that the heaviest part of the storm would pass them by.

Terry walked to the edge of the porch, dipping her head into the wind, forcing herself forward, though it was like trying to run in a swimming pool. Her fingers curled over the rail at the edge of the porch and she squinted into the rain still slashing at her.

Stupid. She should be inside. Warm. Dry.

But inside, she was too alone. Inside, she was reminded that she was a woman apart from the rest of this tiny town at the edge of a storm. Everyone else was with their families. With people they loved or cared about.

Terry had no one.

She'd wanted it that way, of course. For years, she'd done everything she could to keep her distance from anyone or anything that might claim an attachment. She'd loved once and she'd lost and promised herself then that she wouldn't risk that kind of pain again.

Well, it had worked, she told herself now, clinging to the porch railing and watching a watery world of roaring noise and vicious winds. She'd successfully isolated herself.

And she'd never felt more alone.

The family was safe.

Aidan steered his car cautiously down the street, windshield wipers doing their best to keep up with a steady downpour, he looked at the world through a veil of water. Images were blurred, wind whipped, but his mind was clear. Focused.

He'd checked on the rest of the Reilly's. His mom was with Tina and Brian, helping Tina's nana get her house ready. And Connor and Emma were at the church, helping Liam's parishioners batten down the hatches at Saint Sebastian's.

Which left Aidan free to do what his heart was telling him to do.

Go to Terry.

After getting back to base, with a very wet, very angry fisherman, sputtering about lawsuits, he'd headed straight to the Frog House bookstore. With the help of the other local businessmen, he'd managed to board up Donna's place and help Selma tie her shop down as well. Now, they'd done all they could and all they could do was wait.

And there was nowhere he'd rather wait than with Terry.

She'd been there, in the back of his mind, all day. Throughout the rescue calls, throughout all the hurricane preparations, she'd been there, lurking in the shadows of his mind. Reminding him that he had more now to think about than himself. More to take care of than his family.

"Which was damned weird when you think about it," he muttered, steering his SUV around a downed tree and cautiously inching forward, on the lookout for fallen electrical wires.

He hadn't *asked* to care about anyone.

Hadn't *wanted* to be worried about a curvy blonde with a smart mouth.

And yet…instead of hanging around the base as he would have normally—in case they were called out again—he was driving through hell just so he could see her. Reassure himself that she was all right. He'd tried calling her, but the phone lines were down. No surprise. They were usually the first to go in a big storm.

But this was the first time in memory that not being able to make a phone call had turned his insides to jelly.

His fists tightened around the steering wheel as the car was buffeted by wind. He bent his head to look up through the windshield and winced as he watched trees leaning precariously over the street, shimmying as leaves were whipped free, sailing through the air like tiny green missiles.

Aidan made the turn on Elmwood and barely noticed the boarded-up houses and the abandoned look of the normally cozy, kid-filled street.

His gaze locked on one house. He headed toward it as if drawn by a powerful force he had no intention of fighting.

Then he saw her.

Standing on the porch, clutching the railing that shuddered in the wind as if it were a lifeline. His heart thundered in his chest as he watched her blond hair whipping around her head. She lifted one hand to shield her eyes as he got closer and he saw the brief flash of welcome dart across her features as he pulled into the driveway.

He drove as close to the garage as he could, where the car would be protected on one side at least, by the house itself. Then he parked, shut off the engine, set the brake and opened the door.

The wind grabbed it from him, wrenching it wildly out of his grasp and he had to fight to get it closed again.

Once he had, he bolted for the house, long legs striding through the mud and standing water, rain pounding him, wind pushing at him, as if deliberately trying to keep him from her.

But nothing could.

He hit the porch, grabbed Terry and pulled her into the house. When the door was closed and locked behind them, he pulled her into his arms and simply held her, enjoying the feel of her cold, wet body plastered against his.

"What were you doing out there?"

"I couldn't stand it in here anymore," she admitted, holding on to him with a grip as strong as his own. "It felt so…*empty* in here. So quiet."

He laughed shortly and lifted his head, hearing the wind, the rain and the low-pitched voice of the weatherman on the television. *"Quiet?"*

She looked up at him and blew out a long breath. "I felt…alone. And I couldn't take it anymore."

"You're not alone now," he pointed out.

"No." She smiled. "And boy am I glad to see you."

He shifted one hand to touch her cheek, sliding his fingertips across her smooth, pale skin. "Same here."

Her hands moved, from his back to his front, skimming up the front of his now soaking wet T-shirt. Yet, he felt the heat of her touch right down to his bones.

"You were gone a long time."

He sucked in air. "The lost fisherman wasn't easy to find."

"But you did."

"Yeah." He slid one hand along her spine, noted her shiver and moved his hand lower, lower, until he could caress the curve of her behind. His gaze searched hers, for what, he wasn't sure. "J.T. flew all over the damn place. Monk and I were hanging out the hatch and Monk spotted the guy's orange vest."

She inhaled sharply as his hand on her behind pulled her tight against him. Licking her lips, she closed her eyes briefly and whispered, "So he's okay?"

"Yeah. Ungrateful bastard, though." Aidan smiled. "Already talking about suing the charter boat captain and maybe *us*."

"For what?" she asked, clearly stunned.

"He wrenched his neck climbing into the rescue basket."

"Idiot."

"That about covers it." He moved his hand again, this time to the waistband of her shorts. Then he dipped beneath the fabric and scraped his palm over her damp, chilled skin. He sucked in air. "You didn't put your underwear back on?"

She shook her head and closed her eyes again as his fingers kneaded the soft flesh of her behind. "Forgot about it. Got busy…ohhh…"

"You're killing me again."

She smiled lazily. "I don't think so."

He cupped the back of her head with his free hand and threading his fingers through her hair, tipped her face up to his. He bent and gave her a kiss. And another. "I have a feeling this is going somewhere."

"Feels like it to me, too," she managed to say and then swallowed hard.

"So before we get started, you should know I already boarded up the store."

"Oh, good. Thank you."

He grinned quickly. "No arguments? No *'you should have taken me with you'?*"

"Nope," she murmured.

The wind howled again, and the front door rattled loudly as if trying to hold its own against a ravening beast fighting to gain entry.

"We're trapped here, you know. Can't leave in this."

She opened her eyes and looked up at him. "Who wants to leave?"

"Not me, babe."

"You've got to stop calling me 'babe.'"

He grinned again. "I'll work on it. Later."

"Oh, yeah. *Later.*"

Swooping in, he took her mouth with his and showed her just how much he wanted her. How much he'd been thinking of her. How thoughts of her had been haunting him throughout the day.

She opened her mouth to his and when her tongue met his, Aidan sucked in air like a dying man hoping for just another minute or two of life. He tasted her, explored every inch of her warmth, drawing her heat into himself and holding it close, letting it feed the fires licking at his insides.

This.

This is what had kept him going through the long, hard day. The promise of touching her, exploring her, having her beneath him, over him.

His hand on her butt tightened, squeezing, and she moaned into his mouth, squirming closer to him, brushing her hardened nipples against his chest until Aidan was sure she'd left an imprint on his skin right through his shirt.

"Flat surface," he muttered, tearing his mouth from hers.

"Now," she agreed and stepped out of his embrace. Taking his hand, she led him on a quick march through the living room to the hallway and the bedrooms beyond.

Aidan had been in Donna's house before. He knew the layout and he knew when Terry made a right turn, they were headed for the master bedroom. He grabbed her up, unwilling to wait another moment before touching her, feeling her.

She yelped in surprise, then settled against him, running her hands beneath the collar of his T-shirt, splaying her palms against his shoulders, his back. Heat. Incredible heat, speared through him, nearly stopping him in his tracks.

He dropped his head to hers and kissed her again, hungrily, desperately, a man on the edge and ready to jump feetfirst into the abyss.

Then they were in the bedroom and Terry leaned down from her perch in his arms to grab the edge of the handmade quilt covering the mattress and toss it to the foot of the bed. Lacy pillowcases covered the plump pillows and fresh white sheets looked like heaven, even in the gloom.

With the windows boarded up, the room was like a cave, dimly lit, sheltered, tucked away from the storm-tossed world outside.

An island of seclusion.

"Turn on a light," he murmured, swinging her down onto her own two feet. "I want to see you."

A long breath shuddered into her lungs, but she nodded as she crossed the room to turn on a small desk light covered by a Tiffany style lampshade. Pale, ghostly colors danced suddenly around the room, gleaming through the stained-glass shade.

Terry just stared at him. There was no turning back now. And maybe there never had been. Maybe they'd been destined to reach this moment from the instant they'd met. Hadn't she been drawn to him, in spite of her best efforts? Hadn't she felt the magic of his touch in quick, near electrical jolts of awareness every time he was near?

Hadn't she spent the last several hours remembering that incredible orgasm he'd given her and wanting *more?*

While he watched her, she took another steadying breath and quietly, soundlessly, lifted the hem of her dark green shirt up and over her head. He sucked in a breath and she felt his hungry gaze fasten on her breasts, still hidden from him behind their shield of lace.

Slowly, teasingly, daringly, she lifted her hands to the front closure and snapped it open. Then she shrugged out of the lacy fabric and let it fall to the floor behind her.

"Terry…"

She threw her shoulders back and with his gaze locked on her every move, slowly undid the button and zipper of her wet shorts. Then she let them go and they slid down her legs to puddle at her feet.

"If I don't have you in the next couple of minutes," he said, his voice a rumble of sound lower, more demanding and insistent than the thunder outside, "I swear I'm a dead man."

She smiled, feeling a rush of feminine power swamp her, rushing through her blood, making her limbs tremble and her brain shut down. "You're wearing too many clothes again."

He gave her a quick smile that sent a bolt of something delicious straight down to the core of her.

"Guess I am." In seconds, he'd peeled off his shirt, unhooked his jeans and shucked them and his shoes and socks. He let her look her fill, just as he had.

And Terry wanted to *whistle*.

She'd never seen a more gorgeous man in her life. Every inch of him was tanned to a golden-brown and every muscle rippling across his arms and chest and abdomen were sharply defined. And as for the rest of him, his…

"Oh, my."

He grinned and stalked toward her, grabbing her tightly to him, pressing her naked body along the length of his. Hard to soft, heat to heat. She felt the hard, jutting strength of him poking at her and everything inside her went to damp neediness. Her breasts crushed against his chest, her nipples tingled in anticipation even as he took her mouth with his, tangling his tongue with her, tasting, taking, giving.

Her mind whirled.

Her blood raced.

Her body quickened as it had only hours ago, only this time, it was more. More, because she'd had a part of him and wanted all of him.

"Fill me," she murmured, breaking the kiss and nibbling at his neck. "Fill me completely."

Thunder rolled, rain pounded and the wind groaned. The house shimmied, boarded windows rattled and the world seemed to take a breath.

Then he lifted her, as if she weighed nothing. Two big hands at her hips and she was airborne, clutching at his shoulders for balance, looking down into his hungry eyes. She read the passion, the untamed fury and felt a matching need rise in her. His strength cradled her as he lowered her slowly onto the hardened length of him.

"Aidan…" she whispered his name as he entered her, pushing into her depths with a steady determination. Her damp heat welcomed him, and her body adjusted, making room, taking him deeper.

She locked her legs around his middle and leaned back, trusting his strength, letting her head fall and her hair swing wild and wet from her head in a dripping blond curtain.

"Deeper," she crooned, using her legs, hooked over his hips, to pull him closer. "*Deeper,* Aidan. I need to feel *all* of you."

An inferno of need rose up around them, trapping them, drawing them both deeper into the gaping canyon of desire.

He dipped his head to take one of her nipples into his mouth and as his lips and tongue and teeth worked the sensitive tip, a moan slipped from Terry that left her whimpering in its wake.

Every inch of her felt alive, tingling, *desperate.* When he suckled her, she felt the drawing power of him clear to her toes and still, it wasn't *enough.*

Aidan heard that moan and it triggered something inside him that pushed him over the brink of control into the whirlwind of passion. He'd never known need so fierce, so all consuming.

Never tasted passion tinged with desperation.

Never felt anything like this woman he held so intimately.

He tightened his grip on her hips and pulled her down harder onto his length, pushing the whole of him into her depths, savoring the feel of being surrounded by her heat. Lifting his head, he took pleasure in watching the play of emotions on her face. Watching her teeth bite into her full bottom lip. Hearing the whispered breaths and edgy sighs.

Arms straining, muscles screaming, he used every ounce of his strength to set a rhythm designed to drive them both wild. He watched the play of emerald, green and gold light dazzle her pale, creamy skin and lost himself in the wonder of the moment. Her fingernails dug into his shoulders and she lifted her hips in his grasp and then lowered herself onto him again, grinding her body against his as if she couldn't take him deep enough. Hold him tight enough.

His brain short-circuited.

His heart hammered in his chest.

His mouth went dry and his vision blurred until Terry was his whole world. The universe, wrapped up in pale, jewel toned light, sighing, writhing, moaning.

"It's...coming...Aidan..." Whispered, broken words, trembling from her lips as she twisted on him, like a live butterfly on a pin.

"Let it come, Terry," he murmured, tightening his grasp on her hips, plunging himself deeper, higher, inside her. "There'll be another one. Let this one come."

She lifted her head and looked at him through glassy eyes. "Come with me," she ordered, licking her lips, breath coming in short, hard gasps.

Then linking one arm around his neck, she stretched out her other hand, reached beneath the spot where their bodies joined and cupped him, her fingers exploring, rubbing, stroking.

Lights exploded behind his eyes.

Aidan held her tight.

He heard her groan.

Felt her body implode.

And finally allowed his to follow.

Nine

Outside, Mother Nature shrieked.

Inside, Mother Nature celebrated.

Even before the last of the tremors had eased from him, Aidan wanted Terry again, with, if possible, a deeper need than before.

He'd never experienced anything like this. Never known need that couldn't be satisfied, desire that couldn't be quenched. Even now, still buried inside her, his body stirred, eager for another bout. Another surging race through madness to completion.

"That was—" Terry's head dropped to his shoulder "—*amazing*."

He smiled into her wet hair, kissed her head and murmured, "And I don't do my best work standing up."

"Could've fooled me." She lifted her head to look at him. Their gazes locked and he watched as new hunger lit up in her eyes, chasing away the shadows that had first intrigued him.

She moved on him, lifting her hips slightly, only to lower herself again and his body reacted in a heartbeat.

"Again?" she whispered, nibbling at his neck, tonguing his skin, leaving a damp, warm trail against already fevered flesh.

"And again and again," Aidan promised, already moving toward the bed.

One part of his tortured brain heard the howl and cry of the wind, the hammering of the rain. But he paid no attention.

They were warm.

They were safe.

They were stranded.

Here.

Together.

That was enough.

He pulled free of her body long enough to lay her down on the crisp white sheets that smelled of lavender. He'd only uncoupled from her so that he could feel the rush of entering her again. Otherwise, he would have been happy to stay locked within her depths for the rest of eternity.

She moved on the bed, scooting back, sliding her feet on the sheets until her knees lifted and her thighs parted. He looked his fill of her and knew it would never be enough. Reaching out, he touched her center, smoothing his fingertips over swollen, damp flesh, and watched her eyes—those incredible grass-green eyes—glaze over in a mindless daze.

"Aidan…I want you again. Now."

His heart quickened, drumming so loudly in his chest as to be deafening. Every nerve ending in his body sizzled in eager enthusiasm. But this time, he was in no rush. This time, he wanted to draw the experience out—for both of them.

He slipped first one finger and then two inside her, playing with her, stroking her, exploring her. And he watched her move against him, lifting her hips, rocking into his hand while her own hands fisted on the sheet beneath her. Her head tossed from side to side. She licked dry lips and whispered broken, half-hearted pleas as he continued to stroke her body into a firestorm of *need*.

And with every stroke of his fingers, his own body tightened until he felt rock-hard and aching for want of her. Seconds ticked past, and Aidan realized he wouldn't be able to draw this time out much longer than he had the first. Not when need crouched in his chest and hammered at him to bury himself inside her. Not when hunger roared through him and danced on each of her sighs.

Levering himself over her, he slid his hands up, up, her body, over her curves, defining every line of her with fingertips careful as he would be while caressing fragile shards of crystal.

Her back bowed as she arched into him and he dipped his head to taste her. He took first one pebbled nipple and then the other into his mouth, rolling his tongue across them, nibbling with the edges of his teeth. She lifted small hands and cupped the back of his head, holding him to her as he gently tormented her.

"Feels so good," she whispered in a harshly strained voice.

"Tastes even better," he assured her, smiling against her body as he suckled her, pulling on her flesh, trying to draw her essence inside him.

"Aidan!"

His name in a quiet cry of nerves, stretched tight, shuddered through him and he moved to cover her. To push himself home, deep within her. He knelt between her legs and as she parted her thighs in welcome and held her arms wide to draw him in, he slid into her heat again.

Diving deep, he drove himself home with a hunger that grabbed him by the throat and wouldn't let go. He rocked wildly, furiously, in and out of her body, loving the slow slide to heaven enough to put up with having to leave her with every stroke.

She moved with him, instinctively following his rhythm, then setting one of her own. Hands fisted, breaths mingled, sighs twisted in the still, jewel-colored air. She took him, all of him, and held him deeply.

He looked into her eyes and felt himself falling into their depths and knew he didn't want to save himself. Everything he wanted, needed, was right here. In this bed in the middle of a storm that was tearing at the city.

But he wanted to see her, too, so he rolled onto his back, taking her with him, astride him.

She straddled him in the soft light and smiled down at him as she continued the rhythm he'd set, moving, rocking her hips, swiveling her body against his.

She rode him with a quiet power and a tender fury. Flesh slapped against flesh. Heat burrowed into heat. He lifted his hands, covered her breasts with his palms and sucked in a frantic gulp of air when she covered his hands with her own.

Terry looked down at him and felt herself drowning in eyes the color of a stormy sea. She felt the build in her body, knew a climax was shuddering close and felt the rush of expectation tingle through her.

He pulled his hands out from under hers and let them slide down her body, fingertips dancing fluidly over her skin until she could have sworn she felt him touching her on the *inside*.

She kept her hands on her own breasts, squeezing, tweaking her nipples, tugging at them, while he watched her and his eyes went gray and cloudy. A fierce smile curved her mouth as she rocked her hips against him, taking him in as deeply as she could.

Then he dropped one hand to the spot where their bodies joined and touched the very core of her. That one supersensitive nubbin of flesh. He stroked her, once, twice—and her body exploded into a showery storm of brightly colored lights. Her head fell back as she screamed his name into the fury of the storm.

Then he flipped her onto her back and before the last trembling shiver coursed through her body, he'd claimed his own release, whispering her name just before collapsing on top of her.

What could have been minutes—or hours—later, Aidan turned his head on the pillow and looked at the woman lying beside him. In the dim light, she looked like something mystical. Something not quite of this world.

Even as he thought it, he smiled to himself, silently acknowledging that the Irish in him was coming out. With her fair hair and pale, smooth skin, she looked as though she'd been carved from alabaster by a talented, generous sculptor.

But she was real—as he was here to testify.

She turned her head on the pillow and her gaze met his. She smiled. "Well, I guess you've really lost that bet now."

He winced, but couldn't bring himself to mind very much. "Guess you could say that. Man, my brothers will never let me hear the end of this."

She rolled to her side and went up on one elbow to look at him. "Why'd you do it? Why'd you throw away the bet when you were so close to winning?"

He thought about that for a moment. Didn't have to spend much time thinking about it now, as he'd done plenty of thinking about it earlier today. In fact, *all* of today, when he'd been away from her. When he'd had just a small taste of her and was still—as he was now—eager for another. Rolling to his right side, he, too, propped himself up on one elbow and watched her as he reached out to stroke a single fingertip across the tops of her breasts.

She hissed in a breath and sighed it out.

"Because," he said, still shaken by the knowledge, "I wanted *you* more than I wanted to *win*."

"I think that's a compliment."

"Damn straight," he said. "Believe me."

She caught his hand in hers and folded their fingers together. "Why did you want to win that silly bet so badly anyway?"

"To be the best," he answered, without hesitation. "To be the last Reilly standing."

"And now?"

He grinned. "Well, now…Liam will get the ten thousand bucks and he can start getting that new roof for the church." He paused and listened to the still screaming wind and the battering fists of rain. "And judging by this storm, he's going to need a new one. Soon."

"That's good, isn't it?"

"Sure it's good. Hell, I was going to give him the money anyway," he admitted, and realized that she was the only person he'd confessed that small truth to. And he wondered why it was he felt comfortable talking to Terry about his life—his family—everything that was important to him. Then he pushed that question to the back of his mind to be examined later. Much later. "I just wanted to *win*."

"Important, is it?"

"In *my* family? Yeah."

"But you gave it up." She rubbed the edge of her thumbnail against his palm and it was his turn to hiss in a breath.

"And I would again," he assured her.

"For an afternoon like this one," she said, "so would I."

"Glad to hear it."

She laughed, a low, throaty chuckle that set up a reaction that swept through him, carrying new heat, new need.

"Please," she said. "I'm sure you know just what a good time I had today."

"Day's not over."

"Glad to hear *that*," she said and inched a little closer to him. Tipping her head back, she confessed, "Today has been…special, I guess is the right word. I haven't been with anyone in a long time."

He'd guessed that, but he was damn happy to hear it said aloud. He didn't want to think about Terry with anyone else. Also didn't want to think that in a couple of weeks she'd be gone from his life.

So he smiled. "Well, it's been awhile for me, too."

"Poor baby."

"Sarcasm from a naked woman. I like it."

He shifted position, rolling her onto her back and dipping his head to kiss her middle. His tongue dipped in and out of her belly button and slid lower.

She combed her fingers through his short hair, her long nails gently scraping against his skull.

"The reason I told you that it had been a long time for me was that I wanted you to know that I'm not usually this kind of woman."

"What kind is that?"

"You know," she said, sighing as his breath dusted her skin and his tongue swept warm, damp caresses across her abdomen. "The fling type. I'm…more complicated than that." She paused. "Although, after today, you might not believe it."

He laughed against her flat belly. "Babe, believe me, I already knew you were complicated. But thanks for the warning."

Thunder crackled overhead and the wind slammed against the board covered windows. Terry jerked beneath Aidan and he used his hands and mouth to soothe her.

After a minute or two, she started talking again. "There've only been three men in my life. One I loved…one I thought I loved, which is pretty much the same thing." She paused. "And then there's you."

He stilled, even his heartbeat went soft and quiet. Outside, the storm blasted at the windows and doors, searching for a way in. But here in this room, another storm raged. This one in Aidan's heart. Love? Who'd said anything about love?

She laughed. "Don't look so panicked, Aidan. I wasn't proposing."

He gave her a smile he didn't feel.

"I'm just saying," she continued, pushing pillows beneath her head so she could see him clearly, "That this...*means* something to me."

He lifted his head to meet her gaze. And in all honesty, he could say, "It means something to me, too. I don't know what, Terry. Can't tell you that. But it means *something*."

"Thanks."

"For what?"

"For not trying to lie your way out of a tricky situation. For not pretending to be the love of my life. For respecting me enough to give me the truth."

"I'll always give you that, babe."

She smiled. "You know, it's interesting. I'm starting to like hearing you call me that."

"Happy to oblige." He kissed her belly again and moved a little lower.

She sighed. "I'm not looking for love anyway, Aidan. Not again."

That caught his attention. The sorrow, the pain in her voice and he knew that if he looked into her eyes, he'd see those shadows again. The ones that had haunted him from the moment they met.

And he couldn't help himself.

He looked.

Saw the pain and ached for her.

"Who was he?"

She sighed again and this simple release of pent-up breath rattled him right down to his soul.

"His name was Eric."

Aidan hated him already. No doubt tall, muscle-bound and too stupid to know what he'd had when he'd had it. "What happened to him?"

She closed her eyes. "He died."

Damn. Empathy welled up inside him. "God, Terry. I'm sorry."

"It was a long time ago."

"How long?" he wondered, because the shadows in her eyes looked fresh enough to have been born the day before. The pain was obviously still sharp.

She glanced at him and ran her fingertips along the side of his face. "Twelve years."

He blinked. She couldn't be more than thirty now. "You were a kid."

"Not for long." She moved beneath him, arching her body up to his as if to remind him that he'd been kissing her a minute or two ago and she wouldn't mind having him start back up. "I don't want to talk about it now, okay?"

"Sure. Okay," he said, mind spinning, even while his body urged him back to the business at hand.

He dipped his head again, trailing his lips and

tongue across her belly, lower, lower, until just above the triangle of soft blond curls, he noticed the thin sliver of an old scar.

He ran his finger across the faint, silvery line and kept his voice even, as he asked a question he was pretty sure he already knew the answer to. "What's this?"

She closed her eyes, let her hand fall from his head and said, "I had an operation."

"Yeah I get that. What kind?"

She blew out a breath. "Caesarean section."

"You had a baby."

"Yes."

"When you were a kid."

"Yes."

"Eric," he said, feeling his heart sink for her.

"Yes. Eric. My son." Terry's eyes filled with tears and she blinked frantically, trying to keep them at bay. Stupid. She shouldn't have started talking. Opening up a conversation that would inevitably lead them down this path.

"What happened?" Aidan asked and a part of her was surprised that she could hear his soft, low-pitched voice at all, over the freight train of sound just outside the house.

Staring up at the ceiling, she concentrated on the colored shadows tossed from the stained-glass lamp. "Why do you want to know?"

He slid back up the length of her body, flesh

brushing against flesh, hard to soft, warmth to warmth and she was so damned grateful for that *connection,* her eyes filled again. It had been a long time since she'd felt connected to anyone. And that she would find such a feeling in the middle of a hurricane with a virtual stranger, was like a gift.

When his face was directly over hers, his mouth just a kiss away from hers, he looked into her eyes and said, "Because I see shadows in your pretty eyes, Terry." He kissed her. "Have from the first time I saw you. And I want to know what caused them." He dropped another brief, gentle kiss on her lips.

Nodding, she stared up into his deep blue eyes and fell into memory. Fell into the past that she kept too close and yet at a distance.

Running one hand idly up and down his rib cage, she spoke softly, quietly, words tumbling from her in a rush, as if they'd been banked up inside her for too long. "My family's rich. *Really* rich."

"Okay…"

"My older brother was the heir apparent. I was the princess. The debutante, the good girl who did everything right."

He kissed her again as encouragement.

"Until I was seventeen. I fell in love. With the son of my father's friend."

"You got pregnant."

"I did." And she clearly remembered the panic. The fear. The excitement and terror of knowing that she carried a child. Mistakes like unplanned pregnancies just didn't happen in the Evans family. There, everything was planned, thought out, arranged. Babies were neither expected nor wanted.

"The baby's father was scared."

"And you weren't?"

She smiled and patted his back in thanks for his solidarity. "Terrified," she assured him. "When I told my parents, they hit the eighteen-foot ceilings. They told me that I was a disappointment, but that they would take care of this 'episode' for me so no one would know."

Amazing, but her heart could still ache over that long-ago night. Scared, she'd faced her parents, knowing they'd be upset, but secretly hoping for support. Understanding.

She'd received neither.

"They arranged for an abortion. They couldn't have an unwed teenage mother in the family and they didn't want me to marry Randolph."

He snorted. "Randolph. Weenie name."

She laughed, surprising herself. "Randolph *was* a weenie. Didn't mean to be. But he'd been bred to it. And, he was young, too. Anyway…" She shook her head, jostling herself back on track. "I refused the abortion so they agreed to send me to Paris. To stay with my aunt until the baby was born. Then I would give him up for adoption."

"But you couldn't."

A single tear spilled from the corner of her eyes. "I couldn't. He was born and he came out and looked at me as if he knew me. He smiled. And he was *mine*."

Aidan kissed her again and swiped that tear from her cheek with his thumb.

"I told my parents that I was keeping him. They told me I couldn't come home. So I stayed. In Paris with my aunt for a while, then I used my inheritance from my grandmother. Got an apartment and loved my son."

They were heady days. Filled with love and laughter and a sprinkle of fear for the future. But she wouldn't have traded a moment with Eric. Not one second. He was *love*. More love than she'd ever known before. She hadn't realized that she could feel so deeply, so profoundly.

Eric was a tiny, helpless package of love who touched her in ways she had never known existed before him. He was her world. Until...

"Terry?" His voice came, a murmur of sympathy and comfort, whispered close by her ear. "What happened?"

She closed her eyes, steeling herself against the memory, but closing her eyes only made the pictures stronger, sharper. "He was five months old. One morning, he didn't wake me up. I slept until nine and woke up thinking, *Great. He's finally sleeping through the night. Won't this make life easier?*" She bit down hard on her bottom lip, looked him in the eyes again and said, "I went in and said 'Good morning, sleepy boy' and I touched him." She was back in that sun-washed apartment. She could feel the soft breeze slipping in through the partially opened window in Eric's nursery. She heard the gentle tinkle of the wind chimes she'd hung on the terrace. She *saw* her baby. "He didn't move. Didn't stir."

"Ah, God…"

She swallowed the knot in her throat. "I remember thinking. *That's strange.* And I bent over to kiss him awake. He was cold."

"Terry…"

She brought herself up out of the past with a jerk. She couldn't stay there. Couldn't relive the rest of it. The hysterical tears, the screams for help, the sirens and the firemen and the policemen and her neighbors…all looking at her with sympathy. With tears on their faces and dread in their eyes.

"The doctor said it was SIDS. Nothing could have been done. He just…slipped away in the night."

"Jesus, Terry, I'm *so sorry.*"

"I know…"

He kissed her and tasted her tears. She felt his heat, his comfort, his need and let it swamp her, bring her from the past into a present filled with hunger and passion and *life.*

Then he went deathly still, lifted his head and looked at her through horrified eyes.

"What is it?"

"I can't believe I did this...*we* did this. Never happened to me before, I swear."

"What?"

"Talking about Eric made me think of it. Protection, Terry. We didn't use protection. Either time." His features screwed up into a mask of misery. "And now, knowing what I know, I can't believe I let you risk..."

"Hush." She laid her fingertips on his mouth, silencing him. Her own heart was pounding. She hadn't thought once about protection, either, and she of all people should have known better. But it didn't matter. As long as he was healthy, it didn't matter.

"I take the pill. To regulate my periods."

His forehead dropped to hers. "That's good." Then he rose again to look into her eyes. "I'm healthy. Don't worry about that. I'm a careful man."

"That's good to know," she said softly, catching his face between her palms. His deep blue eyes flashed with emotions she was too wrung-out to try to decipher. And right now, it wasn't important. Right now, she wanted to feel that rush of life pulsing through her again. Feel her own heartbeat race. Feel Aidan's body moving on hers.

"I'm healthy, too," she assured him, then stroked his cheekbones with her thumbs. "Now, I want you to make love with me again. And, Aidan..."

"Yeah?"

"Don't be careful of me."

Ten

The next few days passed in a blur of activity. The brunt of the hurricane skipped Baywater, moving along the coast, drenching them in high winds and torrential rain, but sparing the little town what could have been disastrous damage.

Yet, there was a lot of cleanup to do. Aidan's team was kept busy, helping the local police and fire department on several calls. He called to check on his family's safety, but didn't have time to actually get together with his brothers. Until tonight. Between his regular duties on the base and the SAR runs his team was making, he was kept pretty much at a run.

And whatever down time he *did* have, he spent with Terry.

He couldn't seem to get enough of her. Since that first night of the storm, they'd been together every night. Making love, talking, laughing, arguing. He'd never spent so much time with a woman before without feeling the need to bolt.

Always, before Terry, Aidan had kept his distance— at least emotionally. He'd never wanted to *know* a woman beyond the superficial level that allowed them both to enjoy each other. Now though, there was more.

It had sneaked up on him and he wasn't entirely sure what to do about it. Drawn to her time and again, he felt himself being pulled deeper into her life, her world. A corner of his brain continually warned him to back off. To remember that his life was here, hers was in New York. That a former debutante had *nothing* in common with a career Marine.

And mostly, to remember that he wasn't *looking* for forever. That he didn't *want* love.

But that small voice in his mind was getting fainter—harder to hear.

He walked into the Lighthouse restaurant and paused just inside the entrance. He hooked his sunglasses on the open vee neck of his dark blue pullover shirt and let his gaze sweep the crowded restaurant. Families dotted the round, wooden tables, celebrating being together. Celebrating surviving the hurricane.

He spotted his brothers at a back table and braced

himself for the ragging he knew was coming his way. He'd been riding Connor and Brian hard for the last few weeks, so he fully expected to take his share of crap.

Stalking across the crowded room, he stepped up to the table and told Brian, "Move over."

When he did, Aidan dropped onto the bench seat. Shifting his gaze from Brian beside him to Connor and Liam across from him, he took a breath and said, "I'm out."

Whoops and delighted laughter rolled out from the other three men and got loud enough that people at the other tables turned to stare.

Aidan hunched his shoulders. "Jeez. Keep it down, will ya?"

"This is great," Connor said, still laughing.

Brian held up one hand and leaned across the table. Connor slapped that hand hard and they whooped again, just for the hell of it. Liam grinned and rubbed his own palms together as if he were already getting ready to count the money he and the church had just won.

"So what happened?" Brian demanded, giving Aidan a hard elbow to the ribs.

"What? You need a picture? You know damn well what happened."

"Yeah, but what happened to all your big talk about outlasting us?"

"I *did* outlast you two losers," Aidan reminded him quickly. He might not have won the bet, but he'd sure as hell beat out the other two members of the Reilly triplets.

"Yeah, man," Connor said, folding his arms on the table top. "But you only had two weeks to go. I really thought you were gonna pull it off."

"Not me," Brian muttered.

"Terry?" Liam asked quietly.

Aidan just nodded.

"Terry?" Connor repeated, straightening up and looking around the table like a man who's the only one not in on a joke. "Who the hell's Terry?"

"Yeah," Brian added, glaring at Liam. "How is it *you* know about this chick and we don't?"

"You guys don't know everything," Aidan muttered, sliding down in his seat.

"Here you go, guys," a woman's voice said cheerfully, "four draft beers."

The Reilly brothers shut up fast while the waitress delivered their drinks and didn't start talking again until after she was gone.

Aidan reached for his beer and took a long, deep swig. The icy froth hit the back of his throat and eased down the knot of irritation lodged there.

"So spill," Connor demanded. "Who's the new babe?"

"She's not a 'babe,'" Aidan told him, wincing slightly, since he called Terry "babe" all the damn time.

"Where'd you meet her? The Off Duty?" Brian laughed.

He had a right to laugh, Aidan supposed. Usually the women he met *did* hang out at the bar that catered to Marines.

He took another drink, then explained how he'd met Terry. And in telling his brothers, he relived it all. He didn't notice, but his voice softened, his eyes shone and his features lit with warmth.

"She sounds…special," Liam said when Aidan stopped talking.

Snapping his gaze to his older brother, Aidan fought down a sudden, near-overpowering flash of panic. Glancing from Liam to Brian and finally to Connor, he shook his head. "Don't start with me, you guys. Don't make more of this than there is."

"I didn't say anything," Connor pointed out, lifting both hands in mock surrender.

"You didn't have to. I can see it on your face."

"You ought to be looking at *your* face," Brian pointed out and took a drink of his own beer.

"What's that supposed to mean?" Aidan argued.

"Hell, man," Brian said, "holster it. Loving a woman's nothing to be ashamed of." He grinned. "Well, except for Liam."

"Funny," their older brother said and leaned across the table to slap Brian upside the head.

"Hey!"

"Stand down," Aidan told all of them, his voice low pitched but steady and firm. "Nobody said anything about *love* for God's sake. All I'm admitting to is losing the stupid bet."

"Relax, man," Connor said, picking up his beer and gesturing with it. "We've all been there—except for Liam."

"I have to take this from you, too?" Liam growled.

Connor shrugged.

"Seriously," Aidan said, feeling the snaky, cold tentacles of panic tighten just a bit around his insides, "shut the hell up about love. I'm not in love. Don't plan to be in love. You guys can have it."

"You make it sound like a disease or something," Brian said.

"Isn't it?" Aidan countered.

"What crawled up your ass and died?" Connor grumbled.

"Yeah," Liam asked, his voice quieter, more thoughtful. "What's got you so scared, Aidan?"

Instantly he bristled. "Didn't say I was scared, for God's sake. Just said I wasn't interested."

"Don't know why the hell not," Brian said. "Hell, can't imagine not being married to Tina."

"Oh, yeah," Aidan sniped. "You liked marriage to Tina so much, you divorced her *then* remarried her."

"You want to go a round with me?" his brother snarled.

"He's just itchy," Connor cut in, breaking up the tension before it could spiral into one of the Reilly brothers' world famous knock-down-drag-out fights.

"Hell, I remember how it felt. I love Emma, but damned if I wanted to admit it—even to myself."

"Now you're both married," Aidan grumbled. "And what'd it get you?"

"Happiness?" Liam offered.

"No offense, Liam," Aidan said, snapping him a look. "But priests don't get a vote in this."

An angry flush swept up his older brother's face, then faded again almost instantly. "I may be a priest, Aidan, but I'm also a man. *And* your brother."

"*And,* you know jack about women." Aidan took another long drink, set his beer down onto the table and cupped the frosty glass between his palms. Staring at the pale gold liquid, he muttered, "These two at least have a position to argue from. You don't. You don't know what it is to—" he caught himself before uttering the 'L' word "—*care* about someone. To know she matters and also know that you can't let her matter too much."

"Got you there, Liam," Brian pointed out.

"Too true," Connor added. "You lucked out. Didn't have to worry about pissing a woman off and living with the results."

"Who the hell do you three think you're talking to?" Liam demanded, but focused on Aidan, leaning across the table, forcing Connor back in his seat, a surprised expression on his face. "Do you think I was *born* wearing this collar?" he tapped at the white circlet at his throat. "I was your brother first. I was a

man first. Do you really believe I never loved anyone? That I don't know what it feels like to *want?*"

Aidan just blinked at him. It had been years since
he'd seen that flash fire of fury in Liam's eyes.

"Take it easy, Liam," Brian urged, shooting a
glance at the table closest to them and glaring the
nosy woman sitting there a narrowed glance.

"You shut up," Liam growled. "This is between
me and the moron."

"Hey."

"My turn, idiot. You shut up and listen." Liam
pointed one finger at Aidan, took a breath and lowered his voice. "I was in love once."

"What?" All three triplets said it at once.

Liam's eyes didn't flicker. His gaze didn't shift.
Just held Aidan's steadily.

"Her name was Ailish."

"Whoa," Connor murmured.

"I thought priests *heard* confessions…" Brian said
softly.

"I met her in Ireland," Liam continued as if none
of them had spoken. "That last summer before I went
into the seminary."

Aidan thought back, remembering the trip Liam
had taken while trying to decide if he was really cut
out for a life in the priesthood. He'd stayed in their
grandparents' house outside Galway and toured Ireland for a summer. He'd never really talked about
those three months, and the rest of them had let it go,

assuming that Liam had spent those months in quiet reflection and prayer.

Apparently, they were wrong.

Aidan kept his gaze locked with Liam's, unable to look away. "What happened, Liam? If you loved her so damn much, why'd you let her go?"

Liam's breath hissed in and out of him in rapid succession. His eyes glimmered brightly, then darkened in memory. Slowly, he eased back into his seat, still staring at Aidan. "She died."

"Ah, Liam." Connor murmured.

"Damn, Liam…" Brian winced in sympathy.

Aidan held his breath. Sure there was more. He watched his older brother relive old pain and wondered how they'd drifted into this minefield of emotion.

"She drove into Galway city to meet her sister for some shopping," Liam said softly. "An American tourist got confused, drove on the wrong side of the road. Hit her head-on. She was killed instantly."

God.

"I'm sorry, Liam," Aidan said, stunned to his soul. In all these years, his brother had never hinted at the tragedy that must haunt him still. And Aidan finally realized that Marines weren't the only people with courage.

Anger gone now, Liam smiled sadly. "It was a long time ago, Aidan. And I'm only telling you guys now because I want you to know I *do* understand. I know what it is to love a woman so much that she's all you can see of tomorrow."

Silence dropped on the four of them like an old quilt. Each of them lost in their own thoughts, none of them wanted to be the first to speak.

Naturally enough, it was Connor who finally shattered the quiet.

"So, if Ailish had lived," he asked, slanting a glance at Liam, "would you still have become a priest? Or would you have walked away from her?"

Liam's hand fisted around his glass of beer. He lifted it, took a long sip and set it back down again before answering. "I've asked myself that a thousand times over the years," he admitted, then looked from one brother to the other, each in turn. "The honest answer is, no. I wouldn't have. When I met her, it was as if God had sent me a sign, telling me that He didn't want me in the priesthood after all." He sighed again, wistfully. "We planned to be married in the local church. Get a house near Lough Mask. Then when she was gone…"

"Married?" Aidan's voice was a whisper, carrying the stunned surprise all of them felt.

It took another moment or two before Liam smiled again. "I still believe there's a reason for everything—though I've yet to find the reason for her death. But maybe meeting Ailish, *loving* Ailish was supposed to help me be a better priest."

"I don't know what to say," Brian looked at their oldest brother.

"You don't have to say anything," Liam told them all.

An uneasy silence dropped over them. All of them aware now of Liam's private little hell—none of them quite sure how to handle this new side to a brother they thought they'd known.

Finally Brian spoke up again and, thank God, changed the subject. "You are a good priest, you know."

Liam glanced at him. "Thanks. I think."

"No, I mean it," Brian said and took a drink of his own beer. "Which means, I can probably use a few of those super prayers you've got in your stash."

"What's going on?" Connor asked the question they were all thinking.

"I'm shipping out." Brian looked at each of them in turn, then shrugged and grinned. "Next month. Middle East."

Growing up with a Marine father had taught them all that sudden moves were to be expected. Growing up a *family* made them all feel that instant quiver of worry.

"Have you told Tina yet?" Liam asked.

"Nope," Brian admitted. "I'm going home to do that now. That's why I thought I'd ask for those prayers." He grinned again. "Combat's dangerous, but fighting with Tina can be deadly."

"But you'll still be here for our joint humiliation, right?" Connor asked.

"Oh, yeah. Battle Color day. Convertible. Hula

skirt, coconut bra. I'll be there." He gave Aidan a shove. "Slide out, will you?"

"I'll walk out with you," Connor said, "Gotta be getting home or Emma'll hunt me down like a dog."

Aidan snorted a laugh. "See? This is what married gets you. A woman ready to tear your lungs out."

Brian shook his head. "You really *are* an idiot, aren't you?" Then he punched one fist into Aidan's shoulder. "Move."

Aidan got to his feet and Brian slid across the bench seat and stood up beside him. Pulling a couple of bills from his pocket, he tossed them onto the table and said, "See you guys later."

Then he and Connor headed out and Aidan sat back down. "Tina's not going to be happy about this."

Liam shrugged. "She's strong. She'll worry about him, but she'll handle it."

"I suppose." But Aidan wasn't really thinking about his sister-in-law, or even about Brian, soon to be deploying into a combat situation.

Instead he was thinking about his older brother and the love he'd lost so long ago. Looking at Liam, he asked, "Why'd you tell us about her?"

Liam sighed and leaned back in his seat. "I don't know. Maybe I was just tired of hearing about how I don't know jack about women."

Aidan smiled briefly and nodded. "Okay. I can get that."

This news was still too fresh to make much sense

of. He'd always thought of Liam as a quiet, reflective man. Born for the priesthood. Now, to discover there'd been dreams born and lost along the way was a little…disquieting.

"What was she like?"

"Ailish?"

"*Yes.*"

Liam smiled sadly. "Beautiful. Warm. Funny. Stubborn." His voice softened in memory. "She was an artist, too. Damn good one. Landscapes mostly."

A lightbulb clicked on in Aidan's brain. "The painting in your room. The one of the standing stones."

"Yeah. That's one of hers."

Aidan had always liked that painting. Had even tried to buy it from Liam once. Now he knew why his brother had refused to part with it. A simple scene of a circle of standing stones, a dance, as the Irish called them, it had a mystical quality, with soft gray mist spilling across the emerald green grass and twining itself up around the stones like loving hands.

"She was good."

Liam smiled. "I don't need you to feel sorry for me, Aidan."

"What am I supposed to feel, then?"

Liam leaned across the table and smiled patiently. "I just want you to *think*." He pulled money from his pocket, tossed it onto the table and said, "Think about

what you've found. What you *could* have. And think
hard before you let yourself lose it."

Then he left.

And Aidan sat alone, not sure of anything anymore.

Eleven

"**I** can come home early."

"You don't have to do that," Terry said, clutching the phone receiver as she walked around the kitchen, pouring herself some iced tea. "Honestly, Donna, everything's fine."

"No damage to the store? The house?"

Terry sighed. She'd already reassured her friend a half dozen times over the last few days. But she supposed it wasn't easy to be thousands of miles away from home when disaster struck.

"There was a small leak in the bookstore," she told her again. "A *tiny* puddle in the back, by the kids' play area."

"Damn it. Should have had the roof fixed last year. I *knew* that and put it off anyway."

"It's a *very* tiny leak, Donna. Honestly. The store did not float away."

"Okay, okay, I know I'm being a little obsessive…"

"Just a tad," Terry agreed, smiling as she closed the refrigerator door and picked up the glass of tea off the table. Taking a sip, she said, "Just enjoy the rest of your time with your folks."

"To tell you the truth, they're jumping up and down on my last nerve."

Terry laughed, pulled out a chair and sat down. God it felt good to think about something else besides her own situation. Her brain had been running in circles over Aidan Reilly for days—and she *still* had no idea how to handle what was getting to be a more and more complicated relationship.

Of course, to Aidan, it probably wasn't complicated at all, she thought wryly. It was her own fault she'd made the mistake of feeling more than she should have. Now she just had to figure out what to do about it.

"Don't get me wrong," Donna said, "my parents are great. But they spend all their time giving the kids chocolate, which hypes the little tormentors into outer space and then they drive me insane."

A sigh of regret whispered through Terry as she wondered what her life would be now, if Eric had only lived. He'd be twelve now. Almost a teenager. She closed her eyes and tried to imagine that sweet baby face as it would be now, and couldn't quite pull it off.

She'd always wanted children. At one time, she'd assumed she'd have a houseful of them. Now, it looked as though those dreams had been buried with Eric. She was alone. And despite what she felt for Aidan, she was going to stay alone.

Shaking her head a little, she said, "Sounds like things're just the way they're supposed to be then."

"I guess. I'm just ready to be home."

"Yeah," Terry said softly. "So am I."

"Tired of small-town life?" Donna asked. "Ready to go back to Manhattan and start whipping those fund-raisers into shape again?"

Truthfully, Terry thought, but didn't say, *no*. She liked Baywater. She liked having neighbors, even though they were only on loan from Donna. She liked the small-town feel, the slower pace, the sense of community she'd experienced when the hurricane swept through.

And mostly, she liked Aidan.

Instantly that quick grin of his filled her mind. His dimple. The deep, stormy blue of his eyes. The gravelly voice in the middle of the night. The callused fingertips sliding over her skin. His laugh. His humor and strength.

She liked it all.

Oh dear God.

She'd really done it.

She'd fallen in love.

Sitting up straight in the ladder-back chair, she stared blankly at the wall opposite her. Why hadn't she noticed this when there was still time to prevent it?

But then, maybe she'd never had a chance against it. She'd felt something new, something incredibly strong and powerful from the first moment they'd met.

She'd known then that he was different. That he could be dangerous.

She just hadn't realized *how* dangerous.

"Hello? Earth to Terry, come in, Terry."

"Huh? Oh." Shaking her head, she grabbed up her tea, took a long drink and swallowed the icy liquid and felt the chill of it swamp her right down to the bone.

But it wasn't the tea giving her the shivers.

It was the knowledge that she'd given her heart to a man who wouldn't want it.

"Oh, no."

"What? What's wrong?" Donna demanded.

"Oh, I've made a big mistake."

"Sounds bad."

"Couldn't be worse."

"And is the name of this mistake Aidan?"

"How'd you guess?"

"Not really a big jump," Donna admitted, and she couldn't hide the delight in her voice.

"You don't have to sound so pleased about this," Terry muttered, grimacing at the phone she was clutching tightly enough to snap in two.

"Why wouldn't I be pleased? Two of my closest friends find true love and happiness? This is good news."

"Hah!" Terry leaned back in her chair. "As far as Aidan's concerned, we've found sweaty sex and completion."

"And you?"

She sighed. "Donna…I'm an idiot."

"No, you're not, sweetie," her friend crooned. "You fell in love. That makes you lucky."

"No. It just makes it harder to leave."

"You're not going to *stay* and see what happens?"

"Nope." Terry stood up, walked to the window and stared out at the sun splashed backyard. The sky was blue, white clouds drifted lazily across the sky and a puff of wind teased the brass chimes into a soft tune. It was as if the hurricane had never come.

And she knew, that once she was home, buried in work, in the familiar, this feeling for Aidan would go away, too, and it would be like these few weeks had never been.

If a part of her was saddened at the thought, it was just a small part. The hard reality was, she didn't want to love someone again. Didn't want to risk loss again.

After Eric's death, Terry had been lost. Devastated. She'd spiraled into an overwhelming need for risk. She'd put her life on the line time and again, chasing down thrills, adventure.

She hadn't really taken the time then to realize that

she had been, in a way, chasing death. Her own life had felt inconsolably lonely. She'd missed her son desperately and hadn't reconciled with her family enough to find comfort there.

Instead she'd jumped into a whirlwind of activity that was dangerous enough that it kept her mind too busy to grieve. Her heart too full to break.

Until that one morning five years ago. Waking up in that hospital bed, she'd finally faced the sad truth. That she'd become as empty as her world had felt. That she'd chased danger so she wouldn't have to face life without her baby. And that was a slap in the face to the love she'd found with Eric.

Since that morning, she'd changed. Built a life that was based on giving. On helping. On reaching out a hand to those who felt as alone as she once had.

But if she were to chance loving Aidan, wouldn't she be going back into the danger zone? Wouldn't she be handing the universe another opportunity to kick her in the teeth?

"Terry?"

"Sorry," she murmured, still half lost in thought.

"You're really shook, aren't you?"

"Yeah, I guess I am," she admitted, grateful at least to have this one old friend to talk to. To confess her fears and worries to.

"You know what? I'm coming home early."

"You don't have to do that," Terry said.

"I know. But I miss my own place anyway."

"Donna…"

"I'll be there tomorrow or the next day."

"Okay," she said, already planning her return to Manhattan. She wasn't running, she told herself firmly. She was retreating. Quickly. "And, Donna?"

"Yeah?"

"Thanks."

Two hours later, Liam opened the door to the rectory himself.

The housekeeper was out doing the weekly grocery shopping and the monsignor was in the church hearing confessions. Which left Liam to wait for the roofer to arrive and give them an estimate.

But when he opened the door, he didn't find Mr. Angelini. Instead a tall, curvy blonde with summer-green eyes and a quiet smile greeted him. Instantly he knew who she must be.

"You're Terry Evans."

"Father Liam Reilly?" she asked with a smile. "Aidan didn't tell me his brother was psychic."

"Oh, I'm not," Liam said, opening the door wider and waving one hand in invitation. "But Aidan's described you too well to be mistaken on this."

She stepped into the foyer, her cream colored heels making quiet clicks on the gleaming wooden floor. Liam closed the door, then faced her, a beautiful woman in an expensive, beige suit and yellow silk blouse. She looked…uneasy and Liam's instincts took over.

"Can I get you something cold to drink? We have soda, which I would recommend over my house-keeper's hideous iced tea."

"No. Nothing, thanks," she said and walked with him into the living room off the hall.

"Please. Sit down."

She took a seat on the sofa and Liam perched on the coffee table in front of her. There was unhappiness in her eyes and a wistful quality about her that tugged on his heart. Now he understood why Aidan had fallen so fast and so hard. The wonder of it to him was that the man was still struggling so against it.

"What brings you here, Terry?"

She inhaled sharply and looked around the room before shifting her gaze back to his. "Direct. I like that."

He nodded, waiting.

"Aidan told me," she said, "that you were going to use the ten thousand dollars from the bet to replace the church's roof."

He smiled. "Did he?"

She opened her purse, dug inside for an envelope, then pulled it out and studied it. "I don't know if you know this already, but he had planned to give you the money anyway, even if he had won that stupid bet."

His eyebrows lifted. "No, I didn't know. But it sounds like something Aidan would do. He's a good man."

"Yes," she said, running her fingertips idly across the back of the envelope. "He is."

"And you love him."

Her gaze snapped up to his and Liam smiled. Even if he hadn't been expecting it, he would have spotted the sharp jolt of emotion in her eyes. And it made him glad for Aidan. It was high time his brother found something that meant as much to him as the Corps did.

"You sure you're not psychic?" she asked, giving him a wary smile.

"Oh, I'm sure. But if you don't mind my saying so, it's easy enough to read your eyes."

"Great. I'm an open book." Terry shrugged slightly. "I hope Aidan's not in a *reading* mood."

"You don't want him to know?"

"No," she said it softly, firmly. "Neither one of us was looking for this, Father—"

"Liam," he corrected.

"—Liam. What happened between us…well. It doesn't matter."

"You're a lot like him," Liam said.

She laughed shortly. "No reason to be insulting."

He grinned, liking this woman more and more and wanting to kick Aidan's ass for even taking the chance of losing her.

"Anyway," she said, "that's not why I'm here."

"Okay, then why?" he asked, bracing his forearms on his thighs and leaning in toward her.

"For this," she said and handed him the envelope.

Confused now, Liam opened it, looked inside and stared in stunned shock. Her personal check for twenty-five thousand dollars, made out to St. Sebastian's, was nestled inside.

Lifting his gaze to hers, he said, "Not that we don't appreciate the donation, we do. But that's a big check. Can I ask what motivated it?"

She snapped her small purse closed again and folded her hands on top of it. "Ten thousand wouldn't have been enough to get you a new roof, Liam."

"True, but that doesn't explain your generosity."

She inhaled sharply. "Let's just say that I've come to like Baywater." She jumped to her feet and walked briskly across the room to stare out the front windows at the trees that lined the driveway. "It's a nice place. Nice people. I'm going to miss it. And I wanted to help in some way, before I left town."

"You're leaving?"

She turned to look at him nodded, and looked down, but not before Liam saw the gleam of regret in her eyes.

"When?"

"A day or two."

"Does Aidan know?"

"No—and I'd like your promise that you won't tell him."

"Are you going to?"

"I don't know yet."

Sighing, Liam set the envelope down on the table beside him, walked toward her and took both of her hands in his. "Is there some way I can help you?"

She smiled briefly and shook her head. "No, but thanks for offering."

"Are you sure you want to leave?" Liam asked, wondering how in heaven two such stubborn souls had managed to find each other.

She drew away from him and shook her head. "I didn't say I *want* to leave. Just that I am."

He smiled sadly. "That makes no sense at all, you know."

A short, harsh laugh shot from her throat. "Maybe not. But its something I have to do."

"Maybe you should tell Aidan how you feel."

Now she did laugh. "Oh, no." Shaking her head she said, "Even if I was willing to take a chance on love again—you know as well as I do that Aidan's not interested."

"He cares for you."

"Yes. I think he really does." She started past him, headed for the front door. "But it's not love, Father. He doesn't want that any more than I do."

"Are you sure about that?"

"Sure enough."

Liam followed her to the front door. She opened it before he could and then stepped out onto the small porch, shaded by a climbing wisteria vine.

"Thank you again," he said, "for your donation."

"You're welcome, Liam. It was nice meeting you," she said and took the two steps to the sidewalk, leading around to the parking lot behind the church.

"Terry?"

She stopped and looked back at him, bright green eyes shadowed with pain.

His jaw tightened and though his every instinct was to help, comfort, he held himself back—knowing somehow, that she wouldn't welcome it. "My brother's an idiot if he lets you get away."

She shook her head. "Sometimes, Father, getting away is kindest all around."

She left then and Liam stood in a splash of sunlight wondering how in the hell he could wake his brother up to reality before it was too late.

Twelve

Aidan smiled as he pulled into the driveway at Donna Fletcher's house. Dusk was just settling over Baywater and the sky was still streaked with dark reds and orange. A slight wind pushed at the trees and from down the street, came the shrieks of children playing. Next door, Mr. Franklin was mowing the lawn and the older man nodded and waved as Aidan stepped out of his car.

He grabbed the still hot pizza box from the passenger seat, then snatched up a bottle of merlot he'd brought to go with it. Grinning, he headed for the house.

He'd been thinking about this moment all day. Through the work, through the joking around with the other guys, in the back of his mind, Aidan had been planning a nice, quiet night, with Terry cuddled up close beside him.

Funny. A couple of weeks ago, he never would have imagined that a cozy night at home would sound so damn good. But then, a couple of weeks ago, he hadn't yet met Terry Evans.

And ever since he had, his world had taken a subtle shift.

He shook his head and sprinted the last few steps to the front porch. Didn't want to think about what he was feeling. Didn't want to examine anything too closely. Better to just shut up and enjoy it.

He used the bottom end of the wine bottle to tap on the door and when it swung open, his smile dropped like a stone.

Terry stood there, wearing a pale beige suit and high heels. Her makeup was perfect, her hair styled and surprise flickered in her green eyes. "Aidan? You said you couldn't make it tonight."

Frowning, he said, "I got Monk to cover for me."

"Oh. Well."

His brain tried to work. He could almost hear the gears grinding slowly inside his head. She wasn't expecting him, but she was dressed to the teeth and ready for...*what,* exactly?

He glanced past her then and noticed the suitcases stacked in the foyer. Ice settled in the pit of his stomach as he lifted his gaze up to hers again. "Going somewhere?"

Clearly nervous, she licked her lips, pulled in a long breath and said, "Yes. Actually, when you knocked, I thought it was my cab."

"Your *cab*."

"To take me to the airport."

"You're leaving."

"Yes. I'm going home."

"Tonight."

"Yes."

The ice in his stomach melted with a sizzle under a sudden onslaught of fury. She was looking at him as if he were a stranger. She was *leaving*. And didn't look sorry about it.

"Without even telling me?" he asked. "Without saying a damn word?"

She blew out a breath that ruffled the wisp of bangs drifting across her forehead. "Aidan, don't make this harder than it has to be."

He laughed shortly, harshly and felt it scrape his throat. "Not really sure if I could do that."

He felt like an idiot. Standing there in jeans and a T-shirt, clutching a swiftly going cold pizza and a bottle of wine—while she stood there and told him she was leaving.

Shouldn't he have known this?

Shouldn't he have *felt* something? A warning of some kind?

"So what was the plan?" he snarled. "Were you going to call from the airport? Or just let me show up here to find you gone?"

She stiffened and her lips flattened into a grim line. "Donna will be here tomorrow. She could have—"

Another laugh, tighter, harsher than the first. "That's great. You were gonna let *Donna* tell me that you were too chicken to face me."

"That's about enough."

"See? I don't think so."

He dropped the pizza and thought seriously about smashing the stupid bottle of wine against the side of the house. But instead, he tightened his fingers on the neck of the bottle and clung to it like a safety rope. "I thought we had something."

"Really?" she asked, temper clearly spiking inside her now, too. She folded her arms over her chest, hitched one hip higher than the other as she tapped the toe of her shoe against the floor. "And what did you think we had?"

That left him speechless. Hell, how did he know the answer to that? He shoved one hand across the top of his head. "I'm not sure exactly. But whatever the hell it is, it was worth more than *this*."

Disappointment flashed in her eyes briefly and was gone again in an instant. In fact, he couldn't really be sure he'd seen it at all.

"Aidan, go home. This little…interlude is over. Let's just get back to our lives, okay?"

"Just like that?"

Behind him, he heard a car pull up and the short blast of a horn.

"That's my cab."

He turned around to glare at it, and when he looked back, Terry already had her suitcase on the porch and was closing and locking the door. He felt as though he was back in the hurricane. As though the world was suddenly moving too quickly for him to keep up.

He knew he should say something, *do* something, but instead he stood there like a moron as she walked past him, rolling her suitcase behind her, its small steel wheels grinding against the pavement.

He was still standing there when the driver opened the passenger door to usher her into the bright yellow cab. She stopped, hand on the door's edge, to look at him. Then she gave him a ghost of a smile and said, "Goodbye, Aidan."

Alone with his wine and his stone cold pizza, Aidan watched in silence as Terry drove out of his life.

Two weeks later, the Reilly brothers were considering voting Aidan out of the family.

"My point," he yelled as he grabbed the rebounded basketball and took off at a trot toward the end of the driveway.

"Your point because you fouled me," Brian snapped.

"It wasn't a foul."

"It was a *shove*," Connor told him.

Aidan sighed, wiped his arm across his forehead and sneered at his brothers. "Sorry, girls. Didn't know I was being too rough."

"You know," Brian said, starting for him, "I'm thinking it's about time for somebody's clock to get cleaned."

Aidan tossed the ball to one side, braced himself and waved one hand. "Bring it on, tough guy."

"What the hell's wrong with you, Aidan?" Connor demanded, grabbing Brian's arm as he started past him.

"*Nothing's* wrong with me. You two are the ones doing all the griping."

Liam picked up the basketball, bounced it a couple of times and nodded at Connor and Brian. "You two go get a beer. I need to talk to Aidan."

The other two stalked off, muttering darkly and Aidan turned, walking toward the water bottle he'd tossed down an hour ago. Grabbing it, he uncapped it, took a long gulp then fired a warning look at Liam. "I don't want to hear it."

"Tough."

Aidan snorted.

"You miss her."

Aidan stilled. His hand fisted on the water bottle and he stared at it as if it held the secrets of the universe.

"Shut up, Liam."

"Not a chance. You're making a jackass of yourself and driving your brothers to plan your murder. When are you going to admit you love her?"

He shot his oldest brother a hot glare. "This is none of your business, Liam. So back the hell off."

The sun was hot and the air didn't stir. It felt heavy, thick. And too damned crowded around there for Aidan's comfort.

"You're my business, you idiot." Liam moved in close, shoved Aidan and demanded, "Do you think we don't know what's going on? Do you think nobody's noticed that ever since Terry left you've been a complete beast to be around?"

Fury spiked inside him, then just as quickly drained away. Hell. Liam was right. They were *all* right. With Terry gone, nothing felt good. There was no reason to get up in the morning and going to sleep brought no comfort because his dreams were filled with her. Then he'd awaken in the dark with empty arms and a hollow heart.

"She's the one who left," he pointed out in a dark murmur.

"Did you give her a reason to stay?"

"No." He'd wanted to. Wanted to say something that day on the porch. Wanted to tell her…*hell.*

Still clutching the water bottle, he dropped to the shaded grass, drew his knees up and rested his forearms atop them. When Liam took a seat nearby, Aidan started talking. "Just before Uncle Patrick died," he said, peeling the label from the bottle of water, "and left us the money that started this whole mess…"

"Yeah?"

"I went to see him. About a week before he died. Just before I left, he took my hand and he said—" Aidan closed his eyes, to recapture that moment clearly "—the worst part of dying, Aidan, is to die with regrets. Don't make the mistake I did. Do all you can. See all you can. Don't die being sorry for what you *didn't* do."

"I'm sorry he felt that way. He lived a good life," Liam said.

"Yeah, but he lived a quiet life. He never went anywhere, never did anything. I don't want to be that way." He shook his head firmly. "Don't want to die with regrets, Liam."

"And this has what to do with Terry?" His brother asked.

"Don't you get it? If I let myself be in love, I'm tying myself down. Giving up the space to explore, to dare, to risk."

Liam stared at him for a long minute, then shook his head and laughed. "Every time I think maybe you're not a moron, you prove me wrong."

"Thanks," Aidan muttered. "That's helpful."

"Did it ever occur to you that Uncle Patrick might have meant something else?"

"Huh?"

"He never married, remember? Lived by himself most of his life, kept to himself. Mom says he was a shy man in his younger days, so maybe that explains some of it."

"Your point?"

"My point is, Aidan, maybe the regrets he spoke of were more about what he'd missed emotionally in his life. Maybe he regretted never being in love. Never finding a woman to cherish. Never having children."

He hadn't really considered that before.

"Yeah," Aidan said, "but…"

"Aidan," Liam continued, stretching his long legs out in front of him, "you've already done more in your life than most people ever will."

"True."

"Do you really believe, being the kind of man you are, that having someone to love and to love you, would change all that?"

"Well…" His brain was working now, circling around, backing up, going forward again. Trying to shift all of Liam's words into an order that didn't come off making him feel so damn stupid.

It wasn't working.

"Love doesn't *end* your life, Aidan," Liam said, snatching his brother's water bottle away and taking a drink. "It makes it *better*. If you're smart enough to grab it when you have the chance."

"Yeah," Aidan said, feeling the first trickle of hope seep into him like a slow stream in high summer. "But what if she doesn't want me? What if she tells me to get lost?"

Liam snorted now. "Since when do you turn your back on a challenge?" He smiled. "Besides, I don't think she'll turn you away. Before she left, she gave me a check for twenty-five thousand dollars. For the church's roof."

"She did?" Stunned, Aidan stared at him. "Why?"

"She said it was because she liked Baywater and wanted to help. I think it's because she loves *you* and wanted to feel somehow a part of things here, even if she was leaving."

Aidan thought about it for several humming seconds, then jumped to his feet. Glaring at Aidan, he shouted, "Well why the hell didn't you say so?"

Liam laughed as Aidan ran all the way to his car, jumped inside and roared off.

Terry set her teacup down on the polished mahogany table and the click of fine china on wood sounded like thunder in the quiet penthouse. If she listened hard enough, she could probably hear the pounding of her own heart. It was too damn quiet. Too lonely.

Too...*empty.*

But at least it wouldn't be that way for long.

The last two weeks had been a small eternity. Back on her home turf, she'd tried to step right back into her normal everyday rhythm. But it was no use. It wasn't the same, because *she* wasn't the same.

She'd changed. And there was no going back—even if she'd wanted to.

When the doorbell rang, she ran for it. Her socks hit the polished marble floor and she slid all the way to the wide double doors. Laughing at herself, she opened the door and froze.

Aidan stepped inside, closed the door and grabbed her.

Held up close to his chest, she felt his heartbeat thundering against her and she knew she'd never felt anything more wonderful in her life. Being in his arms again set her world right. Everything felt in balance again. As it should be.

As it was meant to be.

"Aidan," She managed to say, "What're you—"

"Just shut up a minute, okay?" He blurted it out, then held her back so he could look at her, staring into her eyes with an intensity that burned right down to the heart of her. "God, you look good."

She smiled and would have spoken, but he rushed right on, not giving her a chance.

"I came all the way here to tell you something." He took a deep breath, blew it out and blurted, "I *love* you, Terry. And I want you to love me back."

"Aidan—"

"Look," he plowed on, outshouting her, "I know why you've protected your heart so long. I understand. About Eric. About all of it."

Her eyes filled with tears, but she blinked them back, unwilling to have this vision of him blurred.

"But you can't do it forever, Terry. I finally understand that. Look, I risk my life everyday in my job. And I never minded before, because I really didn't have all that much to lose. Well now, I *do*. I'll keep taking the risks, because that's the job and it's a risk worth taking. But so is loving you."

Her heart swelled to bursting and her chest felt too tight to contain it. "Oh, Aidan, I—"

"Terry, I'm not the same guy I was when I met you." His blue eyes went dark and stormy, filled with emotion that reached out for her and shook her to the soles of her feet. "You've affected my work, my life. You filled my heart. I don't want to wake up another morning without you. I need you, Terry. And I hope you need me."

"Oh, Aidan…"

"I know love and marriage and all the rest of it is a *big* risk. But I want us to take it together. Can you do it, Terry? Can you love me? Marry me?"

His fingers tightened on her upper arms and she was grateful for his firm grip. Otherwise, she might have melted into a puddle at his feet.

Smiling up at him, she said, "Yes, I love you. And yes, I'll marry you. Today. Tomorrow. Whenever you want. Because I'm not the same, either. You filled me, when I thought I would never be whole again. And the last two weeks without you were emptier than anything I've ever known."

"Thank God," he muttered and pulled her close again. Wrapping his arms around her, he bent his head to the curve of her neck and inhaled the soft, floral fragrance of her. And for the first time since the evening she'd left, Aidan felt his heart beating again.

"There's something else you should know though," she whispered and he pulled back to look at her, waiting.

"I'm pregnant."

Stunned, he blinked at her. "But. You said. The pill. We. You."

She grinned and shrugged. "Apparently, they're not a hundred percent effective."

"Yeah. But. I."

"I was coming to see you, Aidan, to tell you. When you rang the bell, I thought it was the realtor come to list the penthouse."

"You were coming back to me?" he asked with a smile.

"Yeah," she said softly. "I was going to find a way to *make* you love me."

"Babe," he said, inhaling sharply and grinning now to flash that dimple at her. "You already did that."

He pulled her in close again and whispered into her hair. "I'm happy about the baby, Terry. Terrified, but really happy. But are you okay with it? I mean, after Eric. Aren't you scared?"

She nestled in close and felt her fears dissolve in a well of love. She had been scared. When the pregnancy test turned up positive, fear reared up and nibbled on her. But then she realized that if loving Eric prevented her from ever loving another child, then she was cheating both herself and the memory of her son.

"Yeah," she admitted quietly. "I'm a little scared. But I'm also *alive,* Aidan. For the first time in a long time, I'm really *alive.*"

She pulled her head back and looked up at him. "I want to love you, Aidan. Laugh with you. Fight with you. Build a family with you."

He brought his hands up to cup her face and smiled down at her. "You'll never be sorry you took a chance on me, Terry. I swear it."

"We took a chance on each other," she whispered and leaned in to meet his kiss.

Epilogue

Two days later, the sun was sinking against the horizon. Most of the speeches were finished, the Marine band was tuning up and the grounds were packed. There were never enough bleacher seats, so most people just brought lawn chairs and blankets, spreading out across the area.

Battle Color Day, when every Marine dignitary available was on hand for the Corps celebration.

The speeches were mercifully brief, the Drum and Bugle Corps stirred the blood and the Silent Drill team brought the crowd to utter silence.

There was something magical about watching men snap out precision moves, each in time with the other, with no sound but that of a rifle butt smacking into a gloved palm.

There was a sense of pride that rippled through the awestruck, motionless crowd.

A kind of pride no civilian could ever truly understand.

And as the Silent Drill team moved off the field, Tina Coretti Reilly, Emma Jacobsen Reilly and Terry Evans soon-to-be-Reilly, chatted in lawn chairs alongside their mother-in-law, Maggie Reilly.

Tina leaned out from beneath the rainbow striped umbrella, attached to her chair and held up a thermal jug of ice tea. "Anyone?"

"No, thanks, I'm good," Emma said, leaning forward, trying to strain her eyes to watch for a certain red convertible.

"Terry?" Tina asked.

"Yes, thanks." She took the plastic cup of tea and swallowed a sip before saying, "This is all so…"

"Amazing, isn't it?" Maggie said and gave Terry's hand a pat. "I always get teary at the official functions. And I'm so glad you're here with us for this."

"So am I," Terry said meaningfully, "and *this* I wouldn't have missed for anything."

"I hear that," Tina said on a laugh. "The Reilly Triplets in coconut bras?" she laughed again, clearly delighted at the mental image.

"Their friends will never let them forget it," Emma said smiling.

"And neither will we, dear," Maggie said and pulled a video camera out of the straw basket at her feet.

Terry laughed and looked at the older woman with the sparkling blue eyes so much like her sons. "You're going to *tape* them?"

"Of course I am," Maggie said, turning the camera on and winking at Terry. "Never pass up a chance for a little blackmail material on family."

"Ah, the Reillys," Tina said, leaning back in her chair and sticking her feet out to cross them at the ankle. "You gotta love us."

"We *are* fun," Emma admitted.

"Oh," Terry said, as she leaned back to sip her tea and enjoy the moment of solidarity, "I think I'm going to be very happy in this family."

"Look, girls," Maggie called out, excitement squeaking in her voice. "Here they come!"

A shining red Cadillac convertible slowly rolled along the main drive. Liam sat at the wheel, waving to the crowds, an enormous grin on his face.

Aidan, Brian and Connor, all sat on the trunk, their legs in the back seat. Each of them wore a coconut bra, a grass hula skirt and the grim expression of men trapped with no way out.

But as the crowd cheered, the Reilly triplets each lifted a hand in a wave—and met their humiliation like Marines.

* * * * *

SILHOUETTE®
Desire™ 2 in 1

AWAKEN THE SENSES by Nalini Singh

Charlotte Ashton was quiet and shy, but to renowned winemaker Alexandre Dupre, she was an intriguing challenge. He wanted to awaken her senses, and her secret journal told him just how to fulfil her fantasies.

ESTATE AFFAIR by Sara Orwig

Eli Ashton couldn't resist one night of passion with Lara Hunter, a maid at his family's estate. Horrified that she had fallen into bed with a man so out of reach, Lara fled the scene, leaving Eli wanting more.

BETWEEN MIDNIGHT AND MORNING
by Cindy Gerard

When veterinarian Alison Samuels moved into middle-of-nowhere Montana, she hardly expected to start a fiery affair with hunky young rancher John Tyler. But John hid a dark past and Alison wasn't one for surprises…

WHEN THE EARTH MOVES by Roxanne St Claire

After Jo Ellen Tremaine's best friend died, she was determined to adopt her friend's baby. But first she needed the permission of the girl's stunningly sexy uncle—city lawyer Cameron McGrath. Cameron always had a weakness for wild women…

AT ANY PRICE by Margaret Allison

Kate Devonworth had a little problem. Her town paper needed a loan, and her childhood crush turned wealthy investor Jack Reilly was just the man to help. She resolved to keep things between them strictly business…

BUSINESS OR PLEASURE? by Julie Hogan

Daisy Kincaid finally quit her job when she realised that her boss, Alex Mackenzie, would never reciprocate her feelings. But the sexy CEO pleaded for her to return; would the new, unexpectedly close business relationship turn into the private pleasure she desired?

On sale from 21st April 2006

Visit our website at www.silhouette.co.uk

0106/SH/LC130

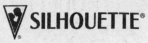

SILHOUETTE®

Desire™

*A family built on lies...Brought together
by dark, passionate secrets.*

January 2006	**Entangled** *by Eileen Wilks*
	A Rare Sensation *by Kathie DeNosky*
March 2006	**Society-Page Seduction** *by Maureen Child*
	Just a Taste *by Bronwyn Jameson*
May 2006	**Awaken the Senses** *by Nalini Singh*
	Estate Affair *by Sara Orwig*
July 2006	**Betrayed Birthright** *by Sheri WhiteFeather*
	Mistaken for a Mistress *by Kristi Gold*
September 2006	**Condition of Marriage** *by Emilie Rose*
	The Highest Bidder *by Roxanne St. Claire*
November 2006	**Savour the Seduction** *by Laura Wright*
	Name Your Price *by Barbara McCauley*

**Visit the Napa Valley in California and
watch the struggle, scandal and seduction.**

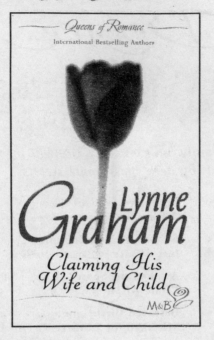